Fern looked
glistening
her trauma.

Whispers of a breeze from the distant mountains and canyons strengthened her. The mountains knew secrets and did not judge.

Fern lifted her face to the sky. "You have no power over me," she told her unknown kidnappers. "I am alive and so are my memories. I will recall them and you will not hurt another woman the way you hurt me."

Feeling alive and energized, she lifted her hands to the sky and twirled, laughing at the feeling of breathing, feeling, simply being alive after months of fear and uncertainty.

"Nothing will hurt me now!" she shouted. "I'm unsinkable."

"Unsinkable in the middle of the desert?" Ryan sounded amused. "Who are you talking to?"

She turned to see him emerging from his truck.

"I didn't hear you pull up," she told him, delighted he was home.

Fern was about to tell him about her revelation when an ominous orange glow flickered in the house across the street. Smoke curled out of the open windows and suddenly gunfire erupted.

Straight at them.

Dear Reader,

Ever wonder what it would be like to be rescued by a handsome firefighter who rushes into a burning building to save you? A stranger who is determined to remain in your life until he's certain you're safe from those who would harm you?

Fern Hensley never wondered. Her entire life has been about survival, from the time when her mother abandoned her over Fern's battle with alcoholism, which she fought and won. She learned at an early age to trust only herself.

When Ryan Colton rescues her from burning to death in an abandoned shack after she's kidnapped, Fern is grateful. But Ryan is more than a firefighter. He's a man of deep compassion who cares, and he knows that Fern is Dark Canyon's best chance of catching the kidnappers abducting women. Once Fern recovers her memory, she can identity the men who took her captive.

Ryan's been burned by love before. Fern has as well. It will take courage, faith and strength for them to overcome the odds and learn to trust that some things in life are meant to be—such as falling in love.

I hope you enjoy Fern and Ryan's story of second chances. Happy reading!

Bonnie Vanak

COLTON'S FIRESTORM

BONNIE VANAK

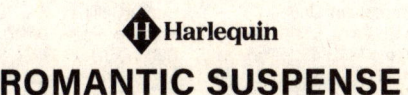

If you purchased this book without a cover you should be aware that this book is stolen property. It was reported as "unsold and destroyed" to the publisher, and neither the author nor the publisher has received any payment for this "stripped book."

Special thanks and acknowledgment are given to Bonnie Vanak for her contribution to The Coltons of Dark Canyon miniseries.

Recycling programs for this product may not exist in your area.

ISBN-13: 978-1-335-47187-1

Colton's Firestorm

Copyright © 2026 by Harlequin Enterprises ULC

All rights reserved. No part of this book may be used or reproduced in any manner whatsoever without written permission.

Without limiting the exclusive rights of any author, contributor or the publisher of this publication, any unauthorized use of this publication to train generative artificial intelligence (AI) technologies is expressly prohibited. Harlequin also exercises their rights under Article 4(3) of the Digital Single Market Directive 2019/790 and expressly reserves this publication from the text and data mining exception.

This is a work of fiction. Names, characters, places and incidents are either the product of the author's imagination or are used fictitiously. Any resemblance to actual persons, living or dead, businesses, companies, events or locales is entirely coincidental.

For questions and comments about the quality of this book, please contact us at CustomerService@Harlequin.com.

TM and ® are trademarks of Harlequin Enterprises ULC.

Harlequin Enterprises ULC
22 Adelaide St. West, 41st Floor
Toronto, Ontario M5H 4E3, Canada
www.Harlequin.com

HarperCollins Publishers
Macken House, 39/40 Mayor Street Upper,
Dublin 1, D01 C9W8, Ireland
www.HarperCollins.com

Printed in Lithuania

New York Times and *USA TODAY* bestselling author **Bonnie Vanak** is passionate about romance novels and telling stories. A former newspaper reporter, she worked as a journalist for a large international charity for several years, traveling to countries such as Haiti to report on poor living conditions. Bonnie lives in Florida with her husband, Frank, and is a member of Romance Writers of America. She loves to hear from readers. She can be reached through her website, bonnievanak.com.

Books by Bonnie Vanak

Harlequin Romantic Suspense

The Coltons of Dark Canyon

Colton's Firestorm

Rescue from Darkness
Reunion at Greystone Manor
Escape from Devil's Den
Desperate Justice

The Coltons of Red Ridge

His Forgotten Colton Fiancée

Colton 911: Chicago

Colton 911: Under Suspicion

SOS Agency

Navy SEAL Seduction
Shielded by the Cowboy SEAL
Navy SEAL Protector
Her Secret Protector

Visit the Author Profile page
at Harlequin.com for more titles.

For all firefighters who risk their lives to keep us safe.
Special thanks to Mike, Tony and Beth,
who know what it's like to save people. Thank you!

Chapter 1

Darkness. So much darkness. Pain. Her leg ached with fierce throbbing, as if someone had battered it with a hammer.

Moaning, she thrashed back and forth. *Someone make it stop. Please!*

Heart racing, she fumbled for an exit, any way out. She had to find her way home, get out of here. Smoke, thick and acrid, filled her nostrils. Coughing, she tried to crawl away from the heat and flames, but something restricted her.

I'm going to die here.

Air, blessed air, whooshed into her lungs. Coughing, she blinked, her eyes watering...

"Fern. You okay?"

Ryan Colton stood in the doorway. Embarrassed to be caught in a nightmare, she blinked and forced a smile.

"Fine, fine. Stupid dream. That's all."

Struggling to get her bearings, she looked around. *Times like this I need a GPS for my life. Some kind of direction.*

Still in Baldwin Hospital in Dark Canyon. Fern Hensley reached past the covers and felt her bad leg. She closed her eyes, forcing herself to center. *You're okay. Safe. Your leg healed. Okay, got it, in the hospital, you'll go home soon to your safe space.*

Except she had no place to be safe. Only here, where they watched over her every minute.

Her home wasn't safe.

Fern opened her eyes to see Ryan cross the room and pull up a chair and sit. A warm palm covered hers.

"You were calling out in your sleep," he said in his deep, soothing voice.

He seemed kind. Concerned. Ryan, the firefighter who rescued her from the fire. She briefly remembered him lifting her up into his strong arms and telling her she had to live, had to fight, his commanding voice seeping into her mind as she fell unconscious.

He'd rescued her from the bad men who'd kidnapped her.

Kidnapped her, but didn't sexually assault her. A memory briefly flared. A cruel voice speaking aloud in the darkness.

"Gotta save her for the online auction. She'll sell better if she's untouched."

Then the brutal pain in her leg when she'd tried to run and they'd beaten her. Couldn't escape.

The fire...

She took a deep breath. At least her throat had healed from the smoke inhalation. The superficial burns on her arms were healed. Her leg, well, the doctors said she'd walk with a gimp, but her leg was perfectly functionable.

Even if inside I am not. Damn, I need a drink.

"Silly dream, nothing more. I'm fine," she lied again, wondering if the smile she forced looked like she was gritting her teeth.

Even sleeping with the light on failed to chase away the darkness inside her. So many times she'd wake up, gasping for air, struggling to breathe as she had back at the burning cabin.

Ava, her counselor and Ryan's sister, assured her the trauma would fade. But with her memory as scattered as jigsaw pieces, Fern wasn't as confident.

She began folding the bed's blanket into triangle shapes. The patterns soothed her for some reason. Maybe because they provided consistency in a world no longer consistent.

Calling her sponsor was a good idea. For the past two years, Belle had talked her off the ledge. But she didn't want to call her in front of Ryan. Bad enough to lie here, helpless, a victim. Much as she liked Ryan, she didn't want him to know her past or her battle with alcohol, even though she had not touched a drop of liquor in seven years.

Ryan's deep blue gaze raked over her body. Professional, assessing, yet she sensed more than compassion. His commanding air and courage fed her hope.

With her kidnappers still roaming free, she felt terrified they might return to finish the job. Maybe this time bring a gun into the hospital to kill her instead of leaving her in the wood cabin to die in smoke and flames.

Jeans hugged Ryan's trim legs, and he wore a blue and white baseball shirt. The clothing fit his lanky body well. Maybe some would call him lean, but she knew the strength in those arms that had snatched her away from death.

"Are you supposed to be working?" she asked.

"I have two days off. I wanted to stop by, see how you're doing."

She played with the covers, smoothed them, glad her hands were no longer shaking. "Thanks. I'm okay."

So many times he'd visited. Ryan was one of the few she trusted.

A brusque knock sounded at the door. Instead of the nurse, Jacob Colton strode into the room. As the lead investigator into her kidnapping, he'd spent a lot of time with her. He nodded at Ryan, his cousin, and studied her.

Fern squirmed, feeling like a bug under the microscope.

"How are you feeling?"

"Okay," she lied.

Not that Jacob wasn't a good guy, but he was a cop and cops always asked questions, probed, wanted answers.

Answers she didn't have but wanted to give him.

Jacob came closer, big and intimidating. "Maybe we can try some more questions. Jog your memory. You were abducted walking home from work. Whoever took you made sure you wouldn't run by breaking your leg."

Ryan frowned and spoke in a no-nonsense tone. "Jacob, is this necessary?"

"It is if we're going to find who did this." Jacob studied her as if he could pry answers from her broken memories. "Remember who hurt you? Anything about your broken leg?"

A faint memory surged. An angry voice, a fist raised to strike. *No, please don't. Don't! Don't hurt me!*

Fern bit back a whimper. Jacob leaned forward, intense and too much in her space.

"Get a memory back?"

Fern's fingers curled into the blanket. *I can't tell him about this. I don't know what memory this is. I feel like it's my childhood, but...*

Too raw and exposed, she shook her head. "No. I'm trying..."

Jacob's expression remained level. He seemed too big, too intense. "Can you try harder? You're the best lead we have now."

"I want to help! I do! But I can't remember!"

Ryan edged closer to Jacob, his expression darkening. "I'm warning you, Jacob, take it easy on her. She's not the suspect."

Jacob glanced at his cousin. "I get it, Ryan. Fern's suffered a great deal of trauma. But we need to find out who did this so we can prevent other women from being kidnapped."

So much pressure. Fern's fists tightened. "I remembered one of them was called Billy. I already told you before, one was Billy. I wish I could remember!" she burst out. "Can't you see I'm trying?"

"Enough." Ryan jerked his head to the door. He looked as if

he might drag Jacob out. A warm feeling of wonder filled her. The sheer command in his voice soothed her agitation.

Ryan was her advocate, and she needed one right now.

"Jacob, outside. Leave her alone."

But Jacob was only doing his job. "I do want to help," she said in a small voice. "I wish I could remember."

Jacob focused on her. "I wish you could as well. What about hypnosis? Would you be willing to speak to someone about that?"

Torn, she bit her lip. Undergoing hypnosis could help them catch her abductors, maybe even find the people who killed that poor woman in Dark Canyon. But ghosts of memories flitted about her mind, vague and threatening.

Ghosts she didn't want to see right now.

"Maybe."

"If you're willing, I'll set something up."

"I—I don't know."

Ryan stood up. "Now, Jacob. Leave her alone. Pushing her isn't going to force Fern into regaining her memory."

"I'm not pushing, Ryan. Fern says she's willing and the hypnosis could work. She's our best chance of catching these bad guys."

"Not if you're going to stress Fern," he snapped.

Cousin against cousin—this was all wrong and it was her fault for not remembering. Families fighting, shouts, screams of pain...

Shoulders shaking, Fern buried her head into her hands. It was too much. She felt like a thread unraveling from a tapestry everyone was trying to sew back together.

Ryan left the room, returning less than a minute with Cassidy, her nurse. Fern raised her head. Cassidy gave one stern look to Jacob.

"Out. Now," she told him.

Jacob looked at Fern. "When you're ready, maybe we can consider the hypnosis."

Cassidy followed Jacob out of her room. Suddenly the walls seemed to squeeze in on her. Suffocating her, pressing her from all sides. She knew she was safe here, but was she really?

Was she safe anywhere?

Ryan gestured to the door. "Sorry about that. Jacob is a good guy, but he can be single-minded."

"It's okay."

"You're not okay. You're shaking."

Damn. Fern blew out a breath, tried to center herself. "I don't know what's going to happen. I can't stay here forever and…"

"It doesn't help having Jacob burst into your room whenever he wants." Ryan glanced at the door again. "You can't go home again. Not until Jacob catches these…"

He bit his lip as if biting back a curse.

Fern offered another faint smile. "You can say it. I'd probably call them worse."

Ryan sat close to her again. "Listen, I'm sure the doctor will discharge you soon…and this hospital must feel like a prison. Would you want a room at my place?"

She stared.

He flushed, and it made him look even cuter. "Just a spare room. I can talk with the police and arrange to have a protective detail—an undercover police officer—watch over the house and make sure you're guarded when I have to work. No pressure. I can only imagine how confining this room is."

Much as she hated being a victim and having no place to go, she felt grateful. The guy had saved her life and was giving her a place to live. A safe place. She placed her hand over his.

Trust. Damn hard to come by these days, but deep inside, she felt the beginnings of it return. Maybe staying in his house, without the constant antiseptic smell of the hospital, nurses coming and going, would help her relax and recall her memories.

It seemed a generous offer, but leaving the security of the hospital would be challenging. Could she trust him?

"I don't know. Where do you live? I mean, why do you think I'd be safe there? Others would know my location, Ryan."

"They won't. I live in a quiet neighborhood and everyone minds their own business. My backyard is fenced for privacy, so if you need fresh air and sunshine, you can sit on the patio."

His intense blue gaze met hers. "I mean it, Fern. You'll be safe there. I promise to do whatever I can to protect you."

Ryan had saved her life. He had been a source of quiet and calm in a dizzying array of frustration and terror over the past three months. While the nurses and doctors, and Ava, her therapist, had been professional, only Ryan made her feel safe. Even Jacob, though he was a professional police officer, made her wary.

Though she wasn't one to gamble, she went with her instincts.

"Thank you. For everything. Yes, that would be great. Are you sure I won't be an inconvenience?"

His hand lingered a moment longer before he pulled it away. "No trouble at all. It will give me a good reason to clean out all that clutter. I have off today and tomorrow, so I have time to get everything ready."

He glanced at the door. "If the doc will sign you out, you can come to my place tomorrow. I'll pick you up."

Fern nodded, but she couldn't erase the fear every present beneath the surface, like a snake waiting to strike. Logically? She was safe, had stayed here in the hospital under another name and no one knew her real identity. The security here was excellent. But moving to Ryan's house, especially because he had to work and she would be alone and vulnerable…

As if reading her mind, he pulled out his phone. "I've been

meaning to ask my cousin Mark to install a new security system. And you have your personal backup Mark got you."

He gestured to the locket given to her, now lying on the bedside table. A panic button in case something went wrong. The pretty jewelry had a button on the back for her to press if she had an emergency and contained a GPS tracking chip.

Fern gave a crooked smile. "Help, I've fallen and I *can* get up."

He grinned, making him look even cuter. Ryan brushed a hand through his light brown hair. Then his smile vanished. "I mean it, Fern. You feel scared or threatened, you press that button."

He glanced around the hospital room. "I know it must feel scary leaving here with so many people around to guard you, but I promise, we'll do everything to ensure you're protected."

Though his words offered comfort, Fern hated feeling dependent. She looked around the private hospital room, her home for the past three months. Ironic how she'd probably coded medical records of people who may have been at this very same hospital after leaving the doctor's office where she'd worked…

Medical coding. The memory returned, making her catch her breath.

"What?" he asked.

"I used to work for a doctor as a medical coder." She frowned, pressed two fingers against her head. "I was walking home from work and then something happened…"

No, don't think about that!

"That's terrific." He gave an encouraging smile. "Little by little, you'll recall everything."

Everything? She wanted to help. She wanted her attackers caught. They had left her in the shack to die a horrific death.

But the idea of remembering everything in her life seemed

overwhelming. Fern had a deep suspicion she'd deliberately forgotten some aspects of her life to move on.

Once she remembered them, would she face even greater pain than the physical hurt inflicted on her?

Chapter 2

The car crash was a bad one. Guy T-boned a truck much bigger than his tiny car.

A stench of fuel and blood filled the air. Bystanders stood nearby, some recording with their cell phones. He scowled, then forced himself to ignore them.

Ryan focused on the job at hand. Make sure everyone was safe, then comfort the victim as they prepared to extract him.

The man's leg was trapped under the dashboard, blood seeping onto the seat. A real mess. But experience taught him the guy's leg could be saved, even though it would take lots of hospital care and physical therapy.

As they removed the man from the car and secured the scene, his thoughts drifted to Fern. Rushing into the cabin and dragging her out of the fire, silently praying she would be okay. The stench of smoke still lingered in his mind.

He felt shock at how shattered Fern's leg was, how much it must have hurt, and fury at who could have done this to her.

He couldn't stop thinking about her and how easily she could have slipped away had he not arrived on scene when he did. Hands and feet tied up, left to die in the fire.

Fern, with her long brown hair, pretty hazel eyes, grit and determination not to be a victim.

By the time the engine and rescue truck returned to the station, he felt worn out, and it was only the beginning of his shift. He was professional, knew his job, but this save had triggered him.

As they removed their turnout gear at the lockers, his buddy Bob Marks kept looking at him.

"What?" he finally asked, in no mood for games.

"Heard you have a lady friend named Fern moving in with you." Bob grinned.

Ryan whirled, narrowing his eyes. "Where did you hear that?"

"Social media."

As he stared at his friend, Bob sighed. "Joke, Rye. Overheard your convo with Ava."

"You overheard nothing, Bob. Keep it to yourself. I don't want people to know where she is."

"Sure, sure. You want to keep it on the DL because it's a big step to have a woman live with you."

The teasing not only irritated him, it made him furious. "Cut the crap, Bob. I have an extra room and she needs to get out of that hospital. She's not moving in with me. I'm giving her a safe place."

Bob blinked and held up his hands. "Whoa, whoa. Sorry, man. Didn't realize you were that sensitive about it."

He sat on a nearby bench and pulled off his boots, throwing them with force into the locker. Ryan heaved a breath and righted his boots, then draped his suspenders over them. He placed his helmet on the shelf in the same place he always did, visor up. Superstitious ritual each time he returned from a call.

Equipment stored, he turned to his friend. Why couldn't Bob get it?

"Sensitive has nothing to do with it. Fern suffered a severe trauma, and she's the best chance we have of catching the ones who did this to her. The bastards who are making our town dangerous for women, *all* women. Get it?"

"Ryan, I was teasing…"

Raw anger bubbled up. "Teasing? How would you like it if Maggie got snatched off the street and beaten? Tied up and left to burn alive in a fire? Had so much happen to her it's a damn miracle she's alive? Couldn't remember half of her life?"

Captain Tom Colburn popped his head into the room. "What's going on? I could hear you upstairs."

Ryan took a deep breath. Bob put a hand on his arm. "Look Rye, I'm sorry. I wasn't thinking."

He shrugged off his hand. "Problem with you, Bob, is you don't think."

Ryan had to get away, cool down, stop reacting, because every time someone mentioned something even slightly derisive about Fern, he went into a tailspin. When he thought of Fern, lying on the floor, flames sweeping over the weather-roughened wood, licking closer to her, it sent him into a rage. How dare someone treat her like that? Tied up and helpless to fight her way free?

There are good people in this world, he'd assured her.

You're one of them, she'd told him.

Always a professional, keeping his feelings stuffed inside, Ryan knew Fern shook him deeply. The exchange with Bob, one of his best buds, proved it.

He was invested in what happened to her.

Fern haunted him. If Noah hadn't been there and Dancer hadn't alerted to her location, she would have died. No rescue. No ambulance growling away to nurses and docs treating her injuries.

Only a body bag.

Steadying himself with a calming breath, he shuddered. Years of saves under his belt and this one woman had turned him inside out.

Another face flickered in his mind. Kate McIntyre, her terrified screams echoing in his head as she twisted, escaping his frantic grip.

Cap followed him outside as Ryan paced in front of the firehouse.

"Rye, talk to me. You have to chill out."

With his shock of gray hair, keen brown eyes and no-nonsense manner, Captain Tom was the heartbeat of the firehouse. Always one to defuse conflict, take charge, Tom was like a big brother. Ryan respected him and never dismissed his advice.

Until today. He was too tightly wound, a coiled spring ready to snap. The crash victim they'd saved reminded him of Fern, pale and stricken by pain. But Fern had been worse.

Cap put a hand on his shoulder. "Rye, what's really going on? Ever since you rescued Fern, you've been involved. Maybe too much."

Oh no, not today. He took another deep breath to calm himself. "How can I *not* get involved? I'm not going to ignore what's going on in town, Cap. I see it everywhere I go. People are scared, and women, they're terrified, knowing a kidnapper and murderer is out there. Fern's alive. She saw her kidnappers. She's our best chance of finding them, but she's too traumatized to remember anything."

"Ryan, we've talked about this. Save the victim and your job ends there. You've already had one incident. I don't want you to have another."

As if he needed reminding. Ryan's insides tightened. Could hear all the talk.

Savior complex. Guilt complex. Hell, his sister, Ava, was a psychologist. No need to remind him what he'd done shortly after taking this job.

I couldn't save her. She slipped from my fingers. I was so close, so close...

Aware Cap's steady gaze was assessing him, ready to analyze him, he forced a nod and a smile, hiding his feelings.

"Okay, Rye. Go talk to Bob. I don't want my team fighting."

He returned inside to find Bob sitting before his locker. "Look, Rye, I'm sorry about this. I won't tell anyone."

"Good." He took a deep breath. "It's okay. Forget about it."

"But I do have to ask, because you are my friend. You certain Fern moving into your guest bedroom is the right thing?"

"Absolutely. She has nowhere else to go. Mark is already working on the security system."

He stated this with more confidence than he felt. Fact was, he had to work and leave her alone. Couldn't be there all the time to ensure she was okay.

What if something happened to her while he was gone?

Three days after Ryan invited her to stay at his house, the doctor finally signed her out of the hospital.

Ryan came to take her back to his home.

Leaving was scary, but she'd faced tougher. Fern struggled to sit up and threw back the covers. She gestured to the bed railing.

"Can you put this down for me? I need to get up."

He obliged and stood back. "I'm here if you need help."

Fern slid her legs over the bedside.

At least Ryan didn't treat her like an invalid. He stood by, ready to assist, but letting her stand on her own. Using her good right leg for balance and leaning on the walker, she hoisted herself out of the bed.

Pain flared briefly as she put weight on her left leg. Fern inhaled a deep breath.

Still watching her, Ryan frowned. "I went to get your meds from the pharmacy to expedite the check-out process. No painkillers. Doc prescribed them, but you refused."

Taking a deep breath, she put her full weight on the bad leg, relieved it held, relieved the pain was nothing compared to…

When you first got injured.

Though Ava, her counselor, had worked with her in trying to get her to recall those horrific memories, now was not the time. Focusing on the goal before her—getting out of the hospital—was far more important.

Fern glanced at him. "No prescription painkillers. I manage fine with over the counter."

Ryan nodded. "If you find you need them, let me know. I can always go to the drugstore to fill them."

He didn't ask why she fought the pain on her own, refusing to rely on heavy medications. Another thing she liked about this guy—he wasn't nosy like some. Nor did he argue with her.

Setting aside the walker, she tested the weight on both legs again and then walked over toward the door. Barely any pain at all now, not if she went slow. Yeah, she wouldn't be racing anytime soon, but at least she was mobile. Fern felt a jubilant surge at knowing she could stand on her own two feet.

She made her way across the room. It felt great to walk and be free from the bed. Balancing her weight, she moved one foot in front of the other. Yeah, she was doing good. Air brushed against her body, now freed from the covers, and her backside felt, well...

Oops.

Suddenly she became aware of the hospital gown flapping open from the back and her butt was showing. Her big butt. Even hospital food for three months hadn't eliminated that problem. Heat suffused her face. Ryan cleared his throat and turned around.

She tried for humor. "Sorry for mooning you. This gown doesn't exactly fit."

"No problem. Nice view."

She turned and saw him blush. He looked even cuter.

"Give me a few minutes to get dressed. I would have been ready earlier, but I slept late because they kept waking me up last night to take my blood pressure. You know, to make sure I wasn't dead when I left here."

Ryan chuckled. "Yeah, I know how hospitals are. I'll be in the waiting room."

Fern grinned as he left. She liked his casual attitude. But being in a hospital had been all about survival for the past three months. Now, knowing she would be staying at Ryan's house, she became aware of her body. A shower would help. Fern felt her hair, dismayed at how scruffy it was. Bedhead. Suddenly it seemed critical to leave clean and refreshed, her hair washed. New start.

Even though problems still followed, attached by invisible strings jerking her downward into a pit of darkness.

I don't need a drink.

But she did need to call her sponsor. Fern walked over to the bedside table and picked up the new cell phone Ryan had bought her.

Belle answered on the first ring, as if anticipating her call. "Hi, Fern. How are you handling everything?"

"I'm okay."

"Don't lie. Talk to me."

She smiled. Belle, always direct, her usual feisty fifty-nine-year-old self, sober now for more than twenty-five years. Her lifeline at times over the past two years, ever since her first sponsor had moved to Europe.

"I'm managing. Scared. I'm leaving the hospital today." Fern cleared her throat. Though many memories eluded her, she knew her voice had deepened from inhaling smoke in the fire.

"I know. Big step. Is your plan in place?"

Belle taught her that having a plan helped to keep a semblance of control, even when life spiraled out of control. Taking responsibility for things within her control was part of AA's twelve-step program. Focus on what the next thing she could do was. Move straight ahead, like taking a simple shower. A shower wasn't climbing Mount Everest.

Her compass was the people helping her along the way. Accepting help wasn't easy, but she needed it.

"Plan is in place," she told Belle. "Shower first, then packing, and leaving with Ryan to go to his house."

"How do you feel about staying with him?"

Ava had asked her this as well. Fern bit her lip. "It's weird. I'm relieved I have a place to live that's safe, but I hate depending on anyone. I don't want to be a big imposition. I feel a little helpless that I can't make it on my own."

"You're not helpless. Look at how far you've come, Fern. You're standing. You're walking. Damn, girl, you're alive. Thank the good Lord you are!"

Emotion clogged her throat. So much gratitude, another important part of the twelve steps. Focus on the gratitude.

"You can do this, Fern. You're one of the strongest people I know, girl."

"You're right. I can do this. Thanks, Belle. I'd better get moving. That shower is calling me."

"I'm here if you need me. Deal?"

"Deal. Bye, and thank you." Fern hung up.

She depressed the nurse call button to get assistance with showering. Not that she couldn't do it herself, but they wanted to stand by in case she needed help.

Belle was right. She was alive and had plenty to be grateful for right now. But in the back of her mind, she couldn't help worrying about what the future held.

Especially with the men who'd kidnapped her still running free.

Fern shivered.

Chapter 3

Knowing Fern was going to stay with him, Ryan had done his best to clean the house. Couldn't do anything about the fact the walls needed painting or the kitchen looked like the eighties wanted their cabinets back, but at least he lived on a nice street in a safe neighborhood.

His house had cathedral ceilings, and best of all, lots of windows letting in natural light. French doors in the living room opened to a big yard, surrounded by a white privacy fence.

Ryan wished he had better furnishings to offer Fern. The guest bedroom was adequate, but the bed was secondhand, picked up at a garage sale. Furniture had been purchased at a scratch-and-dent sale.

On his salary, he didn't have money for the kind of luxurious furniture in his parents' house.

Dad would blame the thrift-store look on Ryan not following in his footsteps and taking a job with the family real estate business. Dad took every opportunity to remind him, *Hey, you can do better.*

But being a firefighter was a dream come true. He wanted to save people, not real estate holdings.

Fern gazed around the guest bedroom. In blue jeans that hugged her legs and her apple-round bottom, a light pink sweater that accented her curves, she sure was pretty. But her trepidation concerned him. He wanted to make her feel comfortable and safe, not scared.

He held her suitcase, the one donated by the local charity who'd also given her clothing and basic toiletries. "Sorry it isn't much, but the bed's comfortable. The quilt is warm, but if you're cold I have extra blankets in the linen closet."

She looked around, nodded. Hard to tell what Fern thought. Her expression was neutral.

"It's lovely. Thank you again. I appreciate you taking me in."

"Where do you want your suitcase?"

Fern's gaze dropped down as she pointed to the bed. "There is fine until I can unpack. It isn't really mine. I mean, it was given to me to get me back on my feet until I can get home again. Everything in my life right now is a loan."

Setting down the suitcase, he knew where she was headed with this. He cut her off. Ava had warned him not to indulge her in a pity party. It wouldn't help Fern mentally heal or help trigger her memory.

"You're not a victim, Fern. Remember that."

She gave a humorless laugh. "Funny, when I went to Florida for a vacation I remember seeing a sign at the airport about reporting human trafficking. I never gave it a second thought and here I am. So, do I report myself?"

He liked her spirit. Probably had helped to keep her alive and fighting. How many times had he seen people in bad situations, people he'd saved from a horrible car crash or lost in the canyon, whom he'd pulled out alive and breathing?

People who fought to live instead of giving up. Fern was that kind of woman.

Jamming his hands into his pockets, he gazed around the room. "Listen, I hate to do this, but I have to work a twenty-four-hour shift that started at seven o'clock. I did get permission to show up to work at eleven, so I have to leave soon. I tried to rearrange my schedule to be here for your first night, but with your delayed release, I couldn't get anyone to switch with me."

"It's okay. I'll be fine. It's great you were able to pick me up."

The staccato sentences didn't reassure him. The way her gaze kept darting around the room, as if looking into every corner for threats, worried him.

"I'll call my sister, Ava, and ask her to spend the night. I don't want you to be alone."

Finally she looked at him. "I'll be fine, Ryan. I have to be alone sometime, right? And I'm not going to be alone. There's a cop outside, nearby, watching the house. Plus this." Reaching into her sweater, Fern pulled out the pretty silver locket from the long necklace dangling from her neck. "I have my emergency GPS finder. All I have to do is double click the hidden button in the back and I send out an SOS to Jacob to tell him my location."

The determination on her face told him she didn't want to impose. Be a burden. Ryan made a snap decision. He hefted her suitcase onto the bed.

"Here, go ahead and get settled. The least I can do is make you a decent lunch."

"I thought you had to work." She glanced at the bedside glass clock that featured a fire emblem. He'd bought it on a whim.

"The boss won't care if I'm a little late." He flashed her a smile. "I'm not much of a chef, but I do make a decent spaghetti and meatballs. Even if my mom says my meatballs are a little too big."

"No problem. I like big balls. The bigger the better."

He grinned wider at the double entendre as she flushed. "Uh, ah, thanks. I'll unpack."

In the kitchen, he set about making lunch after texting Bob and Cap he needed another hour. Bob, as an apology for his words the other day, offered to take his shift until Ryan could arrive at the station.

Both texted back all was fine.

Cap and the others had stopped talking about him giving Fern a temporary place to stay.

Ryan boiled the water and fished in his cabinet for the pasta. He'd been so busy lately, he'd forgotten to grocery shop. Some welcome he'd arranged for Fern.

He turned off the water and walked to her room, knocking on the door jamb.

No answer.

Worried, he poked his head through the door to find her sitting on the bed. Not unpacking, not doing anything except sitting.

"Hey, you okay, Fern?"

She glanced up, touched the bed. "Sorry. I was trying to get my bearings. This is the first time I've been inside a real home in months. Your place is great, it's just that…the last place I was in before the hospital was…not."

Hugging herself, she shivered. "I guess it will take a little adjusting."

Ryan cursed his thoughtlessness. Here he was, worried about food when she was worried about the ground constantly shifting beneath her.

He pointed to the bed. "Mind if I join you?"

Seeing her pale face, sensing sitting next to her would be too much right now, he shook his head. "No, never mind. I think better on my feet."

Her relieved expression was heartbreaking. Ryan took a deep breath, sensing he was treading through a minefield. He didn't want to scare or upset her, but his sister asked him to work with Fern to trigger her memory.

The faster Fern could recall more details of her abduction, the quicker the police could nail the kidnappers. Then not only Fern, but many women in Dark Canyon and nearby towns would be safe.

For now, it was best to stick to essentials.

"I forgot to grocery shop. What would you like for takeout? Italian? Mexican? I'm game for anything," he told her.

A little frown formed between her eyebrows. Made her look thoughtful and cute. "I can cook."

"I don't have much." He paused. "Listen, Fern, you're my guest. I didn't bring you here to cook. Don't feel like you have to earn your keep."

Waving a hand, she left the bed and headed for the kitchen. Fern began opening cabinets.

"I like to cook and I'm good at it. My mom was, well, I learned to make dinner from nothing."

She found a bottle of barbecue sauce and some spices. Next she dug into the freezer and found a package of chicken breasts he'd bought on sale and had forgotten about. Ryan found a container for defrosting the chicken and put it into the microwave.

Fern removed a package of cheddar cheese from the refrigerator.

"Here we go! Cheddar chicken with barbecue sauce. Oh, you have bacon as well. Bacon-wrapped chicken with cheese and barbecue sauce."

He grinned. "A guy's gotta have bacon."

She beamed. Such a little thing, making a meal, yet her enthusiasm told him Fern felt happy to be useful. Intrigued, he watched her set about making the recipe.

Meal preparation was a great icebreaker. It put them on even ground, and she seemed more relaxed.

"We make a good team," he said.

Her expression fell. "You save people and I needed saving."

No pity. "I was talking about the food. I can defrost chicken like a pro."

The smile on her face felt gratifying.

Ryan removed the chicken from the microwave. "I'm really

not a bad cook. Everyone takes turns at the station making dinner. I haven't heard any complaints yet."

She mixed the sauce and poured it over the chicken breasts. "If you haven't had to transport them to the hospital because of your cooking, I'd say you were ahead of the game."

He grinned. "I didn't say that. Never claimed they weren't conscious enough to complain."

After fishing out plates and silverware, he set the kitchen table. Fern wanted plain water and he opted for the same.

Ryan dug into his food. The flavor burst on his tongue. "Wow, this is good, Fern. You can make something out of nothing."

She pinked slightly under the praise. "It's not a big deal. Only a matter of figuring out what ingredients you have on hand can be combined. I learned early in life to economize when doing meal planning. I've survived on less. At the cabin, they gave me a granola bar, and even then I threw it back in their faces… their faces…"

Her expression went blank.

Excitement raced through him. "You remembered?"

Fern glanced at him, looked away. "I guess."

"That's terrific! Remember what they look like? Anything on them? Anything Jacob can use?"

Too late he realized his mistake. He was pushing Fern the same way his cousin and others had done. Fern stiffened.

"I'm not really hungry. You can leave when you want and I'll clean up. Excuse me, I think I'll get unpacked now."

Watching her leave the table, he groaned. Idiot. He'd blown it.

I have to do a reset with her before she bolts. Have to make her feel relaxed, not like I'm applying pressure like everyone else.

He glanced at the kitchen clock. Running late. But Fern came first. She was a priority.

Barely had he started out of the kitchen toward the hallway

when he heard the commotion. Heart pounding, he ran toward the guest bedroom.

"Ryan! Help!" Fern shouted. "Someone's trying to break into my room!"

She screamed.

Chapter 4

This was supposed to be a refuge. Fern shrank back against the wall, quivering as the menacing man at the window peered inside.

Fingers in her mouth, she whipped her head around to search for a weapon and seized the first thing she saw.

Ryan burst into the room, saw her. In his right hand he carried a baseball bat.

"The window," she managed to say.

He ran over as the man staring inside raised a hand. Oh dear heavens, was that a gun in his hand?

"Security," the man outside yelled. "Doing rounds. Can I come in?"

"Badge," Ryan shouted back. "Let me see your shield."

The stranger raised a gold shield. "Officer McCarty. I'm the plainclothes officer assigned to patrol the house."

Lowering the baseball bat, Ryan gestured to the front door. "Ring the doorbell and I'll be right there."

He turned, went to her. "Fern, you okay?"

Nodding, she bit her lip. "I—I—I'm sorry. I saw him at the window and I thought…"

"Not your fault. He should have rung the damn doorbell in the first place before walking around outside." Ryan's gaze dropped to her right hand.

Amusement flared in his eyes. "Were you going to use that on him?"

Fern glanced down at the bedside clock in her hand. Goodness, as if this could hurt someone. Feeling silly, she set it down.

"I've heard of people having time on their hands, but never using it to defend themselves."

His boyish grin eased the tension from her shoulders. Despite her nerves rubbed raw, Fern managed a slight smile.

"Sorry, bad joke." Twirling the baseball bat in his hands, he shrugged.

"I've heard worse." She considered. "Though not in a while."

His grin widened. "I have worse, if you're interested."

Interested? Maybe. She liked his sense of humor and how he used it to defuse a tense situation.

Fern pointed to the baseball bat. "At least you brought something that's useful for defense. Were you expecting to score a home run on the intruder?"

He chuckled. "Something like that. My friends would say it's more likely than me scoring a home run on our softball team."

Fern managed a bigger smile. "Something tells me you're being too modest."

As the doorbell rang, Ryan lowered the bat. "Modesty isn't one of my virtues, but honesty is. Let's go meet this Officer McCarty."

Tim McCarty was a tall, muscled man who wore jeans and a white linen shirt under a denim jacket. He had a serious look, which she supposed went with the job.

"Sorry for scaring you, miss. I was checking out the house. We're renting the house two doors down, and I'll keep an eye out here for you. Another officer will take over the night shift around six."

Tight-lipped, she nodded but couldn't bring herself to relax around the man. Maybe it was his air of authority or how he'd scared her. As long as he remained in the background, she'd be okay.

But this man was responsible for her welfare, so she should trust him. Maybe it would take a little time.

Time, something Fern kept feeling was slipping away. Every day she failed to recall all memory of The Incident, as she referred to her abduction, another woman remained in danger.

One already died. Baby Ella Grace had been left abandoned. Thankfully Ava was now caring for baby Ella Grace. *I'm the key to helping others, but damn, I feel like I'm walking over a minefield. A minefield that can blow up any minute now.*

When Ryan closed and locked the door, she breathed a sigh of relief. Despite the fact she'd barely been here a couple of hours, his home felt like a sanctuary away from a scary world outside. Maybe because it was his home, filled with his personality and calmness and fierce protectiveness.

He gave her a long, assessing look. "You okay? You're a bit pale."

She started with her usual "fine" response and stopped. "I guess I'm a little jumpy. You'd think by now I'd stop being scared of my own shadow."

Ryan shook his head. "After what you went through, Fern, you have a right to be scared. But you're safe here. I want you to know that. And if you need me, I'm a text or a phone call away. I think it's best for my sister to spend tonight with you."

She nodded.

"Sorry there's no food in the house. I have an account at the grocery store, so feel free to order whatever you want and get it delivered. Put it on my bill. They're used to me getting deliveries. Let me give you the grand tour. I know the doc wants you to keep up with rehab, and I have a gym downstairs so you can do the exercises you did at the hospital."

So considerate.

He briefly showed her his bedroom, the largest one. Ryan

jammed his hands into the pockets of his trousers. "Sorry for the mess. I don't sleep well sometimes after a shift, but I need to get my z's, and as a result, well, the bedroom…"

Fern walked over to the windows and the blinds. "You don't have blackout shades? How can you sleep during the day without a room being totally dark?"

He scowled. "I do my best."

"I didn't mean to criticize. Only an observation. I used to work night shift a few years ago when I was in college and blackout shades helped."

He shrugged. "Been meaning to buy some, but it kept getting away from me, with all the other stuff around here. Having a house is a lot of work."

"I'd be happy to help you purchase some."

The long, thoughtful look he gave her wasn't as uncomfortable as others' had been. Not like Ava's when Fern said something during therapy sessions or Jacob's when he grilled her about any details of her abduction.

Rather, it was like seeing her in a new light, ironically, because she knew how important it was to have a dark bedroom.

"Sure, if you want, but it's really not a big deal."

Fern wished she had her own money and access to her bank account. Ava might help with that. Helping Ryan sleep would be a small way to repay him for all his kindness.

The third bedroom he'd converted into an office/library. Bookshelves were filled with medical and science textbooks and crime novels.

"Feel free to borrow anything. I have plenty of light reading available," he told her.

"Physics and medical journals? You call that light reading?"

He grinned. "I'm trying to expand my knowledge. Helps on the job. I'm the senior hazmat technician at the station. Plus it never hurts to know more about emergency medical care."

"I thought there were EMTs and paramedics for that."

"Yes, however, sometimes we're first on scene and have to secure the vic." He gave her a steady look. "Like when I rescued you."

Heat suffused her cheeks. "That's something I can never forget. Thank you again for saving me."

"Part of the job."

His casual comment defused the seriousness of what happened. It wasn't part of his job to give her a safe space to live, or to visit her frequently at the hospital.

Downstairs, she gave an appreciative look around at the equipment, from a treadmill to weights and a lifting machine that looked far too complicated for her.

Opposite the gym was a wooden bar with shelving on the wall holding an assortment of liquor. Fern's smile dropped.

"You like to entertain?" she asked.

He followed her gaze. "Oh that. My dad set it up for me. Not really. A beer once in a while after a tough shift. Some of those bottles haven't been touched in years. I think Dad gave them to me to get them out of his house because Mom was nagging him about them."

Somehow that made her like him more. Ryan wasn't a hardcore drinker like some she'd met, like that guy who asked her out at the doctor's office who came in smelling like vodka and orange juice...

"I used to drink. A lot. I don't drink anymore," she said more to herself than to him.

Whoa, she hadn't meant to admit that to him, but there it was, out in the open. She watched him, ready for the usual uncomfortable reaction. Many people liked alcohol and felt uncomfortable around those who did not.

Ryan looked indifferent, as if she'd told him she disliked a certain color. "I'll have my cousin come over and remove the bottles later. Mark mentioned he liked the design."

"You don't have to do that for me. It's your home, and I don't want to disrupt your routine or anything else. I'm fine, Ryan. I don't drink anymore, but I still go out once in a while to a bar on a date…"

Her voice trailed off as a memory flickered. Fern rubbed a spot on the polished wood counter of the bar. "I was walking home, thinking about this guy who asked me out to this Irish bar…and then…everything went dark."

"Irish bar with a date. Sounds like fun. So who was the guy?"

Such a casual question, but she heard the undertone. Fern tilted her head at him. "That much I remember. A guy I met at the doctor's office. Some kind of salesman."

"Oh." Ryan traced a line along the bars of the treadmill. "Rich, good-looking, huh?"

Was that a little jealousy in his voice? She wasn't the type to encourage it. Fact was, she never had been that type of woman. Hurt feelings weren't her forte, or playing games.

"Not sure about the wealth. He was okay in looks. Average. A little balding. I do remember I agreed on a date because he was nice."

"Did you tell the police about him?"

"No."

"I'll do it. Every guy needs to be checked out, Fern. I'll notify Jacob, and the police may have additional questions. Irish food, huh? I'll have to remember that."

Interesting comment.

"He called me Colleen," she suddenly remembered. "Because he saw at my desk the book I was reading on break about Ireland and its history."

Ryan raised his eyebrows. "Family history?"

Not my family. "Deep dive into the culture. I was fascinated by the Celts. So fierce, like Queen Maeve. Maeve was a mythical warrior queen of ancient Ireland. Strong and brave."

"No wonder you like her. She's like you."

The unexpected praise made her blush. "I doubt it. Maeve slew the men of Ulster with a curse because of a bull."

"Sounds like bull to me," he teased.

She liked this side of him—fun and charming. Ryan tweaked a strand of her hair.

Warmth filled her. "You're like Brian Boru, the greatest and most courageous king of Ireland."

Ryan dropped his hand. "Sounds like a name to live up to. My bet is Brian wouldn't be late for his shift, though. I really have to go."

She followed him up the stairs, watching as he clicked off the basement light. Basements usually bothered her, but his was half finished, with part of it sectioned off into a workshop. Plenty of lighting made it seem less ominous.

After grabbing his go bag and donning his jacket, he frowned. "I really need to leave or I'll be in trouble. But I hate leaving you alone here."

"I'm not alone." Fern gestured to the door. "I have my police protection outside. Besides, the quiet will be good for me. You said the hospital was too noisy, too filled with people."

"Well, if you get worried, or scared…"

Fern gave him a gentle push. "Go to work. I'll be fine. Please."

He nodded. "Ava will be over later to spend the night. I'll be back tomorrow around noon."

For a wild minute she thought he would kiss her. Maybe he thought the same, for he leaned forward.

Ryan pulled away with a solemn look on his face. "Good night, fair Maeve. Remember, if you need anything, I'm a text away."

"Got it. Have a good shift."

Fern stood at the window, waving goodbye as his truck pulled out of the driveway.

For a moment she stayed there, then she dropped the curtain. Lace curtains, feminine and pretty. Not the kind found in a bachelor pad. Maybe his mother or an ex-girlfriend had made them for him.

The house seemed too big, too empty and silent. Well, she'd wanted quiet and now she had it.

For so many months, the hospital had been her routine. Blood pressure checks, physical and occupational therapy and other therapy. Her morning routine had been breakfast, medical checks, everything dictated by the nurses and doctors.

I have to set my own morning routine now.

The idea cheered her. Taking control, instead of having her life dictated by someone else. Maybe tomorrow while Ryan was at work she could make herself hot oatmeal with fruit, use the treadmill and exercise.

Enjoy some light reading to work her brain out as well.

I can do this. I can regain my life back.

Fern busied herself with unpacking, and then repacking what she had unpacked. Her fingers stroked the cheap wig and fake glasses she'd asked Ava to purchase for her.

A disguise to go out in public again. Not that she felt confident enough to try it.

It seemed wrong to place everything into the dresser in the bedroom. This wasn't her home, her refuge, but another temporary place. The sense of displacement depressed her all over again.

She did remove the wooden bear Sassy had given her at the hospital. The sight of it on the dresser cheered her and reminded her of Sassy's friendship. *The bear's name means strength,* Sassy told her.

I don't feel strong right now.

At the hospital they told her returning home was too dangerous. Even someone going to her apartment to retrieve her personal items and clothing presented a threat. Someone might be watching and waiting.

Better to dress in new clothing, live a borrowed life.

A hotel would have been better, but with her attackers out there, not a good idea. Fern sat on the bed, hugging herself.

Ordinary people would catch up on email, watch television or do something perfectly ordinary they enjoyed during downtime, like knitting. Or wood carving.

I had hobbies. I liked...

She pressed two fingers to her right temple. "What did I like?" she asked the empty room.

Surely anyone seeing her now would think she was a little mentally disturbed, talking to herself, trying to remember what she'd liked in the past. Ava would not. Ava was calm and collected and encouraged her to remember the good times.

Because that will help remember everything, including the bad.

She touched the side of her neck and the dollar sign tattoo there. Funny, she didn't remember getting it. And why put a dollar sign on her neck, as if she were a commodity to be sold?

It made her wonder if she hadn't put the ink there. Well, she couldn't worry about that now. Priorities. The tattoo or its origin was not one of them.

Fern got up and walked through the house. Cozy and simple, with big chunky furniture that looked comfortable. Definitely a bachelor home, with Ryan's individual stamp upon it. She paused before a painting of Dark Canyon and a figure climbing the rocks. Oil painting, not bad and with no signature, so most likely Ryan or someone he knew had painted it. Most artists signed their work.

I never signed mine, either.

A memory flickered. Painting. Yes, she preferred watercolors, not acrylics or oils. Light pastels to counter the dark themes in her work. Sassy had encouraged her on this.

Fern touched the painting, forcing herself to follow the memory as if it were a signpost on a road she hesitated to travel.

Art therapy. Classes to help her with the trauma of her childhood and the bitterness still lurking deep inside over a mother who'd abandoned her.

It wasn't all that bad. Remember Fuzzy Bunny? You carried him everywhere, even the fire at that camp where you learned to toast marshmallows...

Her smile faded as the memory returned in full force. Fuzzy, who'd been tossed into the fire by her foster sister.

She glanced at her hands and rubbed a faint scar. Burn mark. So desperate to save Fuzzy, she'd tried to rescue him from the flames, but a counselor pulled her away.

Another one had been called in when Fern launched all her rage and pain at her foster sister, trying to beat her with angry fists.

Yeah, and that ended quickly. Fern had been shipped off to another home, the incident disquieting to the family who'd taken her into their house and were ready to adopt the sister who'd tossed Fuzzy into the fire. They couldn't handle two little girls and had grown fond of the other sister.

I went back into the system like a recycled part.

But there were others out there. People like Ryan, and Ava, and Belle, and certainly Sassy. Cassidy, the friendly nurse at the hospital. Others as well.

The world is a big place, kiddo. You can't stay afraid forever.

She went into the kitchen and rooted through his junk drawer, finding the tape measure. Fern went into his bedroom and measured, precisely, all the windows. She noted the measurements on her phone, but no business could deliver custom-made blackout shades by the time he ended his shift.

No matter. She could make do with supplies.

For the next couple of hours she remained busy, ordering groceries, taking stock of what food Ryan did have—sadly, his pantry looked empty, as if he seldom ate at home or had time to cook—and unpacking.

Fern was about to venture downstairs to test out his exercise equipment when her cell phone dinged a message.

She grabbed the phone, relieved to hear from Ryan. It made being alone in his house less strange.

How are you settling in? he texted.

Fine. I'm ordering you a lot of food. Be prepared for gourmet meals. Do you like fried octopus? she asked.

Green emojis followed. Fern laughed and typed back. JK. Normal food that most guys enjoy—chicken and beef. I noticed you have an air fryer and there's recipes for fried chicken. Thought I'd test it out.

Feel free. I want you to feel comfortable, Fern.

I have a favor to ask.

Go on.

I wanted to start painting again. Thought it would help. Is it okay to set up a space in the basement?

Sure, go ahead. BTW, my cuz Mark is coming over soon. He's the guy who set you up with the GPS emergency locket. He installed security cameras around my house and he's bringing over a surprise for you.

A flutter of unease shot through her. She'd met Mark briefly, but having him here alone with her felt intimidating.

Ever perceptive, he followed with a concerned emoji. You okay with being alone with him?

Not really. She thought about it. Okay if I ask Sassy to come over while he's here?

Having another woman present would help, plus she wanted

to ask Sassy to bring art supplies, help her set up an easel in the basement.

My cousin Sassy who owns the art gallery?

His cousin. Ryan had a lot of family in Dark Canyon.

After she texted yes, he texted back. Sure. LMK when she's there and I'll ask Mark to drop by at the same time. He has a surprise for you.

What's the surprise? A Chihuahua guard dog?

Laughing emojis followed. Never heard of a Chihuahua being a guard dog.

You've never dealt with them. They could scare away a German shepherd.

No dogs. I work too much to deal with them. Surprise is electronic. You'll see. I think you'll like it. Opps. Gotta run—have a call. Take care.

U2, she typed back, not expecting a response.

The texting cheered her, made her more confident. She felt connected, but still, the day was bright and sunny and the thought of exercising inside seemed stifling with the warmer weather. A jacket should suffice.

Maybe she could venture outside, get fresh air, go for a walk. Ryan hadn't said anything about staying in the house. *I'm not a prisoner.*

A short walk while waiting for his cousin Mark. Then she'd call Ryan's cousin Jacob, tell him to set up the hypnosis. Anything to help out with the investigation.

Fern lifted the curtain in the living room.

She looked out the window again and saw a man pedaling by on a bicycle. He stared at the house. Her throat went dry and her heart beat faster.

The guy looked shady, with a ball cap pulled low on his forehead. He stopped right before the house. Stared some more.

Checking it out? Had he heard rumors about the woman staying with Ryan? Maybe wanted to pass on the information to those who'd kidnapped her?

She pulled down the window shade and retreated to the guest bedroom. Stupid of her to think this place was safe.

Nowhere was until the men who'd taken her were caught and brought to justice.

Chapter 5

Sometimes a shift at the station meant the *Q* word, which no one dared to utter out loud because then all of a sudden they'd get call after call. Usually he enjoyed the downtime, using it to catch up on checking equipment, even reading medical textbooks. Ryan found them fascinating.

Today wasn't one of the down days. Nearly as soon as he walked into the station, the alarm rang. Call was for a working fire.

Not pausing, Ryan grabbed his gear, dressing in the truck as they roared off. They arrived at a house in a fairly affluent neighborhood. A man waved them down. Ryan's adrenaline kicked in. He couldn't see smoke, but maybe the fire was inside. Or someone was down, in dire need of medical care.

After the rig was parked, Ryan jumped out. "Sir?" he called out.

"It's too loud!" the man screamed.

"Sir, where's the fire? Are you hurt?" Ryan asked.

"My ears are ringing. Can't you hear that crap?"

Ryan looked around. "What?"

"You deaf as well?" the man yelled. "That music! It's ruining my life!"

Strains of heavy metal drifted from the house next door. Ryan almost laughed.

No working fire. No medical emergency. He glanced at his friend Nick Malone, who shook his head.

"Takes all kinds," Nick drawled.

"You've got to be kidding," he muttered, pushing back his helmet. "We rushed out here for a complaint about music?"

Nick shrugged. "We aim to serve. Saving lives and saving eardrums."

"What are you going to do about it? I have hearing loss thanks to them!" The man pointed at the house. "Damn kids!"

"Long live rock and roll," Ryan told him.

As they returned to the truck, Cap told them there was a new dispatcher on duty, thus the probability for the mistake.

He glared at his captain. "Tell that new dispatcher to look up the definition of 'working fire.'"

"Take it easy, Rye," Tom said. "Everyone makes mistakes, especially newbies. At least it wasn't a real disaster."

"Only a musical one," he muttered.

"Could have been worse," Nick called out as he stashed the paramedic gear. "Guy could have been playing your favorite music, which really sucks."

Ryan cuffed his friend.

Did Fern like music? Maybe he should have told her about his collection in the basement of classic vinyl and the vintage record player he'd bought.

They left the homeowner to the police officer who'd arrived on scene. Soon as he climbed back into the truck, they received another call.

It remained like that until around eight o'clock at night. As they finally sat down at the long table to eat the casserole Cap had cooked, Ryan thought about the impromptu meal Fern had tossed together.

He barely heard the talk around the table. Something about the Salt Lake Urban Search and Rescue Team training.

"Ryan, I'm changing your shift later this month. I want you out of the station in training."

Ryan paused in shoveling a forkful of pasta into his mouth. He set it down. "Why?"

"It's time."

"But..."

"It's spring, Rye. Hikers are already taking to the trails." Cap looked at him. "Utah Task Force One is conducting a rope rescue technician course with departments around the state, and you need the practice."

The food congealed in his stomach. "Cap, I have no desire to become a heavy rescue technician with special ops. Or a rescue specialist on the task forces. So why me? Why not Johnson? He's the one angling to join the task forces. He needs this course, not me."

He waved a fork in the other firefighter's direction. Mike Johnson suddenly looked uncomfortable.

"There was one slot open for our department. Mike offered to give it up this time around so you could train. You've been avoiding rope rescues for more than a year, Rye." Cap leaned back, his gaze level.

Suddenly the other guys at the table seemed fascinated in discussing cooking duties for the rest of the week. Ryan pushed back his plate. He knew why Cap did this. Knew it was logical—hell, he'd do the same if he were in charge.

You need the training because you've avoided rope rescues ever since...

Since Kate McIntyre slipped out of your grasp and fell to her death a year ago.

Never could he forget that moment. Apparently, no one else could, either.

"And if I refuse?" he grated out.

Tom glanced at the others. "In my office."

Fine. He had no appetite left, anyway. As he paced Cap's office, his boss sat behind the desk, steepling his fingers.

"Ryan I'll lay it out clear as I can. You undergo this training. It's mandatory, not voluntary. If you refuse, you'll be subject to disciplinary action, probably insubordination and possible termination."

Stunned, he stopped walking. "You'd do that to me after all my years of service?"

"Not that I want it, Rye. I need every man and woman to follow the rules and orders. Most of all, I need all my staff to be ready to respond to canyon rescues. You know the terrain. Hikers get lost in those canyons or stranded in a crevice, and we need every working firefighter in this station to have rope skills."

"I'm a good climber. I have rope skills."

"And you haven't used them since Kate McIntyre died. It's partly my fault." Cap sighed. "I've been too easy on you this last year. That ends today."

Of course it did. It ended just when Fern moved into his house and he was distracted with her presence.

He flexed his hands, remembering how he'd dangled on the rope. Kate was so close, screaming and screaming and then…

Far easier to run into burning buildings with the proper PPE and save people, like he'd saved Fern, than to face the canyons again and risk screwing up once more. Watching another life slip away.

"You're a damn good firefighter, Ryan. You're our senior hazmat technician and I rely heavily on you. Ever think of taking the lieutenant's exam?"

Talk about a one-eighty switch. Ryan braced his hands on the chair before the desk. "Thought about it."

"Think harder. You're terrific in the field, a bit of a hotshot, but you show real leadership potential." Cap pushed back from the desk. "So I'll put your name into the slot for April?"

Despite the trepidation congealing in his stomach, he managed a nod. "I'll be there."

"Good." Cap's expression turned concerned. "How's Fern settling in?"

"Settling in where?" The fewer people knew Fern was staying with him, the better.

"In your house."

Dammit to hell! "How did you hear? Did Bob say anything?"

"Police who set up the plainclothes officer to watch your house informed me as a safety measure in case something happens and we're needed. Relax. No one else at the station knows. It's a need-to-know basis."

Ryan nodded. "Good. The fewer people who know where she is, the better. With her kidnappers still out there, we can't take chances."

"It's a big responsibility. You sure you're okay with it?" Tom picked up a pencil, tapped it on the desk. "You have a lot of work here, Ryan, and your hours are intense."

"You have a better suggestion? Fern doesn't trust anyone, but she trusts me."

"Because you saved her life." Cap stood. "It's your house and your life, Ryan, but as your supervisor and your friend, I caution you to take a step back and not get so involved. Fern probably already has PTSD, anxiety and fear. She needs professional help."

"She's getting counseling, Cap. Right now she needs a friend as well, a place where she feels safe."

"You have to move on, Ryan. Focus on the job, and don't get involved with victims. It's not fair to you, or her. You don't want her getting a rescue crush on you."

Fern wasn't a victim. Calling her one demoralized her and what happened. It wasn't a rescue crush, either, but a woman struggling to recover from a horrific trauma that could have killed her.

He clapped a lid on his rising temper and managed to speak evenly. "Anything else?"

As Tom shook his head, Ryan's phone buzzed. "Gotta take this. It's my sister."

He went outside, confirming with Ava she was going to stay the night with Fern. Ava was a lifesaver, a true help when it came to Fern. Everyone thought the world of her trying to get Fern to recall her memories.

When it came to Fern's welfare, Ryan wished others would have the same confidence in him.

Fern texted Sassy, who agreed to round up art supplies. As Fern waited for her, Ryan texted, asking how she was doing.

Fern texted him back. Your home is comfortable. Do you paint? I saw the picture in the living room of Dark Canyon. Yours?

Naw. Ex-girlfriend painted it from a photo when I went rock climbing with her.

Girlfriend, rock climbing. So normal. Ordinary. Fern sighed. And you kept it?

It's the only thing that goes well with the colors in the living room and it covers a mark on the wall.

She laughed, more from relief than the idea of him being practical over hanging a painting by his ex-girlfriend.

Gotta run. Call coming in. Make sure to order whatever groceries you need. See yah.

She touched the phone, grateful he'd texted. It made her feel less alone.

Her plainclothes police officer knocked on the door, letting her know he still patrolled but would soon go off duty. He introduced her to his replacement. Officer Paul Jenkins was on duty for the next two weeks. He told Fern he'd taken the assignment because he had a special interest in protecting her, and the overtime would come in handy with his wife having a baby in three months.

Knowing Jenkins was close by made her feel safer.

A little while later, Sassy arrived, toting a sketch pad, easel and watercolor paints and black poster board and tape. Never one to easily make friends, or trust anyone, Fern felt pure relief to see her.

Slim and pretty, with dark brown eyes and long dark hair, Sassy was a talented woman who owned the Zephyr Gallery. Impulsively, Fern hugged her, almost making Sassy drop the supplies.

Her friend looked startled, then set down the supplies and hugged her back. Never demonstrative, Fern felt embarrassed. Maybe it was from all the months at the hospital, or simply realizing that after never having any friends or wanting any, people did care and she needed them.

"Where do you want these?"

"I'll take the poster board and tape. It's for a project. The rest I'll put in the basement. Ryan said I could have a space."

Sassy helped her cart the supplies down to the basement. Her friend gave an appreciative look around. "Forgot what this place looked like. Came over quite a while ago when he had a family gathering, but Ryan works so much I barely see him. Where do you want the easel?"

"The corner over there by the bar."

After they arranged the art supplies, Sassy gave her a speculative look. "How's it working out with Ryan?"

"I'll let you know. Not many people know I'm here, so I'd appreciate it..." Her voice trailed off. Remembering the trauma of her kidnapping erased the joy at being able to indulge in art once more.

"I'll be quiet. Glad I can help. When is Mark getting here?"

A notification on her phone indicated someone had rung the smart doorbell. These days everything was smarter than her. Fern glanced at the screen, recognizing Mark from photos. "He's here now. Great timing. Thanks."

Still, she was cautious opening the door, making sure he recited something only Ryan's relatives would know. Mark nodded at her as she let him in. He carried a large bag and looked surprised to see Sassy and hugged her.

"I'll wait in the living room while you both talk," Sassy told her.

Fern looked at Mark, big, strong, steady. She could see a slight family resemblance. Ryan's cousin didn't intend any harm. Like others, he was here to help.

"I know you have to get back to work. I'm fine. You can leave if you wish," she told her.

Sassy squeezed her hand. "I'll be around if you need me. See you, Mark."

Fern watched her leave, knowing Mark was behind her. But to her surprise, instead of watching her, he was checking out the house. He gestured to her.

"Wanted to let you know I have hidden cameras in the living room, kitchen and hallway and the basement."

He escorted her around the house, showing her cameras in picture frames, the hallway smoke detector, a wall clock in the kitchen and a fake book downstairs.

"They're all infrared, so they work in the dark as well," he told her.

"None in the bedroom?" Fern smiled.

He gave her a wry look. "Didn't want to invade your privacy. Or the bathroom."

So serious, unlike Ryan.

"The DVR monitor is hidden in a cabinet in Ryan's office." He took her there and opened the cabinet. "I set everything up but didn't have a chance to tell Ryan about all the details. You can turn off the cameras from the switches in the back if you feel they're too invasive. Also, I want to install a couple of other cameras, one outside the guest bedroom. Heard you had a scare earlier."

Rubbing her arms, Fern nodded. "Guess I'm a little nervous."

His sudden smile relaxed her. "If anyone deserves to be nervous, you do, after everything you went through. How you survived it is a miracle."

Yet another reminder she was a victim. Not that he wasn't nice, but suddenly Fern tired of it. *I'm a real miracle. Then why can't I remember and get my act together?*

"If you want to install those outside cameras, go ahead. If you're hungry, I can get together cheese and crackers, and there's plenty to drink."

"No prob. I'm fine."

She went into Ryan's office to watch the camera monitors. So many of them. Would a security camera have helped stop whoever kidnapped her? The police had investigated closed-circuit cameras and traffic cameras near her home and found nothing. Nada. Nothing to indicate a crime.

I'm the best source for getting any kind of information about the crime. If only my brain would cooperate.

Staying busy might help. She consulted the local grocery site Ryan used for deliveries and began an order.

By the time she finished, Mark came inside. "All set. Come out into the backyard. I need to show you something."

Mark led her outside to the backyard. A mature elm tree sprawled its branches, just beginning to sprout leaves for the spring, over much of the yard. Appreciating the shade, she followed him to two bird feeders erected on a double shepherd's crook set out in dappled sunshine.

He turned one bird feeder toward her. "Smart bird feeders with cameras on 24-7. Low profile—anyone peeking over the fence wouldn't think much of them. Added protection for the outdoor cameras on the house. Solar panels keep the batteries charged and the system works through Wi-Fi. I added a Wi-Fi extender for the feeders and the outdoor cameras, filled the feeders with seeds local birds like. Give me your cell phone and I'll set up the app and all you need."

In no time, she was watching the bird feeders with delight. In the kitchen, she gave him a bottle of water for the road as the doorbell indicated the grocery order was out front.

Mark helped her carry everything inside and put away the groceries. Then he went into the living room, returning with a pink laptop bag.

"The bird feeders aren't the surprise. This is."

Her heart beat faster as she set the pretty pink bag on the kitchen table and unzipped, withdrawing a slim brand-new laptop. Fern stared at him with awe. "This is mine?"

"Yeah. Heard they wouldn't let you have one in the hospital due to security worries about you being tracked or hacked. I set it up with a top-notch antivirus, plus a great VPN, everything you need, and a medical coding software program. Not sure if it's the one you use, but…"

Fern set down the computer and threw her arms around him. "Thank you! This is terrific!"

Pink tinted his cheeks for a minute, then he nodded gravely. "You're quite welcome. I know what it feels like to be cut off."

He looked around the house. "Ryan is a great guy. He could have taken the easy road to money, well, easier, by working with his dad. Instead he chose to put his life on the line all the time as a first responder. We have more in common than some of my other cousins."

He was recently home from the military, Fern remembered.

Like Ryan, Mark served others and had his own experiences and probable brushes with death. Her respect for him grew.

"Thank the good Lord you and Ryan do. Otherwise I might not be here."

Ducking her head to hide her emotions, she opened the laptop. "Can you walk me through it briefly?"

In no time, she had accessed the medical coding software. A memory flickered. "I think I know this program. At any rate, it will keep me busy learning, or relearning. Thank you so much!"

Mark nodded, distant once more. "Thanks for the water. Tell Ryan I said hi and I'll call him."

She locked the door behind him and leaned against it with a happy sigh.

A new laptop, security cameras, plenty of food and her art supplies. Tension slid off her shoulders. Life was looking up.

First, her project. She found scissors—Ryan's junk drawer was surprisingly organized, a fact she appreciated, being an organized person herself—and began to cut the poster board to the correct measurements.

In no time, his bedroom was shrouded in darkness. Only the lamp on his desk cut through the blackness.

Pleased with the results, she put away the supplies and went outside with a pencil and her sketch pad.

Fern sat on the patio, staring at the phone bird app. A notification showed a video of a pretty yellow bird with a black head stopped at a feeder, pecking at the seeds. She pressed the identify button.

American goldfinch.

So soothing, watching a bird go about its business of finding food. Normal. A good reminder life went on. It was cool enough, but not too cold. Perfect for sitting outside and sketching. She took the pad Sassy brought over and moved a chair close enough to the feeders to watch but not scare off birds. Lots of action at the feeders this time of day.

Smiling, she began to draw. This was a good routine to begin reclaiming her life.

A few more goldfinches arrived at the feeder. The colors were amazing, the birds energetic as they fed. Almost absently, she filled in details.

Absorbed in her work, she barely noticed the setting sun. Fern glanced up at the lavender and rose gold streaking the sky behind the mountains near Dark Canyon. Gorgeous colors. Ryan was lucky to have a view of such a magnificent landscape from his backyard.

She went inside to get water and returned with the glass, setting it on the table next to her chair.

As darkness began to shroud the yard, she sat back with a happy sigh. Drawing made her lose track of time and place. Fern clicked on the light app on her phone to view the sketch pad and results.

Birds flying into the sunset, distant mountains that would look terrific with purple shadows. Something else as well. Odd. Small in the right corner.

Fern sipped more water and leaned closer to inspect what she'd drawn. A face, tight and drawn, the mouth in a sneer.

Only her death grip on the cell phone kept her from dropping it. The glass dropped to the concrete patio, shattering the silence. Leaving the canvas outside, Fern jumped up, ran into the house and locked the door. She ran around to all the windows, pulling the shades and making sure everything was locked up.

Sliding down the wall, she hugged her knees.

For a long time, she remained there, her breath coming in a terrified whoosh, her heart racing.

She couldn't be certain, but deep inside she knew.

What she'd drawn was a face recalled from memory.

It could be one of the men who'd kidnapped her.

Chapter 6

After years of fighting fires, Ryan was used to the rush of adrenaline, the clear-eyed focus on the job. Not this call.

It came as darkness fell and set him on instant alert. Riding in the truck, he controlled his breathing, relying on his training.

Residential fire, which meant possible victims inside. Maybe children. Pets.

People often ran back into a burning house to rescue loved ones and pets. These kind of calls, especially at night with limited visibility, were harrowing.

Automatically they went over the information given by the dispatcher. Hydrant close by, good news. Bad news was the house was approaching fully engulfed.

When Engine 69 pulled up to the curb of the scene, he jumped out to hear screams. As Cap began giving orders, a woman ran up to Ryan.

"Please, please hurry! My little girl Carolyn's inside. She insisted on finding Wobbles!"

"Wobbles?" he asked.

"Our dog!"

Damn. Ryan looked at Cap for orders.

Cap nodded. "Ryan, Bob. Primary search."

As the other firefighters got a line on the house and began hosing down the flames, Ryan and Bob donned their self-contained breathing apparatuses, hoods and then their helmets.

Sounds of his own breaths filled his eardrums as Ryan and Bob went into the burning house. Flames shot out the back rooms. Pitch-black inside—even the light on his helmet barely cut the inky darkness, making it hard to see. He heard the guys on the roof, cutting holes in the attic to vent the smoke and heat from the house.

If they didn't find Carolyn soon, the whole ceiling could collapse, trapping them and the girl and her pet. Through the acrid smoke and darkness cut by orange flames, he could see barely anything.

The memory flickered of running into the cabin, finding Fern unconscious on the floor, barely alive. A feeling of panic, erased by automatic professionalism kicking in, as he hauled her over his shoulder to rush outside.

Praying she would be okay.

Carolyn would not die here today. He couldn't let that happen. Not an innocent child who only wanted to rescue her pet.

"Fire department, call out," he yelled. "Carolyn! Fire department!"

"Carolyn! Fire department, call out!" Bob screamed. "Carolyn, where are you?"

Through the roar of the fire, he heard faint sobbing. Holding the portable heat camera, he found a heat sig through the smoke. Carolyn. They ran forward to find her coughing and sitting on the floor of the living room. The fire advanced, getting closer.

Ryan motioned to Bob. But the girl screamed and struggled. "My dog!"

He pushed Bob. "I'll find him. Go!"

Bob grabbed the girl and hauled her outside as Ryan combed the room for the missing dog. Using the camera, he searched through the smoke and saw something on the floor emit a heat signature.

Something with four legs.

He grabbed the animal as the guys trained water on the flames through a broken window in the living room.

Carrying the limp dog, he made it outside. Face blackened, her anxious mother hovering, Carolyn tore off her oxygen mask administered by the paramedics.

"Wobbles!" she sobbed. "Is he alive?"

Ryan grabbed the special pet oxygen mask. The conical shape fit over the dog's snout. Nick ran over to see what he needed.

"Portable O2," he told Nick.

Nick brought over a bottle, and Ryan began administering oxygen to Wobbles.

"I'll take care of Wobbles if you promise to get back to the paramedics and let them help you."

Cap pushed back his helmet and gave him a long look, but the girl stopped sobbing and hovered.

"Is Wobbles gonna be okay?"

He watched the dog's chest rise and fall and nodded.

Regular oxygen masks could deliver less than 20 percent of much-needed oxygen to dogs and cats suffering smoke inhalation. This special mask, which his rig carried, was designed to save the lives of much-loved pets.

At budget time, he'd lobbied to get one per engine, with Cap's backing.

The dog began breathing, and Ryan kept the mask on as the other guys trained water on the flames.

"Thank you," Carolyn whispered. She coughed.

"I've got Wobbles. Now you have to get back to let the paramedics help you, okay?" he told her.

As he kept helping the dog, watching the pet begin to struggle against the unfamiliar mask, Carolyn returned to the rig. Her mother rushed over, tears streaming down her face.

"Thank you. I don't... I don't know how I could live with myself if my daughter died."

"Part of the job." Ryan nodded at the dog. "Wobbles should be on oxygen for at least a few hours due to smoke inhalation. There's an emergency pet hospital not far from here. You need to transport him."

"I have to look after Carolyn."

Ryan looked down at the dog on the ground. "Can a friend or neighbor take him?"

Another woman stepped forward, introducing herself as a neighbor and offered to take the dog. Carrying Wobbles over to her car, he waited for her to open the sedan's back door.

"I'm Carrie Armstrong," the woman told him. "I'll make sure he gets to the hospital."

"Keep the mask on him, and I'll drop by the hospital later to retrieve it," he advised.

He felt good about saving the dog. Yeah, some people might say that it was only an animal, but he did not. Carolyn would recover quicker, and the loss of her home was bad enough without compounding it with the loss of a beloved pet.

The neighbor took a long look at him. "I know you. You're that firefighter who was on duty when they brought in Kate McIntyre from Dark Canyon. I saw you at the hospital when they brought her in and tried to revive her."

His stomach gave a sickening lurch. "You knew her?"

"She was my student at the climbing school," Carrie told him. "Horrible what happened."

Gone was any sense of feel-good emotions, replaced by a swarm of fresh guilt. Ryan placed the dog in the back of the woman's car. "Remember, keep the mask on him."

He slammed the back door and walked off.

"Good save, Rye," Cap told him.

"It was okay. Bob got the girl."

Shrugging, he watched the car drive away, feeling like a total loser.

Cap noticed and pointed to the engine. "Rye, fire's almost out. Why don't you stand by and help with the overhaul?"

Simply because a blaze was extinguished didn't mean they finished. The overhaul was tough labor, tearing down walls and sifting through debris to make sure everything was extinguished. Last thing they wanted was for the fire to rekindle.

"Sure. Guess I'm good for that." He glanced at his captain. "That woman taking the dog to the hospital? She was there when Kate McIntyre was brought in."

Cap issued an order into his shoulder mic and turned to him.

"How many times do we have to tell you, Ryan? Kate's death wasn't your fault," Cap said gently. "Nothing could have saved her. This is why you never get involved with a victim, Rye."

A reminder he should not be involved with Fern as well. Ryan's mind reeled.

He saved a dog. Why the hell couldn't he have saved Kate that day in Dark Canyon? Was he also making a mistake by getting involved with Fern and trying to help her, and in the end, he would hurt her as well?

Fern couldn't move. All she could do was grip her legs, huddled into a corner of the living room. Flashes of memory zinged by, a man with a baseball bat hovering above her, his face twisted in rage...

Gonna get you, bitch, for doing that. You'll regret it. No one messes with me.

Pain exploding in her leg, her cries turning into screams...

Darkness shrouded the entire house. When the doorbell rang, she still couldn't move, or talk, only listen to the sounds of her breath coming in and out in little whispering pants. Helpless.

If someone broke inside, she was toast. Fern tried to move and could not budge.

She'd left her phone outside with the smart doorbell notifications. Anyone could be at the door. A delivery person, Ava or a serial killer. But she couldn't move. Fern managed to pull her arms away from her legs. Nothing more.

The doorknob rattled and she heard the door creak open.

"Fern? It's Ava. I'm coming in. Are you okay? I have a key to the house and I'm coming inside. Can you call out?"

Somehow she managed to find her voice. "Here."

A light snapped on. More lights. Ava's sweet, wonderful face came into view as her counselor squatted down in front of her.

"Hi, honey. I'm here. Would you like a cup of chamomile tea?"

Tea. So normal and ordinary. Something a friend would offer upon coming over, a friend who would find the house's guest greeting her with a smile, not cowering in a corner, terrified of her own shadow.

Fern shook her head and flexed her fingers. Slightly numb, but working.

"May I help you to stand?" Ava asked.

Fern managed to lift her hand. Ava gently helped her get upright, letting her lean against the wall.

Ava went into the living room and patted the sofa. "Come, sit by me. Ryan's couch is much more comfortable than his floor."

Fern swallowed hard and got to her feet, her legs feeling like cooked noodles. She made it to the sofa, sitting at the far end. This drill was familiar. Ava was trying to establish a safe space. Glancing at the clock on the fireplace mantle made her startle. It was well after seven at night.

How long had she been sitting in the dark, too terrified to move?

Some progress.

"How do you like my brother's house? He may be a bachelor, but he did a great job decorating."

Hard to breathe. Think.

Ava looked at her. "Remember your exercises, Fern. Breathe. In. Out. Remember your mantras."

Fern took a deep breath and did what she asked. *You're safe now. This is a safe space. You are in control. No one is going to hurt you or make you do anything you don't want to do.*

A few minutes later, she felt well enough to talk. "It—it's a nice house. I like it."

"I remember when he bought it. Our dad was appalled he spent money on such a fixer-upper. But Ryan's done a great job restoring it."

Seems like your brother enjoys restoring things, and maybe I'm one of them? Fern took another deep breath.

"I know I locked the door. I'm glad you have a key, Ava."

Ava pulled out a key fob. "Ryan gave me a house key back in the days when I helped him with a furniture delivery when he was on shift. I kept it."

Her impish grin helped Fern relax a little more.

"Can you go outside? I left my cell phone there and my sketch pad. You need to see what I drew."

Ava glanced at her. "You okay with me leaving you alone right now?"

Nodding, Fern pushed a hank of hair behind her ear, her hand less shaky now. She focused her attention on a photo of Ryan and his family on the fireplace mantle. Normal and ordinary.

Ordinary was good. Could she ever feel ordinary again? Have a home of her own and a job, without fearing her own shadow?

When Ava brought it back, Fern felt enough in control of her body and her mental state. She took the sketch pad from Ava.

"I like it here. Your brother is kind, and I deeply appreciate what he's doing for me. So is your cousin—he brought me a laptop. I feel safe here."

"That's terrific, Fern. What did you want to show me?"

Grateful her hands no longer shook, Fern set the pad down on the coffee table and pointed to it. "This. I was drawing the birds outside and before I realized it, I drew this face. It—it scared me so much I ran inside and I couldn't move. Why did I do this?"

Ava studied the drawing. "You feel safe and you're more in control of your emotions. By relaxing, your traumatic memories are returning. It's rather like getting ideas when you're in the shower."

Fern shuddered. "Some idea. Should we call the police?"

Ava nodded. "I'm proud of you for thinking like this, Fern. You're getting stronger."

Stronger, when all she could do was huddle in the corner? She didn't feel stronger, but right now, she'd take all the encouragement she could receive.

"Have you been keeping up with making your lists of things you're looking forward to once you regain your memory?" Ava asked.

"No." Words stuck in her throat. She found it hard to think of something so ordinary as making a list when a cruel face stared at her from the confines of the sketch pad.

"How about we put the kettle on and make a cup of hot chocolate and then call the police? I know how much you enjoy hot chocolate."

Fern gave her a wry look. "You're trying to talk me off the ledge."

"You're already off the ledge. I'm merely giving you fortification for when you talk to Jacob, since he's lead on the case. Speaking of which, do you have any food? I came straight from work and I'm starved. Make something you like and we can eat together."

Minutes later, Ava had called Jacob and Fern had made a charcuterie board with cheddar cheese, Brie, prosciutto, grapes and whole wheat crackers. They sat in the kitchen, drinking hot chocolate and grazing.

"Is the drawing a good indication my memory is returning?"

Fern asked after eating a bite of Brie. She turned over the sketch pad, not wanting to see that face unless absolutely necessary.

"Could be. It's important, but we can't be sure what kind of memory is returning until we discover who you drew."

Toying with a grape, she shook her head. "I feel bad for Ryan. He was nice enough to offer me a place to stay and get back to normal, but looks like my normal is far from normal."

"Stop it. You are normal, Fern. You're strong, remember?"

"You sound like your brother."

Ava smiled. "He's one of a kind. Hero complex."

"I don't think so. I think he's terrific, and thank God he is a hero or I wouldn't be alive today," she burst out.

Blinking, Ava gave a little smile. Fern's suspicions flowered. "You baited me into revealing how I feel about staying here."

"Perhaps. Do you feel safe staying here or would you rather return to the hospital?"

Fern knew regaining her independence remained a priority in her recovery. Independence meant regaining her memory as well, and in the hospital with everyone hovering, she couldn't focus on anything except the trauma and fear.

"I like it here for now," she said with caution. "Ryan has been a most generous host. Do you want to know my feelings about that?"

The last sentence she uttered with a little sarcasm, because much as she liked Ava, everything was subject to analysis. Ava knew she was being baited, judging from her expression.

"Right now we need to focus on you and this drawing. It could be a major clue to your memory returning."

Some memories she might not want to return. Though she didn't recall every detail, Fern knew her past was shady. She drank heavily as a teen and finally got herself straightened out, thanks to understanding foster parents and Alcoholics Anonymous. At least with Belle, her sponsor at AA, she'd learned to forgive herself.

But forgiving herself didn't mean she wanted those memories back any more than she wanted to be the old drunk Fern again, drowning her sorrows in a bottle of cheap vodka.

"If it's a memory from my questionable past, I'd rather not have that one back. I do want to help find the jerks who did this to me and stop them from hurting another woman."

Ava sipped her hot chocolate and set it down. "Those memories, good and bad, are part of you, Fern. You can't simply put them away in a locker and pretend they don't exist. You can help heal from them, but you have to acknowledge them first."

Fern sighed. "You make sense, but that doesn't make it easy."

"It never is. It's hard work putting your life back together. But it's worth it, Fern. You're worth it. Never forget that."

One reason she liked and trusted Ava was the woman had been frank and upfront with her from the beginning. Ava told her about the types of therapy she wanted to try to help Fern.

"What's the next step in my therapy?" she asked. "You mentioned a desensitization approach, getting me to return to the place where I was held. Must we?"

"One step at a time. The fact that you feel strong enough to live outside the hospital is an important first step to your recovery of your memory."

Ava gave another of her million-dollar reassuring smiles. "Now, while we wait for Jacob, why don't you show me the new laptop Mark gave you?"

Food had fortified her, and by the time she showed Ava the laptop, Jacob rang the doorbell. Confidence filled her. Maybe the face she'd drawn was an important clue to her kidnapping.

While Ava made coffee for Jacob, who asked for the caffeine, Fern talked with him. Odd how now she felt more comfortable with him at Ryan's house than at the hospital.

"I was sketching the birds and sunset and didn't realize I drew this face." Fern handed Jacob the pad. "I'm sure it's a guy from my past, only I don't know who he is. But the image was so scary it immobilized me for quite a while with fear, so whoever it is, he sure isn't Santa Claus."

Jacob flashed a rare smile. "Some kids are terrified of Santa." He studied the sketch. "Great detail. You couldn't remember anything about him, anything else such as hair color, or identifying marks?"

"I wish I knew." Fern rubbed her head. "I think it was one of the guys who hurt me, but I can't be certain. My memory is still fuzzy."

Jacob nodded. "May I take this? I can make a copy, run it through the national database to see what pops up."

What if it were a face from her past and not the man who'd abducted her? "One thing really bothers me. I lived in Oso. How did the kidnappers know where to find me? I mean, I don't live around here or near the place I was found, so…"

Jacob exchanged glances with Ava. "It wasn't by chance, Fern. Whoever took you had been observing you for some time and waited for the right moment."

A chill raced down her spine. Any semblance of feeling safe and confident fled. "Someone was stalking me, you mean. I'm no one special."

Jacob sipped his coffee before answering slowly. "That's what we're trying to determine. But you fit the profile. You don't have family or many friends. You're a loner."

Her lower lip wobbled, and she fought her emotions. "You mean because I like being alone I was a target for these monsters?"

"We can't tell for certain. It's an ongoing investigation."

Cop talk. They all talked like that, in circles. She pressed a finger to her temple, suddenly wishing Ryan were there to help her find her center. Ava was great, and she trusted her, but Ava's motive was to help her recall her memory.

If drawing a face from memory wrung out all the terror

stuffed deep inside her, why would she want to regain those memories?

"Maybe you're both wrong. What if this guy I drew wasn't the kidnapper, but someone I liked?"

Ava shook her head. "Fern do you think you would have had such a violent reaction if it was someone you liked? Let Jacob do his job. We have to determine if this is one of the men who kidnapped you."

She didn't like the speculative look Ava gave her. "Or what? Who else could it be?"

"Someone from your past, perhaps. Someone you don't want to recall, but on a subconscious level, you did. We need to do some tests to make sure," Ava told her.

Somehow she knew what this meant. "You mean hypnosis."

At Ava's nod, she sighed. "I want to undergo hypnosis. I want to help. Can't you understand that I want to do anything I can to find these guys so no other woman will get hurt?"

"Then we can set up the session as soon as possible. Day after tomorrow okay?" Ava asked. "I promise I'll be there the entire time."

"Can Ryan be there as well?"

Blinking, Ava glanced at Jacob. "If you want and he agrees and isn't working."

Ryan's presence would give her a sense of balance, of backup. Right now she needed stability in this upside-down world.

A few minutes later Jacob left with Ava promising to call him with a time for the hypnosis. Ava helped her clear the table.

"I need to get my overnight case from the car," Ava told her.

Fern took a deep breath. "I don't need you to spend the night with me, Ava. I'll be fine."

Ava frowned. "Fern, you've had a scare…"

"I'll have more of them in the future. I need to start being on my own. There's plenty of security cameras, and I have a phone, plus Officer Jenkins two doors down from here."

"Are you sure? It's not a problem for me to remain here until Ryan gets home."

"I'm positive. Besides, I need the space. If I need you I can call you. You know I have your number."

Ava nodded. "I'm proud of you, Fern. You've made a lot of progress, and the hypnosis may seem intimidating, but it's a huge step forward in your recovery."

When Ava left, Fern finished doing the dishes and tidied up. Though it wasn't even ten o'clock, she felt exhausted. After making sure the house was locked up, checking the DVR to see the cameras functioning, she got ready for bed. Control was important to her therapy, so Ava had helped her pick out a cute pair of pink and yellow floral pajamas.

Yet an hour later, she still lay in bed, unable to sleep.

Try as she might, she couldn't relax. The unfamiliar surroundings unnerved her. But she wasn't going to capitulate and call Ava.

On impulse she went into Ryan's bedroom and grabbed his pillow. Fern brought it back to her bed, hugging it, breathing in his scent, and felt herself finally begin to relax.

She wasn't crushing on Ryan. Nope. Not at all.

The hypnosis session hovered in the future like a mandatory root canal. What would happen when her memory returned and she found out about all her past?

Fern dreaded knowing.

Chapter 7

Because he needed to work a full twenty-four-hour shift, Ryan didn't get home the following day until noon. His stomach grumbled, reminding him he hadn't eaten since the previous night. Breakfast had been abandoned for a car crash, and by the time they returned to the station, he had no desire for whatever congealed mess was left on his plate.

He rang the doorbell and spoke into it to alert Fern he was home because she certainly didn't need any more frights.

"Ryan! Please, can you use your key? I'm in the kitchen."

Dare he hope she might have ordered food, something simple he could use to whip up a quick meal? Smells of something delicious wafted from the kitchen. After locking the door, he followed his nose.

Fern stood at the oven, beaming. She wore a red-and-white-polka-dot dress that looked faded and worn, and had tied around her waist the apron his sister had given him as a gag gift one birthday.

It read If Something is Burning, Call the Fire Department. Wait, That's Only Me Grilling.

It was such a domestic scene that he had to blink to make sure it wasn't a dream, because lately, he'd thought about what life would be like to have someone waiting for him at home after a tiring twenty-four hours.

"I figured you'd be hungry after your shift and made a

chicken, potato and vegetable casserole. It's been warming in the oven."

Would it look impolite if he salivated all over the floor? Ryan's stomach gave an appreciative grumble. He felt embarrassed, but she nodded.

"As I thought. I've been monitoring your police radio, and I know how busy you've been. Sit down. Would you like decaf tea or sparkling water? I saw you had some water in the fridge."

"I can get it."

"No, sit, relax, please."

Soon they were both sitting at the kitchen table, Ryan with a sparkling water and Fern with tea as they dug into her casserole. He moaned as he tasted it.

"Whoa, this is amazing. Thank you so much, but you didn't have to do it. Honestly, Fern, I don't expect you to do anything for me."

"I was hungry as well, and it's a waste of good food to make a casserole for one." Her cute, pert nose wrinkled. "Or make one of those frozen meals you have, that are probably petrified by now."

All he'd had time for lately was cooking a frozen dinner. "Fern, cooking for me is not…"

"Please, Ryan."

The soft plea in her voice made him glance at her. "What's wrong?"

"I need to do this. Establish some kind of routine. I've felt so lost for months, and this feels good. Normal. I enjoy cooking. Please don't tell me not to do it."

Never had he thought about a simple task helping her. Ryan nodded. "As long as you let me clean up."

She smiled. "Deal."

He asked about her day and how it went with Mark. Fern toyed with her casserole. Finally she glanced up.

"I heard you saved a life again in a fire," she told him.

Ryan shrugged. "Bob was the hero, saving the little girl, Carolyn."

"You're the hero. I'm sure Carolyn would have been devastated without her pet. You helped her as much as your coworker did."

"Guess so." He shook his head. "Then there are the ones I can't save, as much as I try. Those are the ones who haunt me, the ones I can never forget. Is it worth it?"

Fern's gaze remained steady. "Every shift you're out there, Ryan, fighting the good fight. Sometimes the end result isn't what you want, or hope or pray for. You did your best, and you have to leave it behind so you can fight another day."

Seeing him stare at her, she flushed and added, "At least that's what I had always believed when I was getting my act together. There were days when I didn't think it was worth it to get up the next day. Good people convinced me to never give up."

"I'm glad they were there for you," he said, meaning it.

"I don't mean to be a conversational downer, but I need to tell you about the sketch I did."

He ate while listening, letting her talk in halting sentences, not pushing her, knowing it had to be tough to talk about it.

She finished and added, "I told your sister I'll do the hypnosis tomorrow afternoon, but only if you're there. I—I am sorry to involve you, but I'd feel safer."

"Hey, no problem." Ryan drank some water. "Be happy to help. I don't have plans. I work a 24/72 shift, so I'm off for the next three days. I have some stuff lined up, but those appointments are flexible."

Instead of looking relieved, lines etched her forehead. "You need to know…it's not going to be pretty, Ryan. Because as I understand, from what I researched on hypnosis on my new laptop your cousin was kind enough to give me, the memories recalled may not be cut-and-dried, but stuff from my…ah, murky past."

"I understand."

"I wasn't a Girl Scout. Not even close. Much as I wanted to be one, it wasn't my destiny." She gave a grudging laugh that nearly broke his heart because he sensed the pain the laugh hid.

"So it could get ugly, and if you feel uncomfortable being there, please, let me know. I'll do fine with Ava. I trust her. Even your cousin Jacob, well, he's starting to grow on me." She laughed again. "Not like a fungus, either."

Such a great sense of humor, considering what she'd been through. Yet another display of Fern's courage.

After they ate, he insisted on helping her clean up. Soon as the dishwasher was loaded, he felt the crash coming on him.

"I need some sleep." He yawned. "Sorry to ditch you."

She nudged him toward his bedroom. "I have a surprise for you."

What kind of surprise? Normally a woman indicating a surprise in the bedroom turned him on. Not with Fern and what she'd endured. He liked her, and part of him wanted to know her better, but an intimate relationship was a bad idea.

For now.

When he walked into his bedroom, Ryan's jaw dropped. Blackout shades, sort of. He wanted to jump up and down with pleasure, except he was too damn exhausted.

He walked around the bedroom. Not only had she put up blackout shades, but she'd changed the sheets. Fresh sheets! A sense of happiness swept over him, along with vague unease. Did she think he expected this of her?

"Thank you." He turned and saw her hanging by the door, a little hesitant as if she disliked intruding.

"Fern, you don't have to do this. You're not the housekeeper, and I don't want you feeling like you have to cook or clean or do things for me."

Her eyes looked solemn. "I know. But that's what friends do for each other, right? I mean, it's been a long time since anyone cared about my welfare, and I wanted to help you out however I could. It's not a big deal, Ryan. Not compared to you sharing your home with me, which is something I can never repay you for."

She gave a pretty little sigh. "Let's not even mention how you saved my life, in more ways than one."

He would have liked to continue the convo, but suddenly the meal and the drop in his adrenaline nudged aside all desire to talk.

"We'll talk about this later." He yawned.

"Sleep as long as you like. I'll be downstairs in the basement. Night."

When she closed the door behind her, he undressed to his boxers, snapped off the lamp and crept between the freshly washed sheets. She'd even used fabric softener so they smelled a little like the outdoors he loved.

Fern smelled like that, he realized as he closed his eyes. Flowers and sunshine.

Ryan fell asleep, drifting into a dream of a field of flowers, Fern scampering through them and laughing, erasing the dark shadows from her pretty eyes.

By the time he woke, it was well after six. Ryan yawned, stretched and dressed in sweats and a T-shirt, hoping Fern was okay. He felt bad for abandoning her, but damn, he had been tired.

Thanks to her efforts, he slept the best he had in weeks.

He found her downstairs, painting. Fern looked absorbed in her work. Much as he hated to disturb her, he needed to exercise.

"Thanks to you, I slept great. Sorry to bother you, but I need to work out."

Fern wiped her hands with a rag. "No bother. I need to get my PT done as well. Mind if I use the treadmill?"

"Go ahead. Today's my weight day." He looked at the weights. "Let's get down to business."

As an incentive, he put a vinyl record on the vintage player. The eighties music made her laugh, and she began walking faster to the beat.

The music accompanied the weights going up and down on his machine and the treadmill's hum. Having a pretty woman work out alongside him pushed him a little further.

One reason he'd never worked out with past girlfriends. Ryan knew how easy it was to overdo it by showing off.

He took it down a notch, focusing on his breathing and reps, only to glance up and realize Fern did the same. Ignoring him, centering her concentration on her own cardio.

Finally she climbed off, panting. "Wow, I'm really out of shape. Need a break."

Though he could keep going, Ryan decided it was a good idea to stop. He chugged the water he'd brought downstairs while Fern drank the sports drink she had by the easel.

He should really push himself today, though. Knowing he had rope training presented him with a good incentive. Ryan returned to the weights as Fern began painting again.

By the time he finished with his reps, Fern was absorbed in her work. Curious, he set the weights down, wiped off the sweat and went over to her.

"Mind if I see?" he asked.

Fern shrugged. "It's not good. More therapeutic than pretty."

She'd painted the orange twists and turns of Dark Canyon, with a burning yellow sun overhead.

"I remember this much," she said slowly. "It was cold, oh so cold. I could see the canyons rising above me, like prison walls. I remember I always enjoyed hiking there and now…"

Setting down her paintbrush, she took a deep breath. "Talk to me about something else. Are you always this dedicated with weightlifting?"

"Part of the job and training. I have to keep up with my workouts." He returned to the bench and sat. "My gear, just the turnout stuff like the helmet, coat, pants, gloves, weighs about fifty pounds, and the SCBA…"

At her puzzled look, he explained. "Self-contained breathing apparatus, which I use to breathe in a fire. That weighs around thirty pounds. Then you add in the equipment to get people out, like an axe…"

When he finished, Fern's eyes widened. "Wow. You gain about seventy-five pounds by fighting fires. No wonder you have to keep in shape."

With a rueful look, she glanced down. "Especially when you have to carry someone as heavy as me out of a burning building."

"Hey. Stop that. You're beautiful."

The skepticism on her face angered him. Why did women who weren't model thin think they were fat? Fern had gorgeous curves.

"I need to lose weight."

He walked over to her and touched her cheek. "You need to focus on yourself, regaining your memory and not losing weight. You're perfect the way you are."

Silence. Fern kept staring at him as if he were an alien dropped down from outer space. Ryan dropped his hand and backed away. Maybe this physical proximity proved too much for her.

"Please don't call me perfect. It's not a good word. Perfect to everybody means there is nothing wrong. It's a high standard to maintain."

"I never thought about that."

"I have, only because I've tried being perfect. It's exhausting. Being perfect in foster care with the first two families who took me in. Tried to be as little trouble as possible. Made my own meals, helped with the laundry, never complained, tried to do well in school, even picked up after my foster brothers and sisters. Well, perfect didn't cut it."

Ryan listened. Much as he wanted to provide comfort, he could not.

"If I helped with laundry, I used the wrong fabric softener. If I made meals, I wasted food and got yelled at for disrupting their plans. Perfect is a huge responsibility. No matter how hard you try, you can't be perfect because something always goes wrong and you get punished for it. I learned to settle for average and hopeful."

With all the family problems he thought plagued him, it was nothing compared to Fern's past. His father nagging him to find a better career, make more money, join the business was little compared to getting punished for trying your best.

"Thank you," he said quietly. "Thank you for sharing that. I've always tried to be the perfect firefighter. You're right. It is a hard standard to maintain, almost impossible."

Her expression brightened. "You are a great firefighter. You have courage and an amazing skill set. I'd say if anyone was close to perfect, you were."

Tension filled the air, a sweet tension he didn't mind. The impish light returned to her eyes.

"Of course, since you're a man you can't be perfect because you don't ask for directions. Men never do."

"I have a good GPS." He puffed out his chest in pretend outrage. "Men *are* perfect."

At her eye roll, he laughed. "Back to work."

Glad things were right between them again, he returned to the bench press. He didn't want to make her uncomfortable, but weight issues with women upset him. Too many of them judged themselves by impossible standards.

Fern went to the treadmill and sighed. "You're very sweet. And you are right about my weight. It's the least of my troubles for now."

Time to change the subject. "How's the leg? You okay on that setting?"

"Slow and steady. My PT gave recommendations, which I plan to follow." Fern glanced at him, and he saw grit and determination on her face. "Eventually I'll be strong enough to run if those bastards try taking me again. I don't ever plan on being a victim again."

You're not a victim. Words stuck in his throat. No matter how many times he told her, Fern wouldn't believe it.

She had to make herself believe it first.

Chapter 8

Hypnosis wasn't a cure to recovering all her memories, Ava told her. They sat in an office with the hypnotherapist the following day. Neutral colors and a comfortable cream-colored sofa and armchair soothed her, in addition to the presence of Ryan. Jacob and Ava sat in chairs at the edge of the room.

Usually, an audience would unnerve her. Not now, with her on the fringe of recovering what her mind refused to remember.

Brenda, the hypnotherapist, had a kind face and professional air. "My job is to help you recall memories your mind buried, Fern, but there are no guarantees. Memories are tricky things. You may recall false memories or even change existing ones. It's not foolproof, but I'm going to work with you to avoid any false memories your mind conjures to protect yourself.

"Think of hypnosis as adjunctive therapy to what you're undergoing with Ava. I want you to relax. I can't make you do anything against your will. Only help you. You're in a safe place."

A wry smile touched her mouth. "You can't make me bark like a dog? Or you can only make me bark like a big dog and not a yapper?"

A chuckle from Ryan, a censuring look at him from Ava. Brenda smiled. "No barking. Now I want you to sit back and get comfortable."

Fern settled on the armchair, leaning back against the scatter pillows. She propped her feet up on the ottoman.

"I'm going to do progressive relaxation induction, Fern. It's a method of helping you completely relax. Take three deep breaths and close your eyes," Brenda told her.

Though her heart raced and her palms felt clammy, she did so.

"Now I want you to think of someplace calm and serene that brings you joy…"

Brenda's soothing voice washed over her like a gentle rain. Gradually Fern felt the relaxation spread from her toes, up to her head. On and on Brenda's voice droned like the hum of rain on a tin roof.

She heard suggestions. Brenda nudging her to return to the place where she'd been held captive, reassuring her she was safe and nothing and no one could hurt her…

Fern stepped back into time and memory.

A face, sneering and ugly, looming over her. Had to protect herself because no one else was there for her. Bill. Going to hurt her, stifle her screams. Fight back! But immobilized with terror, she couldn't move, her body wouldn't cooperate. Legs that kicked and ran were useless.

Something hard and cruel descending. Pain exploded in her legs.

She tried to scream, nothing came out. Felt like someone wrapped her in chains.

I'm going to die.

Fern opened her mouth to scream. A voice called out as if from a distance, commanding her to wake up.

Wake up, Fern!

Her eyes flew open. Ryan staring at her. Ava concerned. Jacob grim. Brenda composed, but worried.

Judging from their expressions, she'd stunned them.

Stunned herself as well. Fern studied her hands, unable to lift her gaze.

"It wasn't one of the guys who kidnapped me. The man I

remembered was one of my mother's boyfriends. The guy in the sketch I did. Bill. He—he...wanted to hurt me when I was ten. Same name as the kidnapper I remembered. Guess I got confused."

She gave a little laugh. Laughter was a good self-defense. "You'd think the guy who kidnapped me would have the courtesy of having a different name so I could keep them straight."

"Fern, it's going to be okay." Ryan's voice was gentle.

Shame crept over her. "I... I'm sorry it didn't work."

Then words failed her once more. The memories she recalled were dark and grim, but of little use to the case.

For she had recalled parts of a childhood she had desperately tried to forget.

Ava asked to speak to him in private before they left.

He had a bad feeling about this. Ryan followed his sister into the hallway and closed the door, leaving Fern alone with Jacob and the hypnotherapist. Much as he loved his sister, she tended to worry too much about him. Like their mother and father did.

Maybe if I chose a career selling pre-owned vehicles, they'd be happier.

"What's going on? You weren't expecting this to be magic and suddenly Fern would recall everything and everyone would live happily ever after."

Ava gave him a level look. "Please stop the sarcasm. You're insulting her profession, and mine."

"Sorry," he muttered.

"I had a talk with Mom and Dad. They're worried about Fern living with you, and after what happened, I tend to agree with them. Dad has offered to pay money to put Fern in a rental house with round-the-clock security. They've already leased the home."

What? His parents, especially his dad, had sometimes interfered in his life, but never to this extent. "You agreed with them? Since when did you start taking their side against me?"

Ava assumed what he thought of as her "counselor face," the smooth look she gave clients. He'd seen her give it to Fern. No trace of what she was feeling, enabling the patient to express their own emotions without being influenced by Ava's.

"Ryan, it's not a matter of taking sides. They're worried about Fern staying with you because of the trauma she suffered."

First his captain at the fire station, now his family. Was everyone against Fern being around him?

The woman *had* suffered tremendous stress. It deeply bothered him that people in his circle were more concerned with his welfare and not hers.

"Listen, Ava, I'm not the one who was held captive in a wood shack and left to starve and then burn to death. Show a little sympathy for Fern, will you?"

"Ryan, I have a great deal of sympathy, and compassion, for Fern. If I didn't, I wouldn't be working so hard to help her."

Sensing the frustration in her higher-pitched voice, he sighed. "I know."

"Fern has a dark past and psychological issues, ones you may not be able to handle with her in the house when you're alone."

"You make her sound like a serial killer."

A withering look from Ava had him regret the words. "It's for her sake as well, Ryan. Have you ever heard of bonds formed over trauma?"

Now it was his turn to scowl. "I'm a firefighter, sis. It happens. People I rescue form attachments. Romantic ones. Common with first responders. We're seen as their saviors. Usually it's women who eye me as a romantic partner. Since I've rescued their lives, I'll automatically make them feel better about everything else. It never lasts, and I know how to handle it."

"You can handle it professionally through your work. But

now you're living with the woman you rescued. It's altogether different, Ryan."

Couldn't argue with that. He knew it as well, had known it from the moment he'd considered asking Fern to occupy his guest room.

Yet Fern was different. Not clingy or starry-eyed because he'd risked his life to save hers, even though that was his job. Quiet and self-effacing, and strong, she didn't cling, as Mom put it, "like a kitten climbing the drapes."

Something about the woman pulled at him. Though he couldn't be certain it wasn't his desire to set her life right after such a devastating experience, he also knew it went much deeper.

Ava scrutinized him. He hastened to reassure her. "Look, I appreciate your concern…"

"No, you don't. You want me to butt out." She shook her head. "You have that same stubborn look you had when we were much younger, and you insisted you were firstborn and Mom and Dad found me in a bin in a secondhand store because no way we were related."

He had to grin at the memory. "Yeah. I do want you to butt out. In a nice way. In return, I promise if I feel like Fern staying with me is detrimental to either of us, I'll make safe, alternative arrangements for her."

"Not in a secondhand store, I hope."

Ah, there was his sister's good humor. He put an affectionate arm around her shoulder. "Nope. Fern and I are friends. Nothing more."

"Are you off next Saturday night or do you work?"

"Off." He mentally went over his schedule. "For now, unless an emergency arises, like a hazmat fire."

"Good. Then come to dinner at Mom and Dad's next Saturday night. It will set their minds at ease."

He wondered about that. "As long as they can keep it quiet

that Fern's staying with me. I won't risk anyone finding out, not with her kidnappers still roaming free."

"They will. Mom said it's only family. Chay and Ella Grace will be there, of course."

This was a good opportunity to show his parents his relationship with Fern was merely friendship, as well as set their minds at rest. Once they got to know Fern, with her quiet strength and humility, he was certain they'd like her.

"Okay. We'll be there. Can't wait to see Ella Grace again. Now, will you quit worrying about me and focus all your concerns on your fiancé? He's the man in your life who deserves the attention."

The radiant glow on Ava's face assured him love was real. For a fleeting moment he envied his sister. His relationships were always brief and shallow. He longed for deeper.

"How *is* Ella Grace?" Ryan felt a tinge of guilt he hadn't spent much time with Ava's soon-to-be adopted daughter, his only niece. At least this family dinner would resolve that issue.

For a few moments Ava raved about the little girl, who'd been found abandoned at the fire station. Then she glanced at the closed door.

"Fern must wonder what we're doing out here. Take her home, keep an eye on her. Even though her memories haven't returned, a few may, now that hypnosis has occurred."

Like shaking loose rocks and setting off an eventual avalanche? He hoped not. "I can handle it."

Ryan dropped a quick kiss on Ava's cheek. "Thanks for caring," he said, meaning it.

She gave him a look far wiser than her years. "Odd. I was about to tell you the same thing regarding Fern."

During the entire drive home, Fern had been quiet. The hypnosis had shaken her up, and Ryan knew what she needed. Fern could use a dose of normal and ordinary. Not being poked and prodded and examined like a bug under a microscope.

He enlisted her help chopping vegetables for dinner, teasing her about how she liked cutting the tomatoes into quarters instead of halves. He liked the becoming blush tinting her cheeks, and when she teased him back about the lack of greens, Ryan felt relief she finally relaxed.

"My parents invited us over to dinner next Saturday. Ava, Chay and their baby will be there. You game?" he asked.

Fern looked doubtful. "Are you sure they want me there? You don't have to bring me, Ryan. It's your family, and you probably want alone time with them."

Always considerate. He gently gripped her shoulders. "I'm certain. Come to dinner. My mom is a terrific cook and you'll get to meet baby Ella Grace. She's a sweetheart."

She bit her lower lip. "If you're certain…"

"I am." He gave her an encouraging smile. "It will be fine."

Fern gave a little nod, though doubt remained on her face.

After a healthy dinner of grilled chicken, spices, corn and roasted tomatoes, Ryan asked her about watching a movie with him. Fern looked delighted.

"I'd love it."

"I'll make the popcorn. You choose the movie," he told her.

"If your popcorn skills are as good as dinner, you've got a deal."

Soon they were in the living room, and Fern picked up the remote to turn on the television.

"There's a rom-com on the DVR. Can't go wrong with that."

"Chick flick."

"Oh yeah? What's your preference? I didn't see any NASCAR or monster truck smash shows on. Or do you prefer some chest-pounding guy reality show where they run through the woods naked and try to make dinner from squishy bugs?"

At her teasing tone, he grinned. "How about the fishing channel?"

Her expression fell and he laughed.

Her eyes sparkled. "Besides this one is about an unwanted houseguest so you can identify with the main character."

"You're not unwanted," he protested, reaching for a handful of popcorn.

"And you don't have a house in the Hamptons. Lucky you. If you lived there, I'd probably never leave."

She laughed as he tossed a piece of popcorn at her. Fern put the kernel on the table and flicked on the remote. She scrolled through the channel guide.

"Hey, here's something on live television. A special on Ireland. You game?"

At his nod, they settled in to watch. Ryan felt a sense of peace. Hell, he hadn't been this comfortable with a woman in a long time. Dates, yeah, he'd dated plenty. But relationships were not easy, mainly because when the women realized he was a dedicated firefighter who sometimes went into burning buildings and faced a risk of not returning, well, they said their goodbyes.

Not that he blamed them. Except for Kim, his last girlfriend, he'd settled for having fun, casual dates and breaking it off when he sensed the women grew distant. Better for everyone.

With Fern he didn't feel the need to excuse his job. She understood what it was like at the end of a tiring shift, when all he needed was his bed and sleep, not dancing all night or being someone's arm candy at a party. Forget modesty. He knew he was good-looking, which attracted women.

Fern didn't seem to care about his looks. She did seem to care about his welfare, and it was refreshing.

Much as he knew his captain and his family were right about not getting involved, he might as well enjoy her company. Sooner or later she'd recall her memory and the house would fall silent once more.

Besides, this wasn't a date. It was watching a movie with his house companion.

Yeah, right. If that were the case, why did he feel tempted to slide his arm around her shoulders?

Fern pointed to the lush landscape shown on the wide screen. "So beautiful. I promised myself when I was younger, I'd go there someday. It was my little secret, my reward for making it from one day to the next."

Ryan glanced at her. "Making it from day to day? You said you were in foster care. What kind of childhood did you have?"

She rubbed her temple, a move he recognized her making when things troubled her or she tried to recall a memory. "Not a good one. Let's just leave it at that. I've had enough today of trying to remember things. What about you?"

Ava mentioned Fern had a lot of issues, so he didn't want to pressure her. "The usual. Dad said I wasn't doing as much as I could, achieving grades to his standards. I was more into hiking, rock climbing, sports, the stuff Dad couldn't understand. One reason I became a firefighter. I like the physical aspect of it."

"Did you want to be a hero?"

A hero? He watched the screen, trying to lose himself in the fascinating Brian Boru establishing himself as the last true high king of Ireland. "I'm no hero. I only do my job. Real heroes don't get paid to save people."

"Hey."

Firm pressure on his arm. Fern gave him a look he'd never seen before from her. "Stop denigrating yourself. Job or not, you are a hero. You put your life at risk every time you ride on the truck. You tackle life-threatening situations most people would run away from."

High praise. He'd heard it before, shrugged it off. Yet coming from Fern it sounded more sincere.

"Okay, I'll stop it and we'll bask in our mutual admiration society."

Damn, her smile could make a man's heart race, make him think he could be a warrior king like old Boru. Ryan munched on more popcorn, glad a boring commercial showed on the television.

One would be hard-pressed to find hemorrhoid supplies sexy or heroic. Though he might admit to having ex-bosses who were like hemorrhoids.

He grinned.

"What's so funny?" she asked.

"Ever work for someone who is a pain in the butt and you wish you could dunk them in hemorrhoid cream?"

Fern sputtered out her drink. "You're bad."

"The worst. Just ask around the station. They'll agree."

"Such a high honor. Ever get a trophy?"

"They didn't have one large enough to fit through the door. Like my head."

Laughing at her eye roll, he tossed a piece of popcorn at her.

"Hey, keep doing that and I'll make you clean up. After all your hard work popping…"

Fern went quiet, staring at the screen.

He looked at the television. A family gathered around a blue van, loading vacation supplies. The father was talking about how roomy it was inside.

Fern's breath caught. In a flash, she went from relaxed to deer-in-the-headlights scared.

Instantly he pressed Pause on the remote. "You recognize that person?"

Her hands shook and her breathing became rapid and shallow. "I…"

Closing her eyes, she seemed to struggle to control herself.

"Easy," he soothed. Ryan remembered what Brenda the hypnotherapist had said during Fern's session. "Deep breaths.

You're in a safe space. I'm here with you right now. No one is going to hurt you."

Her eyes opened and she stared at the screen. Ragged breathing filled the room and a pulse jumped in her neck, but a little color finally suffused her face.

"I recognize the van. Not the guy. That van... I remember the van. Dark blue. Back windows tinted so you couldn't see inside. It pulled up as I was walking and the door slid open, exactly like on the television. Two men's voices, and one was tall and he grabbed me. His hand was rough... I looked down and I saw black leather boots, like biker boots."

Depressing the pause button, he let the commercial play. Such an innocent advertisement for a family vehicle. Not so innocent for Fern, who'd become an unwanted passenger.

Reaching for his cell, he depressed the camera button and snapped a photo of the television screen. Ryan texted it to Ava.

"We need to tell Jacob and Ava. This is critical, Fern. You're remembering!"

"I'm scared."

He paused in texting his sister. Fern's lower lip wobbled. Here he was, all excited about this clue, and she was scared out of her mind.

"Ryan, can you hold me, please, before you tell Ava? I feel like the ground is slipping out from under me."

He set down his cell and wrapped his arms around her, feeling her body shake. Much as he knew this was a bad idea, it felt good to hold her. Provide some slim comfort.

Warning bells sounded in his mind. He heard his sister's voice and the voices of Cap and friends urging caution.

Heard his own conscience scream at him.

Saving Fern won't bring Kate back. She's dead and it's your fault.

You're getting too close. Can't cure her of everything she's endured. Get in too deep and you can do more harm than good.

As if Fern needed more harm.

Chapter 9

Going to be a late night. Why couldn't she have a normal life like other women? Watch a program with a cute guy, relax and have some fun, instead of ending up a shaky mess...

Over a stupid television commercial.

You have an obligation to other women to remember what happened to you. That's more important than feeling normal. Don't be selfish.

While Ryan phoned his sister and cousin, she excused herself to the guest bedroom—she still couldn't think of it as hers, her bedroom was back in an apartment she wasn't certain she'd ever call home again.

Fern stared at her cell phone, wanting to call her sponsor. Not that she longed for a drink, no, she needed to talk to someone who understood her past and never condemned her for it. Normally she'd go to a meeting, but meetings were prohibited while she was in hiding.

The closer she got to remembering the past, the more scared she became. Bad enough she knew she had a murky, troubled childhood. Worse were the looks of pity or disgust. That much she did remember—people distancing themselves from her because Fern Hensley was a problem child. The kind of kid who grew up and ended up pregnant, or homeless, or in jail, or passed out in some dark alley, an empty bottle of vodka clutched in one dirty hand.

Her shaking fingers dialed Belle's number. Her friend immediately answered. "Hey, kid, you okay?"

"No." Fern relayed to Belle what happened.

"Do you want to have a drink?"

"No." She squeezed the cell phone so hard her knuckles whitened. "I want my life back. But I'm scared, Belle. I'm scared once I fully regain my memory, people will look at me like a pariah because I know there's bad stuff in my past."

Fern gave a little laugh. "Not that people wouldn't stare at me in pity now anyway, knowing I got kidnapped in a sex trafficking ring."

"Who are you afraid of pitying you? Ryan?"

Silence gave them both the answer. "Has he indicated in any way he feels sorry for you?"

"No." Fern thought about the enjoyable time they'd spent together today. "Far from it. When I'm with him I feel normal. He treats me like any other person. It's refreshing and I like it."

"He gets you."

Hearing it from her friend and sponsor clicked on a light. How had she missed this? Ryan understood her and spoke her language. Not like a victim, or like fragile glass, but like an ordinary woman.

"He's becoming my person. You once told me everyone needs a person. I don't want to burden him."

"Seems to me Ryan doesn't regard you as a burden. He could have easily passed along the responsibility to someone else and washed his hands of you. He likes you, Fern. He's one of the good ones."

Ryan was a good guy. What happened if he found out she had not been a sterling member of society? Would he lose all respect for her?

"He is. I don't know if I deserve him. I—I never told you my history."

That much she did remember.

"Fern, you know me by now. I don't need to know, Fern, to know you're a good person as well. I never judge people by their past, only their present, and I bet Ryan is the same."

Belle's voice gentled. "You deserve to be happy, Fern. Lean on Ryan for support. People can be jerks, but they can also be wonderful."

So true. She released a deep breath. "Thanks, Belle. I have to go now. I'll be in touch."

By the time she went into the living room, Jacob and Ava had arrived. Ava was in the kitchen, making tea.

No amount of chamomile tea could decrease her nervousness. Sure did help having Ryan sit next to her on the sofa, his big, strong presence a rock of comfort.

Life was about choices. She faced a few now. Going forward and facing her fears with courage, or hiding from them.

Women in Dark Canyon and other nearby towns depended on her recovering her memory. Every bit of information helped, painful as it might be for her.

Ava brought out a tray and handed a mug to Jacob, curls of steam rising into the air. "Coffee for you, and tea for the rest of us."

Fern shook her head. "I'm fine. I'd rather get on with this."

Jacob hesitated. Ryan gripped Fern's hand. "Whoever it is, you'll be okay."

Her heart sounded too loud, and everyone looked at her. Fern pulled her hand away from Ryan.

"I was walking home from work. Usually I drove, but my car had a flat and I'd left it back at the apartment. It wasn't a long walk. Silly me, my head was elsewhere." She gave a bitter laugh. "Living alone, I was aware of my surroundings at all times and how vulnerable I could be as a woman, but this night all I could think about was my upcoming date."

Frowning, she tried to remember. There was something else,

something critical, but it slipped through her mind like sand through her fingers.

She pressed fingers to her temples. "I remember he was cute. Funny. I was so looking forward to going to this Irish bar to meet him, listen to this terrific Celtic band playing there.

"It was cold, so cold, and I walked fast, and I didn't even think about anyone following me." She spoke faster now, trying to purge the fear. "It wasn't until this van pulled up to the curb… The streetlights showed it was dark blue, and I heard a door open and turned.

"Two men jumped out… I can't remember their faces but one grabbed me. Like someone zapped my brain into waking up, I tried to run, but the tall one grabbed me, and I heard him call a name. Billy, remember I told you I recalled his name? I kicked and screamed and looked down. He had on…"

Fern closed her eyes, willing to see the black biker boots.

"These leather boots with square toes. They were like biker boots, with a chain, and then I felt this prick on my arm, and I screamed but no sound came out. Th-that's all I remember."

Tears slid down her cheeks. Fear and absolute panic—oh, she remembered them as well. The feeling that she was being sucked into a vortex of danger, and she could try clawing and fighting her way out, but it was useless.

Her life was no longer her own. No control.

Barely registering the feel of Ryan's warm palm covering hers once more, she took a calming breath.

Jacob looked intense, but his voice softened. "I know this is tough, Fern, but any details help the investigation. Do you remember anything else about the van? Sounds, like was the motor running rough? Was it a panel van without windows? Scratched or dented? New? Anything about the man who grabbed you? Was he short, tall, skinny or muscled? When he grabbed you, did it feel like his arms went down or were they level to your height? That gives us an idea of how tall he was."

Fern took another breath and closed her eyes, willing to recall the horrid moments.

"I—I remember thinking before everything went dark that I needed to recall everything...in case someone rescued me. The van had windows, dark windows. That's why the commercial we saw tonight reminded me of it. Like a family van you'd see on vacation with a bunch of kids in it, or going to soccer practice. Except this van had a dent in the passenger's side like someone hammered it.

"The guy, the guy..." Fear gripped her in a tight vise, making it hard to breathe.

"It's okay, Fern. You're safe."

Words Ava used all the time, yet this time Ryan said them. Ryan, who had been there when the fire roared and despair had seized her as she thought no one would find her and she'd die there all alone.

Another deep breath, smelling Ryan's citrus aftershave. Not overpowering or cloying, only refreshing...

"He smelled!" Her eyes flew open. "His coat... He had on a coat, and it smelled like skunk, and I couldn't understand why he'd use aftershave like that..."

Jacob glanced at Ryan and a smile touched his mouth. "That's great, Fern. Good detail. High-potency cannabis contains a bigger amount of THC and smells like skunk."

A flutter of hope beat inside her, tiny butterfly wings. Encouraged, she nodded. "Yes! I've smelled it before, and I had this crazy wild thought that maybe he was too stoned to do much, but then I felt this pinprick on my neck and everything went dark."

Judging from the excitement on Jacob's face, this was a very good thing. "Can you track someone if they smoke pot?" she asked.

"We can access the businesses that sell it and ask for their video footage and send out a description of the suspects, along with any details you provide. Are you up to sitting with a sketch artist now to have her draw any details you can remember?"

Fern balked, shaking her head. Too much. "I told you, I don't remember details!"

"Okay, I understand. You've given us something. Thanks," Jacob said.

Ryan's hand slid over hers. "What about her drawing, Jacob? Did you find out anything?"

He nodded. Fern's stomach tightened. "What did you find out?"

She was proud her voice remained level. Calm.

Ryan's cousin nodded, set his mug down on the coffee table. "We got a hit on the face you drew. But it's not one of the men who took you. Guy's been dead for five years."

Was it possible to feel relief and disappointment at the same time? "So he's not one of the men who kidnapped me. But he must have a criminal record if you discovered his name. Or at least be in the system."

As Jacob stared at her, she added, "I know about this from a friend of my foster parents. He was a prosecutor. That much I do remember."

I wish I could remember more important things.

"Yeah." Jacob exchanged glances with Ava. "He's probably from your past, which is why you drew him. Those memories are surfacing."

All the bad memories. Were there any good ones? She had vague recollections of some, but her life had hardly been ideal. Far from the childhood Ryan experienced. His parents, strict as his father might be, sounded loving. Judging from Ryan's interactions with Ava, his sister, the entire family was close.

"I need to know who he is. Every single memory I recall helps piece together my life," she said evenly.

Jacob nodded.

"Like I said, we ran the portrait through facial recognition, which only works if a person is in the system. Fortunately, the object of your sketch was, the man you remembered during hypnosis. His name is Bill. William F. Conners. He was arrested for petty theft and larceny in Salt Lake, died about five years ago in a botched robbery attempt on a convenience store. He listed as his next of kin a woman named Olivia Hensley. Your mother."

Ryan, Ava and Jacob all looked at her expectantly.

"He's dead. You're certain of this?" she asked.

At Jacob's nod, Fern rubbed her temple, the memory sharp and uncomfortable. But she could deal with this—she had support, and the face no longer terrified her.

Bill, her mother's old boyfriend, was in his grave and could no longer hurt her. Fern swallowed hard and gathered her courage. Admitting this to these people, who had ordinary, normal lives, was tough. But these were good people and they would not judge her.

"William, no, he went by Bill. He was my mother's boyfriend. He's the guy I recalled in Brenda's office. He…tried to hurt me."

She gave a bitter laugh. "Did more than try. Slapped me around a few times, especially when he got drunk."

Despite the air conditioning in the living room, she felt soaked with perspiration.

Silence hovered in the room for a moment. Fern couldn't bear it. She looked directly at Ryan. "My life was pretty screwed up from childhood, Ryan. Knowing my background, you sure you want me to stay in your house?"

Ryan scowled and gripped her shoulders. "Hey, hey, stop it. You are not your mother. We all have problems with our families. My dad thinks I'm a loser for not joining the family business and making a million dollars by my thirtieth birthday. The important thing is you're starting to remember, Fern. And in remembering, you know you got past that lousy upbringing and became the woman you are today. Strong and independent, not taking crap from anyone."

Embarrassed at the curtain of her past pulled back, she felt naked and exposed. Ryan could reassure her all he wanted, but facts were facts.

She didn't look at him. Or anyone else. "I'm really tired. I'd like to go to sleep now, if you don't mind."

Grabbing her bag, Ava was the first to stand. "It is getting late. Fern, we have an appointment tomorrow in the morning, but because it's so late, I'll push it back a couple of hours. I'll be here at ten."

Her therapist hugged Ryan. "If you need me, I'm a phone call away."

An almost cryptic warning. Was Ava afraid she might have a breakdown and her brother couldn't handle it?

Fern blocked the doorway with her body. She had to show these people she wasn't a hot mess, but could handle her own problems. "Ava, I'm fine. I'm not going to fall apart. Or hurt myself or anyone else."

Pointed, clipped, decisive. All the things Ava wanted her to become.

Ava looked her up and down and a little smile tugged at her mouth. "You're not the one I'm concerned about."

With a quick glance to Ryan, Ava reached around her and slipped out the door.

Jacob followed, advising her to call him if she remembered anything else.

It had been a long day. Promised to be an even longer night.

To her surprise, Fern slept through the night and awoke refreshed and ready for her session with Ava. Ryan's sister showed up at ten while Ryan was out running errands. Clever of him to arrange his schedule around this.

When Ava left, Fern turned her attention to work.

Somehow she knew her life before "the event," as she thought of her abduction, had been normal. Normal for her, anyway. The laptop before her represented a world of possibilities. A window to what others regarded as ordinary.

After powering it on, she stared at the icons. No one warned her against going on social media, yet she knew it was too dangerous. Hackers infiltrated all the time, could discover her IP address and even trace her back here.

Even the secure VPN was no guarantee. Not when you dealt with men who would do anything to get her back into their clutches. Sell her to the highest bidder.

Fern shivered. She clicked onto the software program for medical coding. Letters, numbers, diagnosis. Felt familiar. Comfortable, like soft slippers instead of walking on gravel. Or Lego pieces.

She needed to attend a meeting, be around others like herself struggling with alcohol. Meetings were forbidden while she remained concealed, so this was a balm to her soul.

Numbers and logic always suited her. In a world with a mother who abandoned her, foster families who mistreated her, Fern found comfort in math and numbers. When she couldn't make sense of why she was ill-treated and no one seemed to love her, the numbers were there. Constant, logical and nonemotional. Numbers made sense. She could create a world where she didn't have to worry about pleasing a foster mother who scolded when she failed to scrub away every spot from a faded linoleum floor or yelled when she spoke too loudly.

Numbers were quiet perfection. She learned to study in silence, marveling over their complex yet simple logic.

People seldom made sense.

Numbers always made sense.

Fern was absorbed in learning about insurance coding a diagnosis for a complex heart problem when the doorbell rang twice, then a third time. Typical signal for Ryan, yet to make sure, she glanced at her phone.

So sweet of him to alert her, instead of walking into the house. After all, it was his house, but his consideration relaxed her.

An hour later, he called out he was going out for a run. She envied his freedom. Despite the comfort of his house, she began to feel a little cooped up.

When he returned, Ryan popped his head in the doorway of the office.

"Hey, don't mean to disturb. Wanted to know if you're ready to take a break. I finished running six miles, and after a shower, I was thinking of relaxing out back with a cold sports drink and great company."

In navy blue sweatpants and a blue hoodie with the Dark Canyon Fire Department logo, he looked cute. The kind of guy she'd give a second look if they passed on the street.

Her smile faded. Ryan wasn't any guy. He saved her, and she had read about the hero complex in one of his books on firefighting. Getting attached was a bad idea.

I can't make things any harder for him. I have to keep him at a distance. Ryan's been terrific, and sooner or later, he'll be out of my life.

Like all the others who'd drifted in and out of it. A revolving door of foster families, friendships, men.

Safer to be alone. Less chance of heartbreak.

"Thanks, but I need to finish this."

Fern sensed his disappointment as she returned her attention to the screen.

The sooner her memories returned, the sooner she could get back to her life.

Even if that life had been filled with loneliness, it was a safe haven.

Chapter 10

They didn't eat together that night. Ryan told her he was supposed to meet the guys for dinner. Before leaving, he instructed her to make sure she pressed her panic button if anything went wrong.

She refused an offer of takeout, mainly because she wasn't hungry. Plenty of leftovers in the freezer, she told him.

The house seemed so quiet without him.

Two hours later, he texted he would be home soon.

Restless, unable to focus on anything, she put on her coat and went outside into the front yard. The neighborhood was quiet. She had a police officer staying two doors down watching over her.

No reason to feel anxious or worried.

Yet the hypnosis session unlocking those childhood memories made her feel ashamed and exposed. Not her fault. She was a survivor. Life was short, and no way did she want her captors to have any more power over her.

It was about time she stopped thinking of herself as a victim and took charge of her life. Memories or no memories.

Fern looked at the dark sky, the stars glistening overhead, silent witnesses to her trauma. Whispers of a breeze from the distant mountains and canyons strengthened her. The mountains knew secrets and did not judge.

Fern lifted her face to the sky. "You have no power over

me," she told her unknown kidnappers. "I am alive and so are my memories. I will recall them, and you will not hurt another woman the way you hurt me."

Feeling alive and energized, she lifted her hands to the sky and twirled, laughing at the feeling of breathing, feeling, simply being alive after months of fear and uncertainty.

"Nothing will hurt me now!" she shouted. "I'm unsinkable."

"Unsinkable in the middle of the desert?" Ryan sounded amused. "Who are you talking to?"

She turned to see him emerging from his truck.

"I didn't hear you pull up," she told him, delighted he was home.

Fern was about to tell him about her revelation when an ominous orange glow flickered in the house across the street. Smoke curled out of the open windows and suddenly gunfire erupted.

Straight at them.

Acting on instinct, Ryan shoved Fern downward. He fumbled for his cell, dialing 911.

Fern buried her face into her hands and didn't look up. Chances were those rounds would never reach the street; still, he wasn't taking chances.

The guys responding to the call needed a warning.

"I've got a 10-0 here across from 1900 Maple Avenue. Working fire, house engulfed. Tell the first responders to use extreme caution until the scene can be secured. There must be several rounds of ammo cooking in there."

Other neighbors had come outside to watch the fire. Ryan glanced down. "Stay here and don't move."

Scrambling to his feet, he ran to the street and shouted for them to stay back, yes, the fire department had already been called. Officer Jenkins, the plainclothes police officer watching over the house, ran over.

"Fern okay?" he shouted.

Ryan nodded. "See if you can talk sense into the lookie-loos and get them off this damn street."

Fern peeked upward at him through splayed fingers. "Serves me right for telling the universe nothing can hurt me. Though I didn't think my challenge would end up firing bullets. Still, I knew about the Titanic. You think I'd learn to avoid statements of absolutes, such as 'unsinkable.'"

They watched as smoke poured out of the house and orange flames rose higher and higher. Ryan felt bad for the owner. Guys were trying to get a handle on the beast, but they couldn't risk getting too close.

"Is anyone inside?" Fern asked from behind him.

"Doubt it. My neighbor, Simmons, has been on a business trip for a couple of weeks, and he lives alone."

Lots of people milling around now, with police cordoning off the area for safety. He glanced back at Fern. Orange shadows danced on her troubled expression.

He spotted a police officer headed in his direction. "Stay here. I gotta talk to this guy."

Ryan went to the sidewalk, glancing back at Fern hovering on the stoop. Fern was seemingly torn between going into the house and remaining out here with him.

The officer removed a notepad. "You called it in?"

"I did. Spotted the smoke and heard the gunfire."

The cop asked question after question. How much ammunition was inside, weapons, where were most of them located.

"The house is vacant now. Owner runs a business selling guns, attends a lot of gun shows around the country, so I guess he stashed them in the garage," Ryan told him.

Remaining outside wasn't a good idea, not with all these neighbors milling around and now… *Oh damn, here comes a news truck.*

Turning, he went to gesture to Fern to get inside. Relief filled him as he saw she'd already left.

Seeing Fern on the late local news would not make Jacob, or Ava, happy. *Hey, we're trying to hide her, and less than a week with you and her photo is all over the television!*

Could be funny if it were not true. Ryan gave the cop a pointed look. "Can I go now? I'm on shift tomorrow and need my z's."

Like firefighters and nurses, cops understood about first responder shifts and the importance of quality sleep. The officer nodded, said he had Ryan's number if he had more questions.

But when Ryan reached the front door and rang the bell for Fern to let him in, she didn't answer.

He tried again. Nothing. Ryan texted her. No response.

Don't panic. Yeah, try telling his accelerated heart rate the same. Fern had to have fled inside the house. Only a few feet had separated them. Why wasn't she answering?

A nasty thought winked on and off like a faulty neon sign: *What if someone snatched her while you were busy talking with the cop?*

He couldn't go there, but like trying to forget the word *elephant*, it remained implanted in his mind, flashing over and over. Cussing, he rang the doorbell again. Nothing.

He called Fern's cell. It went straight to the generic voicemail Ava had set up for her.

Ryan walked around one side of the house and the other. Both gates were locked. He'd taught her the combination. Now he tried it and went into the backyard.

No Fern.

The back door was open. *Whew. I'm overreacting, she probably stepped inside for a moment...*

Minutes later, after a thorough search of the entire house, including the basement, sweat rolled down his back. The April air outside as he ran out the door did little to cool him off.

Fern wasn't anywhere around the house or the yard.

Okay. *Panic now.*

Chapter 11

Where could she have gone? Terrible thoughts shot through his mind as he continued searching in front of the house. The crowd had dissipated, thanks to the police officers controlling the scene.

No Fern.

As he was about to admit defeat and ask one of the cops for help, he saw a woman approach the house, hugging herself. Relief mingled with anger.

"Where the hell have you been? You can't disappear like that, Fern. You know how risky that is, being out here in the open!"

"I'm sorry," she burst out. "I wasn't thinking."

"No, you weren't. Do you know how damn worried I was? How I started thinking someone grabbed you again right under my nose? I brought you here to keep you safe and protect you."

Putting his anger on pause, he stopped and looked at her. Fern didn't make any noise, not even a protest.

Moisture swam in her eyes, and he was the reason. Yelling at her. Stupid of him, so stupid, when she needed reassurance. Ryan took a deep breath to apologize when she nodded meekly.

"You're right. Absolutely right. I should have told you where I was headed, Ryan. Instead, I thought only of myself. Time to stop doing that. You and the others have been wonderful to me, and how do I repay you? It was selfish of me to not let you know what happened."

For the first time he noticed she was trembling inside her coat, her hands shaking slightly.

"Why did you leave?"

"I—I don't know if I should tell you... Please don't be mad anymore."

Ryan gentled his voice. "Fern, I'm not mad. But I need to know why you left the yard and where you went."

"I had to save him from being trampled."

Slowly she opened her coat to reveal a button-like nose. A whimpering dog peeked out at him.

"Everyone was so busy looking at the fire. He was so scared and darted out in front of the cars and no one was helping him. I had to follow him and get him. I think he's hurt."

Ryan peered down at the dog and saw an injured paw. Looked like a burn. "Yeah, he needs a vet."

"He came right to me." She stroked the dog's head. "I was wondering... He has no tag, but the vet can see if he's chipped, and if he's not, instead of putting him in a shelter... Those shelters are so cold and lonely. I totally understand if it's an imposition."

An adorable, injured dog with Fern and her big beseeching eyes. How could he say no?

Ryan sighed. He had no room in his life now for a dog or more complications, but he sensed Fern needed the dog. "Maybe. He needs vet care first and probably a good foster home, but maybe later."

Her expression shuttered. He could almost read her mind. Yet another disappointment.

He gentled his voice. "Let's get him checked out at the animal hospital first. Good thing you saw him or this little guy might be in real trouble."

She handed over the dog, who snuggled against him as if seeking warmth. "I started calling him Bumper because he kept bumping my hand with his nose."

Bumper. Ryan glanced at the house. With the fire under control and almost extinguished, traffic on the street diminished. He couldn't risk Fern coming with him...

"I know I'm not supposed to leave the house, but if I wear a hat and maybe glasses, no one will recognize me. Can I please come with you? I need to see how he's doing."

More than anyone, he understood the need to follow through with a victim you'd saved from harm. "I'll give you ten minutes."

By the time they returned from the animal hospital, they were both worn out. Fern admitted her disappointment over Bumper staying with a foster family once he recovered, but she understood.

Ryan almost caved in to having the dog at the house. The little pup had gotten to him as well, licking his nose as he placed him on the exam table for the vet. But with Fern hiding from the criminals who abducted her, trying to regain her memory, and his intense work schedule, he feared he couldn't give Bumper the proper attention and care the pup needed to recover from his time on the streets.

At work the following day, the Dark Canyon fire investigator told Ryan the fire had been deliberate. An empty gas container had been found in the backyard. A broken window at the back indicated someone got inside and started the blaze, setting oil-soaked rags in the kitchen and candles nearby.

They were investigating the homeowner to see if this was a case of insurance fraud, but considering Simmons had thousands' worth of ammo and guns stored in the house, it made no sense. Surely he would have removed them before setting the fire himself.

The puppy had been a stray. Neighbors reported seeing him hanging around Simmons's garage. Poor fellow had probably gotten burned when the fire spread. Investigators found a hole in the garage siding, which explained how the dog had gained access.

And fortunately he escaped the fire, though not without injury.

Ryan had little time to consider it, because he agreed to work back-to-back shifts when one of the guys had a family emergency. When he finally got home after work, all he could do was crash and sleep. There was barely time to exchange greetings with Fern.

Ryan felt bad for her, isolated here in his home. A week after the fire, he sensed her extreme frustration. She was no closer to making gains in her memory. When he returned home from checking on the dog at the veterinary hospital, he found her outside, staring absently at a canvas. Soft yellow light illuminated the patio in the pitch-blackness.

"You'll be happy to know that Bumper is recovering fine. Vet says in another week he can be released to a foster home until he's adopted."

"That's good."

Her voice sounded listless.

"Why are you out here in the dark?" He draped his jacket over her shivering shoulders.

"Guess I lost track of time."

"What are you working on?" he asked, pulling up a chair.

"Nothing special now. I can't get it together."

"I hear creativity is like that. Comes and goes."

"One reason I liked working with numbers and codes. They're stable and I don't have to imagine anything."

Curious, he looked at the palette of colors by her side. "Can I see what you're working on?"

A slight shrug. Ryan went to look at her work. A landscape, with vivid sunset colors. Not vivid. Almost angry.

"Why did you start to paint if you enjoy math so much?"

Fern picked up a paintbrush and stroked the bristles as if

petting a cat. "Painting helped save me, in a way. It kept me going through a series of bad foster homes. Oh, it wasn't painting then, but drawings and doodles. I'd sketch out my feelings."

He could only imagine how dark those drawings were. Ryan knew pain, and grief, but nothing like what she'd experienced. He still had a loving, though interfering, family, and caring co-workers. She'd been all alone.

"I can't imagine what that was like. I know what it feels like to lose someone you love, or make a mistake that you always regret, but nothing like what you've been through."

She set down the brush and looked at him, really looked at him, with those huge hazel eyes that seemed to sear through his soul.

"Don't compare my life experiences to yours, Ryan. Everyone is different and everyone experiences grief differently. Some people mourn the loss of a beloved pet more than they do a parent who was never supportive. We don't compete in the pain Olympics."

He managed a crooked smile. "Wise words."

"Partly your sister, partly me." Fern's gaze darted to him. "I should tell you something. I had a toxic childhood. My life was never normal or even close to it. I was bounced around from foster home to foster home when my mother abandoned me when I was ten."

Ryan's steady blue gaze centered on her. He knew this was important to her, and he gave her his full attention.

"My mom was a drunk who wanted her abusive boyfriend more than me. She left me in the middle of the night. I had a lot of setbacks. And then I started drinking. Heavily. Got into trouble. I was headed down a bad path.

"When I was fifteen, I got into a foster home where I felt loved for the first time in my life. My new parents were reliable, dependable and when they made a promise, they followed through."

Fern sighed. "They were wonderful. Never put up with the trouble I gave them, but they were fair and taught me discipline. Gave me boundaries and respect and made me feel like I could make something of my life."

She looked away, as if ashamed. "I'm an alcoholic, Ryan. The Englehearts, Delia and Joe, didn't lecture me about drinking. They got me into a teenage Alcoholics Anonymous program and stuck by my side the entire time. I could never repay them for their support and belief in me."

"You're a recovering alcoholic." His admiration for her increased. "You manage it well. Is it why you refused pain meds in the hospital?"

Fern nodded. "I'm always afraid of slipping. I've learned to do without. You can do almost anything you set your mind to, Ryan."

"Almost anything," he agreed.

"The Englehearts treated me like their own daughter. They let me stay past my eighteenth birthday, when I aged out, as long as I got a job and paid some rent. Their rent payments were low enough to enable me to use my job to pay for community college. They moved away a couple of years ago, but always kept in touch until they were killed in a car crash."

"I'm sorry," he said gently. "After everything, that must have been devastating."

"It was." She sighed. "Do you ever want to feel happy, feel more than a glimmer of pure joy, but when those glimmers come, you seize them and hold on to them with all your might because you're so afraid the next moment will bring something that hurts to your core?"

His chest tightened. Ryan managed a nod. Yeah, he knew what that was like, and sometimes he felt he didn't deserve the happiness coming his way. Why should he go on with life when the woman he'd tried to save lost hers?

He'd failed at the job, and it seemed like he could never make up for the loss.

Ryan swallowed past the lump in his throat. "I know what that is like, Fern. You're not alone in these feelings. They suck."

Her lower lip wobbled. "They do indeed suck. Big donkey donuts."

Then the spark returned to her eyes and she grinned. "My favorite swear words."

He couldn't help it. He laughed, the sound shattering the grimness in the air. For a moment he regretted losing the intensity and connection, but it was worth seeing her smile. Hell, he'd climb the aerial ladder ten times carrying one hundred pounds of weights for one of Fern's sweet smiles.

Sweet might be the wrong word. Sweet reminded him of a young girl, innocent and carefree. Fern was a woman, an old soul, who had been through a lot.

"You have a sunshine smile," he murmured.

Her smile dropped. "What do you mean?"

Okay, awkward moment. But he needed to be honest. "When you smile, it brings sunshine to dark places."

Pink suffused her cheeks, a becoming shade on her. He felt tempted to reach out, stroke the softness of her skin. Almost subconsciously, he lifted his hand to her face.

Fern didn't flinch or jerk away. She watched him, not with wariness like a frightened animal, but with darkened pupils and anticipation on her face.

He stroked a line down her right cheek, marveling at the satiny smoothness of skin, delighting in the flush, the little sigh she made indicating she enjoyed his touch. Fern leaned forward as he dared to cup her cheek in his palm. Even better.

Whoa, this was great, feeling her soft skin, seeing desire swirl in the darkness of her eyes. Ryan swallowed hard against the urge to push forward, do everything he normally would with a woman responding in kind to the chemistry between them.

Lean in closer, brush his lips against hers, gauge her response and maybe go deeper, bonding them together in mutual passion.

But this was Fern, who'd endured plenty of heartache. Slow, even slower, his instincts cautioned. Now wasn't the time to experiment and tease and taste and see how far he could take this.

Ryan dropped his hand. Was she disappointed? He couldn't tell.

Fern turned away. "I have dinner in the Crock-Pot. When you're hungry, help yourself. I already ate."

"I'm starving. Thanks. Don't stay out here too long. Temperature's dropping."

She nodded. "Thanks for your jacket."

Knowing she wanted to be alone, he went inside. As he ate, killing two glasses of tea with the delicious stew she'd made, he thought about how she must feel right now.

Fern had to suffer from cabin fever. Too dangerous for her to go out in public with her abductors still at large.

He consulted a map on his cell phone as he finished dinner. Her apartment was more than an hour's drive from here. Maybe taking her there would trigger a memory. After calling Ava and discussing it with her, he went outside to talk to Fern.

She sat on the patio, staring at the fence like a zoo animal pacing its enclosure, looking for escape.

Ryan pulled up a chair. "How would you like to do something fun? I'm off for the next three days, and I need to get out for a long drive now that winter's over. You could wear your wig and glasses as a disguise and we can visit Oso, drive by your apartment, see if you remember anything."

Paleness on her face and the grip of her fingers on the chair's armrests told him her terror of returning.

"I want to help, Ryan." Fern swallowed hard. "If it's best for me to go back, and that will make me remember so they can prevent this from happening to another woman, then let's do it."

Such courage. New admiration filled him. Fern's strength

inspired him. She'd endured so much trauma, and yet instead of thinking of herself, she strove to help others.

"We won't stay in Oso long. We'll continue to Durango. There's a terrific walking trail along the Animas River I think you'd enjoy. It's far enough from here that no one will recognize you."

The hope and dawning excitement on her face was like watching a butterfly emerge from its cocoon. Fern glanced around.

"Drive to Colorado? You'd do this for me? It's your day off, and I'm sure you have errands, things to do with your family and friends. If you change your mind at the last minute, I'll understand..."

Her voice trailed off. Ryan squatted down before her, making sure their gazes were level. "Fern, I know a lot of people have disappointed you in the past. I don't make promises I can't keep."

Not anymore. Not since the day Kate had slipped from his grasp. Couldn't think about that tragedy. Fern came first. She needed this.

Hell, I need this as well.

"The drive will do us both good. We can take my dad's Jeep. Take the top off as we're going through the mountains. Maybe even do a little exploring and off-roading."

The smile tugging her mouth upward radiated pure joy. "I've never been off-roading but always wanted to try. Didn't know you liked it."

Oh yeah, he liked it. Ryan grinned. "I took the Jeep off-roading a couple of years ago and had a little problem. Dad refused to let me drive it after that."

"Will your dad let you borrow it?"

His grin widened. "I kept an extra set of keys he doesn't know about."

"Why do I get the feeling you were a troublemaker when you were young?"

"Still am."

At his wink, she laughed. Felt good to see her spirits lift and hear her laugh, as clear and enchanting as the distant toll of church bells.

"Tomorrow morning then. Leave around five thirty for my parents' house and get breakfast on the road."

"That early? Won't you wake up your parents?"

"Not if I'm careful."

He grinned as she laughed again. It was going to be a great day tomorrow. He felt it in his bones.

Ryan had a mischievous side she liked. Before dawn, they left. He parked his truck in the sweeping driveway of his parents' house. Ryan keyed the code to the garage door and backed the Jeep out as quietly as a thief.

The vehicle was older and smelled like grease and tacos. He grinned at her wrinkled nose.

"Dad uses it for working on odd jobs and off-roading. I think he also sneaks out for his favorite taco truck when Mom's not looking or she'd lecture him on the dangers of raising his cholesterol. I'd have cleaned out the tools from the back but I didn't want to waste time or risk waking them up."

They stopped for gas, and while the vehicle filled up, he gave her a sheepish look. "I'm texting Mom that I took the Jeep and not to worry. Don't want her thinking someone broke in."

"Someone other than her son, you mean."

"Well, if you put it that way."

Soon they were on the road again, heading to Oso. Too cold to take the top off, they opted for the vehicle's heater instead. Bundled into a soft down jacket, a long-sleeved shirt, jeans and pink suede boots with plush lining purchased courtesy of Ava, Fern began to relax. Ryan let her select the music and she used

Bluetooth to connect a soothing jazz station to the sound system. Seldom an early riser, Fern felt grumpy, despite the delicious coffee he'd brewed for the road. After a few sips from her insulated tumbler, she began to appreciate the surroundings.

The first light of dawn streaked across the leaden sky, transforming it into a brilliant blush of pink, purple and orange, accented by indigo clouds. Like an artist's brush, the colors stretched out on the horizon. Mountain peaks in the near distance silhouetted with dawn displayed their craggy edges. Fern imagined waking up in the canyons, watching the sun touch the sharp rocks and twists and turns, turning them to fiery orange.

"It must be beautiful to hike in there and see the sunrise," she mused.

Ryan glanced at her. "I've camped before in the canyons. It's fantastic this time of year, before the summer begins and the tourists invade. Feels like you're the only person in the world when the sun climbs over the mountains and shines down on the valley."

"Peaceful. No one around to tell you what to do or how to feel."

He nodded. "It's soothing. You and nature, nothing else. Except you have to be careful because of spring flooding. Those canyons can turn into raging rivers in minutes. I always carry a weather radio to keep up on the rainfall in the mountains."

Fern shivered. "I'm more afraid of fire than water."

Reaching over, he squeezed her hand. "I understand."

Thinking of the cabin as it burned, how she could have perished in the fire if he hadn't pulled her free, twisted her guts into a knot. Couldn't think that way. She was here, alive, and on the road to recovery.

He pulled away and focused on the road leading to Oso.

I understand. Two words meaning a lot to her. No questions or probing, like from Ava or others who only wanted to help, but sometimes she only wanted silence to explore her own thoughts, not pressure from having to answer them. Fern leaned back and cracked the window. Crisp, cool air flowed inside, the delicious balm of sagebrush and pine carried on the wind. The desert seemed to shimmer with life, and she could imagine the creatures hiding in the brush beginning to venture out, looking for food as the sun warmed the land.

Utah had incredible sunrises. Different from the ones she'd experienced while on a vacation in Florida. More dramatic, and in a way, serene.

Ryan hummed along to a tune as he drove. "There's a roadside diner about thirty minutes from here. Sound good?"

Absently she nodded and traced a line on the window. "Did you hear back from your mom yet?"

In answer, he depressed a button on the Jeep's display screen. A text message sounded over the speakers.

"Ryan, your father's going to have a meltdown when he finds out you took the Jeep. I won't tell him if you don't. Enjoy and please, this time, stick to paved roads."

Fern smiled. What a wonderful mom. "I like your mom. She sounds like fun."

"She's definitely less uptight than my dad, but they're good parents. Dad's stricter and more worried about my future as a firefighter. But once in a while he stops pestering me to join the family business."

"At least you have someone who cares about your future."

The words slipped out before she could catch them and snatch them back. Ryan glanced at her again.

Embarrassed, she asked about the diner and what kind of food they had. Fern busied herself looking up the restaurant and scanning the menu offerings.

By the time he pulled into the parking lot of the Roadside Diner, her stomach was cheerfully announcing breakfast time. The pink neon sign sputtered on and off, but enough cars and trucks out front assured her this was a popular destination.

Smells of frying bacon and rich coffee made her salivate as they walked inside. The counter was filled with men, including some grizzled truckers who barely glanced at them. Ryan asked for a quiet booth in the back and sat watching the door. Fern's gaze darted around. Though no one paid attention to her, it was unnerving being in public like this.

Maybe it wasn't a good idea.

Ryan leaned forward. "I'm not leaving you for a minute, Fern. No one's looking at you. Please, try to relax."

"I'm not nervous."

He gave a pointed look to her hands, gripping the table's edge as if it were a life raft.

"Well, okay, maybe a little. Only because I don't know if this place has good coffee and I need my caffeine fix."

Mischief danced in his blue eyes. "It's a diner. They have to have good coffee or they'd go out of business."

After their food arrived and Ryan dug into his eggs and ham, she was able to lose a little tension and study the restaurant. It had been so long since she'd been around this many people. Most diners seemed intent on their meals. Only one or two men at the counter gave her a second glance.

Ryan slung an arm over the back of the booth. Even relaxed, he remained watchful, as if her bodyguard.

"You're right. No one is paying attention to me," she told him.

"They should. You're the prettiest woman here."

The compliment warmed and unnerved her. Not used to them, Fern rolled her eyes. "I'm the only woman here, besides our waitress, and she's more important than me."

"Because she has the magic juice." He pointed to his now empty mug. "Wish she'd deliver more over here."

Fern waved her hands over their mugs. "I can make her appear. All I need to do is have a mouth full of food and she'll stop by to ask what we need. It's my secret talent."

Barely had she said the words when their waitress appeared with a pot of coffee and filled their mugs. "Where you guys headed?"

As Fern compressed her lips, not wanting to answer, Ryan nodded his thanks. "Going to Cortez, maybe look around Mesa Verde. Tourist stuff."

Relief filled her. Of course he wouldn't talk about their plans.

"Be careful on 491. Heard from Hank—" the woman inclined her head to the counter "—some nutcase in a van speeding like a bat out of Hades nearly ran him off the road an hour ago. Guy was doing at least ninety, as if running from the cops. Some jerks think they own the road and learn too late big rigs like Hank's can't stop or turn on a dime. Someday someone's gonna smash into that ass and he'll find out too late."

Fern's eyes widened and her breathing hitched. "What... kind of van?"

They exchanged glances. The woman frowned and called out, "Hey, Hank! Got details on that ass who almost ran you off the road?"

Dressed in a leather jacket, his waterfall belly spilling over a belt, Hank ambled over to them. He pushed back a worn ball cap. "Green, I think. It was dark. Guy was driving like a dickwad."

"With windows on the sides instead of panels?" Ryan asked.

Hank frowned. "You know the guy?"

"Doubt it. Want to know what to look for as we get on the road. Don't want an accident."

"Van had dark windows. Not a panel van, I think. Hard to tell because I was too busy controlling my rig." Hank squinted at him. "Hey, I know you."

Sensing Fern's discomfort, Ryan shook his head. "Don't think so."

"I know so. Never forget a face. Three years ago outside Dark Canyon. My rig caught fire after I crashed and you pulled me out. Saved my hide. You're a fireman." Hank grinned and hooked a thumb at him. "Hey, everyone! This guy's a hero. Fireman who saved my sorry ass in that crash."

Hoots and hollers about said ass followed, along with waves and thanks.

Hank stuck out a meaty hand and Ryan shook it. "Thanks, man. Let me buy you and your lady breakfast."

"Just doing my job."

The trucker gave him a serious look. "If it weren't for you, I'd be toast, literally. Never been so scared in my life. Thought I was going to die in there. Because of you pulling me out, I slowed down, learned to appreciate life. Please, let me buy your breakfast."

Fern looked at the sincerity on the man's face, felt the gratitude. Hank wanted to do something in return. She glanced at Ryan. Ryan sighed, and nodded.

"Thank you."

Then his gaze turned speculative. "I could use your eyes and ears. If you or the other truckers you know see that van again, can you call this number? My cousin's looking for it. Guy might have been involved in a hit-and-run."

Fern exhaled a long breath.

Hank copied the number on his cell. "Sure thing. I'll spread the word. Gotta run, but I'll leave money with Sal for your bill."

"Thanks."

"No." Hank looked serious. "Thank you. Stay safe."

They finished their breakfast in silence. Ryan left a generous tip on the table. As they left, a chorus of thanks followed.

On the road, Fern felt introspective. He glanced at her. "You okay? You haven't said a word since Hank mentioned the van."

"I was thinking about Hank and how you saved him." She gave a little laugh. "Being in there, I was so caught up in worry about being in public, would anyone recognize me? It's easy to get wrapped up in your own problems and focused so much on yourself that you fail to see other people have personal issues as well."

"True. But self-care is important, Fern. You have to put yourself first."

"You don't." She shook her head. "You weren't thinking of yourself when you pulled him out of the burning truck."

"Of course I was. Every time I go on a call, I think of myself. Getting on my bunker gear, making sure my head's on straight so I can focus on the job. Oxygen mask on yourself first, remember?"

Traffic began to increase. She thought about the van Hank mentioned. Nothing to worry about, not really. How many vans were on the road? Some people lived in their vans, converting them to campers. Didn't mean anything.

Still, she couldn't quite relax. Ryan gestured to the radio. "Why don't you put on some music you enjoy?"

Fern didn't answer. Movement in the side mirror caught her attention. Acid churned in her stomach and she felt sick.

"Ryan, can you go a little faster?"

"What's wrong?"

"I think we're being followed."

Chapter 12

Going on the road with him had seemed like a happy outing, a chance to escape the house and breathe fresh air. Now Fern wondered if it was a huge mistake.

"Which vehicle?" He glanced at the rearview mirror. "The black sedan behind me?"

"Two cars back." Her heart raced. "Blue van. He's been behind us for a few miles now. Right after we left the diner."

A blue van at night could look green. She wondered if this was the same van that nearly ran the trucker off the road…or contained her kidnappers. Anything was possible.

Anything could happen. Tension gripped her.

Dust flew up as he pulled off the roadside and sat, engine running. Ryan's fingers tightened on the steering wheel.

"Let's find out if this guy is following us."

Palms clammy, she waited, watching a line of cars pass, along with a blue van. Panel van, no dark windows. Fern exhaled.

"Guess I'm a little paranoid."

"I wouldn't call it that." He waited for a break in traffic and pulled back onto the road. "Cautious. I'm glad you noticed. Better to be aware than unaware."

Yeah, she'd already been unaware and that had cost her when they took her captive. Fern scrolled through her phone and changed the music to eighties rock. Ryan laughed.

"Interesting choice."

"I know you like it. Saw your vinyl collection."

A vinyl collection seemed a safer topic than the fear gripping her since the mention of a van nearly running the trucker off the road. That combined with returning to her hometown made her feel as if she were returning to a nightmare.

"Do you think they would still be out there in the same van? Billy and the other guy, I mean."

Ryan shrugged. "I don't know. For all we know, they might have ditched it and stolen another one."

Terrific. So any of the vehicles on the road could be her kidnappers.

"Don't think like that," he said suddenly. "Fear can immobilize you. The best thing you can do for yourself is to recover your memory so we can find these jerks and put them behind bars. Tell me about your job."

Fern consulted her phone and the GPS. Not far from Oso now. She knew a diversionary tactic when confronted with one, but she would play along. Much as she longed for him to turn the Jeep around to the safety of his home, she knew this was best.

She'd been through a lot in her life and would get through this as well. Self-reliance was best.

"I loved my job. It was time-consuming, but I was working on the laptop yesterday on the coding software and remembered how much I loved it. Like Hank, I was so absorbed in my work that I didn't have much of a life."

"Work can get like that," he agreed.

Staring out the window, she remembered numbers and codes and medical terms. "All I ever wanted was to do the best job possible, maybe even to prove I could make up for failing in the past. Coding isn't easy. You have to know the patient's problems as diagnosed by the doctor, and subsequent treatment. The tests ordered by the doctor, and the diagnosis. It means interpreting doc speak, as I call it, plus labs and radiology results, so I can apply the proper codes for insurance. In some cases, I saved patients a lot of money by researching their conditions and knowing the codes so insurance will cover the costs."

Fern sighed. "It's not as action-packed as your career. I don't go racing into fires to rescue people."

"It's not all that," he told her. "A lot of it is training, always trying to keep up so I know the latest tech and methods. Sometimes it's inspections. Some days it means sitting around the station, waiting for calls. On those days I try to work out, read journals. I like to expand my knowledge in case I'm first on scene and have to assess the med sitch."

"Your work is more critical," she said.

"I'd say your job is as lifesaving as mine. I save lives and you save their peace of mind."

"Well, I don't know about that."

He looked intense. "I do. I remember being on a call to a home where the kids, teenagers, were alone and the mom was out working. Their dad had died from cancer and the mom was working two jobs, one to help pay down the medical debt. Mom could barely afford food on the table and a lot of her income went to pay the bills. If you had been there, coding her insurance, I bet she wouldn't have as much debt."

The words gave her a pleasant jolt of warmth. "Most would find my job boring or only be concerned about how much money I make. What happened to the mom? Did you have to call the authorities?"

"Yeah, we did, but we got her into a program with day care, and I worked with the insurance company. Turns out a lot of the procedures were coded wrong, so insurance did end up paying. So see? Your job is critical."

She knew Ryan was one of the good guys, but going the extra mile to help a stranger added another star to his rating. She gave a faint smile.

"Maybe if my mom had someone like you watching her back

when I was little, she could have received the help she needed. Maybe if I had direction in my life, I could have avoided some of my problems. Do they make a compass for guiding your life?"

"Would be nice," he agreed.

Fern sighed. "Thanks for helping those kids, Ryan. Probably no one else bothered or cared."

He gave a modest shrug. "I was only doing my job."

No, you were getting involved. Like with me. You always seem to go the extra mile, and other guys wouldn't care, say it wasn't their responsibility. Or bother taking the time.

It seemed too intimate to voice her thoughts, and she sensed he was uncomfortable with praise. Like her, Ryan didn't like the spotlight, but preferred being behind the scenes.

It made her like him even more. Not good, because she couldn't afford to get attached to this man. He had his own life to live.

She glanced at the GPS again. Closer now, the cheery white Welcome to Oso sign making her palms sweat and her heart race. Welcome, yeah, she was welcome. Last time she was here, a horrible man named Billy and his partner pulled her into a nightmare. Seemed like she could never awaken from it, try as hard as she might.

The small town of Oso seemed eerily quiet as Ryan pulled his car onto Main Street. Fern clasped her hands in her lap, the knuckles white. Every face they passed on the sidewalk made her wonder—could they be involved? Did they know something?

She'd lived quietly, seldom interacting socially because life was easier that way. No one needed to know she was an alcoholic. Once an alcoholic, always one. Invitations to parties where people would be drinking were politely turned down. She'd only worked up the strength to date again, looking forward to the date at the Irish bar because she'd heard the food was authentic Irish and the people were unpretentious and the music lively.

Why did this happen to her? She never hurt anyone.

You're a loner. Words Jacob uttered came back to haunt her. Raised in the foster system, no family, few friends.

That's why I became a target.

Ryan suddenly pulled into an empty parking space on Main Street. She stared as he switched off the engine.

"What's going on?"

He pointed to the store out front. "Stay here. I'll only be a minute. Lock the doors."

Though most of the shops were open, she had no idea why he suddenly had an urge to shop. She waited, turning her head from pedestrians passing the Jeep.

A few minutes later, he returned and slid into the driver's seat. His grin seemed infectious.

"Got you a gift." He handed over a small paper bag.

Removing the small circle from the bag, she glanced at him. Then at the storefront that read Camping Supplies.

"I don't understand. What is this for?"

Maybe he wanted to go hiking with her?

"It's a compass. Pocket one, like kids own." Ryan's smile dropped. "So you will always know where north is and you can find your way through life. You're a strong woman, Fern. But even strong, independent women need help to find their direction once in a while, especially after they're given a second chance at life."

He looked away. "Guess that sounds silly."

Impulsively, she threw her arms around him. "Thank you," she choked out, barely able to whisper the words. "It's a wonderful gift. Thank you."

No one had ever been as thoughtful to her as Ryan. The little compass meant more than two dozen roses.

He hugged her back and released her. "Now for the hard part. You ready?"

Fern nodded as he started the Jeep and pulled out of the parking space. After clipping the pocket compass onto the necklace with her GPS tracking pendant, she tucked it back inside her shirt. The two items nestled against her breasts, a reassuring reminder she was not alone.

Still, she couldn't help a shaky breath as Ryan turned off Main Street, following directions to the Oso Care Clinic on Sage Lane. Familiar streets and buildings flashed by, each seeming innocuous, but triggering her fears as if monsters lurked on Sage Lane. She forced herself to focus on Ryan's steady presence beside her.

When he found an empty parking space and pulled in front of the clinic, she could barely breathe. Her hands clenched together as her heart raced. The brick building stood like a sentinel to her nightmares. Pedestrians passed on the street, strangers to her, but perhaps not. Could she have known them? No one gave a second look to the Jeep. A young mother hustled her child inside the clinic.

Such an ordinary day, with ordinary people. But nothing was ordinary in Oso to her anymore.

She swallowed hard. *If I ever get my life back together—no, Ava said don't think that way, you* will *get your life back together—how can I ever return here? Work here without thinking it could happen again?*

A gentle palm covered hers, warm and strong. "Fern, if this is too much for you, we'll leave. Your welfare comes first. You come first."

You come first. Words of conviction. Ryan meant it. She glanced at him, and something in her tight chest eased. No one ever put her first. People had been clamoring for her to remember, remember! You have to do it so you can help other women.

Even Ava, as supportive and wonderful as she was, hadn't been this convincing.

Not only had Ryan given up a precious day off to drive her here, but he remained with her through the process. He could have asked his sister or Jacob to make the trip, excused himself with the dozens of chores and errands awaiting him.

She turned in the seat. "Thank you. I—I needed to hear that."

Gently he rubbed his thumb over her trembling palm. "Fern, you need to lean on those wanting to help. You're not alone."

Alone had been all she knew. Alone meant no heartbreak when someone let her down, made promises they couldn't keep. Ryan was a good guy, but after this was all over, he would be gone.

Same as everyone else in her life.

Pulling away her hand, Fern swiveled back to the window, tracing a line on the glass as she stared at the clinic's sign. Familiar, and yet it was only a clinic, a building. Buildings couldn't hurt her. People could and they did, but she felt a grain of hope she could control this. From deep in her core she gathered all her strength and determination. Ryan risked his life every time he went to fight fires.

His courage and convictions fueled her. If he believed in her, then she could do this.

Closing her eyes, she willed the memories to bubble up from the depths.

"I closed that night," she said suddenly. "I asked to stay late to catch up on patient files. I had a key, so no one worried about me working after hours. We had an older man struggling with his insurance and finding the right coding would pay for his procedures, but it meant researching the diagnosis. By the time I left the office, it was dark.

"Billy... I can't remember his face. But the taller guy...a tattoo." Suddenly she could see the details as clearly as the sign on the medical building. "It was a compass on his outside wrist.

I remember that because I was walking north and I scratched him, fighting him, and he raised his hand with the ink on it and, and, one of my last thoughts was funny how he was pointing north, like the compass was a real one."

Tears welled in her throat. "I wanted… I wanted so bad to stop them from taking me. I didn't understand, I wasn't anybody, I'm a nobody, and I fought, I really fought, you have to believe me. I tried so hard in the cabin to get free, and Billy hit me so hard I screamed, and it felt like I was going to die there."

As a sob rose up, she squeezed her eyes shut, trying to control the emotions, but it felt like plugging a dam with bubble gum. For months she'd resisted crying, afraid once she did she would never cease. Impossible to stop now. Fern began to cry, big ugly crying she hadn't done since she was younger and everything went to hell.

Two warm arms encircled her as Ryan pulled her against his chest. "It's okay, Fern. Let it out. I know you fought. You're here now, and no one is going to hurt you again."

For a moment she cried as he stroked her hair, murmuring assurances.

Finally she lifted her head. With the edge of a thumb, he wiped tears from her cheek.

"You can't promise I'll stay safe because you can't be there every minute, Ryan." Fern pulled away, scrubbed her eyes with an angry fist. "No one can make that promise."

"Fern, I can promise…" He heaved out a breath. "You're right. I can't promise that. But I'll try, dammit. I'm not going anywhere."

After finding a tissue in her purse, she blew her nose and wiped her eyes. "I'm such a wreck. I hate crying. Makes me feel weak."

Ryan blinked. "You, weak? You're one of the strongest people I know, Fern. Crying is normal. Everyone cries. Sometimes it's the only way you can deal."

"I bet you never cry. You're a guy."

"Men have emotions, too."

Oh, she knew they did, but big, tough guys had emotions of anger, not tears. At least the tough guys she'd known.

"Men cry. We seldom admit it, though." He rubbed the back of his neck. "I've cried at times after a rescue went south. Do it after the job is over because you become useless if you do it while working. You shove down the emotions and deal with them later in private."

Fern blinked and studied him. "You cried? When?"

Hard to believe he actually cried. But Ryan was different. His compassion and honor were coupled with a wiry strength, both inside and out. He lacked the cruelty of men she'd known who only knew how to make others cry.

He blew out a breath. "Seriously? You need to know?"

"I'd like to know. Maybe I'd feel less of a sobbing mess if you told me."

The interior of the Jeep suddenly seemed like a cocoon, shielding them from the outside world. No one could overhear them, nor did those passing by on the street give them a second glance.

After exposing herself, she needed to know she was normal.

He gave her a grave look. "One time? Well, after you were brought to the hospital and I saw you unconscious for the first time. You were a mess, and they weren't certain you'd make it. They were sure you would die. I found a private room and cried there for a couple of minutes. You were so pretty and fragile lying in that bed, and it killed me inside to think of you taking your last breath, and I hadn't saved you in time."

Fern sucked in a shaky breath. "I didn't know."

Jaw tight, he looked out the window. "Yeah, well, now you do."

Another surprising revelation about him. She forgot about her own distress and looked at him, really looked at him. With his light brown hair cut short and burning blue eyes, he was cute, but Ryan went deeper than looks. Soul deep.

Why had their paths crossed? Oh sure, he'd saved her life, but any of the firefighters could have pulled her from the burning cabin. Yet he was the one who hauled her out of there.

He offered his home as a refuge.

Belle, her sponsor, once told her destiny could really screw you up, but things did happen for a reason. Fern had refused to believe her. The idea of fate mucking up her life was scarier than all the horrors she'd endured. Control was critical. She had to have some control over her life, over something, rather than believe she was a patsy to some mysterious and unknown force.

Yet now she wondered. Something connected her to Ryan, and the feelings she experienced were not gratitude or appreciation. They went deeper.

Scary as hell to think she was starting to care for him. When you cared for someone, anyone, they left. Or did worse.

It was her turn to comfort. Fern put a hand on his arm, resisting the temptation to remain aloof and detached. Maybe aloof was better in the past for avoiding pain, but he'd risked telling her his feelings and opening up to her.

Besides, aloof never got her anywhere. Maybe if she hadn't been so isolated, she could have avoided being kidnapped. *I'll never know.*

"Thanks for telling me. Knowing you cried makes me feel less alone, makes trying to remember those horrid days in the cabin less frightening. I don't feel so much like a freak."

His gaze turned intense as he swiveled toward her. "You're not a freak, Fern. Don't ever think like that. You're a strong woman who suffered a horrible experience thanks to bad guys who think they can do whatever they want and escape the law. Well, they can't. They'll get caught. The more you remember, the closer Jacob and the police will get to capturing them."

"A lot is riding on my messed-up memory. But what if it stays like Swiss cheese and all the pieces remain missing?"

Ryan touched her cheek again, a single caress of his thumb against her wet skin. "You'll remember. I have faith in you."

"You do?"

"Always have, from the moment I brought you out of the cabin. You're pretty, Fern, but you have a fighting spirit, more than anyone I've ever met."

The intimacy of the Jeep, their mingled breaths and this conversation made her heady. For a wild moment, Fern wanted to lean close, seal her mouth against his and kiss him, as if a single kiss could wipe away the past.

She actually leaned forward when he consulted his cell phone, the sweet moment gone, for now at least.

"Damn. So busy talking I forgot to call Jacob. I promised the moment you remembered anything, any other details, I'd call."

Ryan glanced at his cell, frowned. "I can't get a signal here. Soon as we get service, I'll call."

There went the intimacy and connection between them. Back to business. Fern's stomach tightened. Of course he said those things to assure her because the most important thing was recalling her memory to track down Billy and his accomplice.

She wasn't anything more than a witness to her own kidnapping. When all was settled and the men behind bars, she'd return to her fragmented routine. Ryan would return to his. They'd be free to move forward.

Except for the first time in months, she didn't want to move forward. Not if it meant Ryan would vanish from her life. If that was selfish, so be it.

Maybe it was time for a change—to be selfish—and put her own needs first.

Chapter 13

"Where's Fern?"

Ava glanced up from her laptop at her worried mother. "Mom, what are you doing here?"

"Where's Fern?"

Last thing she needed on this hectic day at work, with all her patient concerns piling up in a mountain of paperwork, was her mother to sound like a parrot. Okay, she probably needed reassurance.

"Ryan's taking good care of her. They're together."

"That's why I'm here." Sherry planted herself in front of Ava's desk. "You're her psychologist. You're the one treating her, not your brother. You're the one responsible for her."

Ava sighed. "Mom…"

"I need to know where they are, Ava. I called Ryan's cell, and it went straight to voicemail."

This was more than simple motherly concern. Ava leaned forward. "What is it, Mom? What aren't you telling me?"

"I don't want to worry you…"

"You already are, so tell me."

Sherry stopped pacing. "I was at Jacob's house and overheard something, and Ryan needs to know, especially if Fern is with him."

"Heard what?" She wanted to be patient, but Sherry was stirring up all her emotions.

"I knew it was a mistake for your brother to take her into his home. He's such a good man, and this…"

"Mom! What is it?"

Sherry twisted her wedding ring. Now she knew how worried her mother was.

"She needs to come back to Dark Canyon right away. He—oh dear Lord."

Fear riddled her mother's voice. Ava went over to her, rubbed her shoulders. "Mom, slow down. Tell me what's wrong."

"Jacob… One of his team was investigating Fern's kidnapping and found information on the dark web. He tried to reach Ryan, but Ryan's cell went to voicemail. No one can reach him."

Ava felt her stomach tighten. "What kind of information?"

"It's terrible, so awful."

Patience was usually her strength. Not now. "Mom, what did he find out?"

"It—it was a website for trafficking women. Fern's photo was on it, and she…was listed for sale."

Break it down, bit by bit. "We knew she was kidnapped to be sold because of the sex trafficking ring they're investigating, Mom. This is why Fern had to be kept under guard and her location kept as secret as possible. It's why a plainclothes police officer is staked out in Ryan's neighborhood."

"It's not the same information," Sherry burst out. "Whoever put her photo up there added an update that she is missing and there's a reward for information leading to her return. They're planning to go after her again."

Not unexpected. Still alarming, but with Jacob on the case, Ava felt confident things were under control.

"They want her back, of course, because they counted on making money from her. It's nothing really new, Mom. I know you're concerned…"

"They had a buyer for her. Jacob's team found out on the dark web. A man overseas was willing to pay a healthy six figures for her, maybe more. But there's a catch. The reward of cryptocurrency is good only if whoever is sheltering her is eradicated."

Blood drained from Sherry's face. "They want to make sure there are no witnesses. Ava, your brother is in danger. Whoever took Fern will kill him to get to her."

Now it was her turn to feel panic. "How much is the reward?"

"Fifty thousand dollars."

Her brother had a price on his head. Many unscrupulous, desperate people would risk killing Ryan to get Fern and the money.

"Jacob said the description of Fern added she can be singled out by a brand on her neck. A black dollar sign on the side of her neck."

Ava's blood ran cold. She'd seen this symbol on Fern's neck, but Fern thought she'd gotten the ink when she was younger. "A dollar sign is a typical tattoo of someone being sold in sex trafficking. Fern must not have remembered getting tattooed."

They needed to reach Ryan. Right now. Every minute counted.

"Still no service." Ryan frowned at his phone. "How did you live here with such crummy reception?"

Fern laughed. Such a normal question made her feel almost ordinary, as if this weren't the town where men had snatched her off the street to become someone's sex slave. "It's a dead zone. A lot of this area of Oso is, which is why I installed a cell phone booster at my apartment. I always had to use a landline when I was at work because the reception isn't great…"

Her voice trailed off. No cell service. No way to call for help.

Her gaze met his grim one. Ryan set his phone down. "They must have known and that was part of their strategy. No time to react, not even dial 911, not that you could even try because it's a dead area."

Dead area. Fern hugged herself. A memory surged. Blood pouring from her nose as she howled in pain, kicked again and again. Billy hovering over her with meaty fists, screaming at her.

"Teach you respect, you little bitch! Next time you do as I say!"

Shivering, she rocked back and forth. "I can't believe this happened to me. I've fought my whole life because no one believed I was worth fighting for. It wasn't until the Englehearts took me in as their foster child that I started to believe in people."

No words from Ryan. No hollow assurances, or murmured condolences. Sitting there, he listened. Really listened, unlike others who couldn't wait to talk after she finished. Few people had that skill set. Ava was one.

Her brother was another.

Fern stared at the building. Voicing this aloud felt almost as painful as those long-buried memories. "It took a long time for me to think I could be loved. Be worthy of love. The Englehearts helped me fight, restored my confidence. But when those…jerks abducted me, it set me back years. Like that children's board game, Chutes and Ladders? I had climbed a ladder to a boring but productive life, and slid down a chute as if I was that ten-year-old girl again."

Still nothing from Ryan. The silence grew too painful. He could think anything of her, including regret he'd offered to drive her here to jog a memory she didn't want returned because it was too painful.

She rubbed her arms. "Say something. Tell me something, anything."

The door to the clinic swung open, and a little girl, about five, perhaps, walked out with her mother. The girl's arm was in a sling.

Ryan gestured to the child, walking past them with her mother. "See that girl? Looks like she broke her arm. Can you imagine the trauma she suffered, getting hurt that badly?"

Unsure of where this was headed, she nodded.

"Kids are resilient. They bounce back. But no one tells you when you're young, or when you grow up, that your mind isn't hardwired to set aside the trauma. Set it aside and believe you deserve to have good things happen to you. That there are people in this world who believe in you and your potential."

His hand rested on her shoulder, giving it a gentle squeeze. "I believe in you, Fern. Several of us do as well. You deserve to have good things happen. Not wait for the next disaster."

She bit her lip. "I want to believe it. I can't move forward until I go back, and it's so scary to go back."

"You're not alone. I'm here with you. So is Ava. Cassidy. Sassy. Mark. Jacob. You have friends and people who want to help, not hurt you. We're with you every step of the way."

Much as she longed to believe him, Fern couldn't. She had to do this herself.

She pulled away. "You're great, Ryan. You have no idea how much I appreciate what you've done, what you're doing. I don't want to drag you into this anymore. You have your own life, your own issues."

"Hey." He gripped her hand in a gentle but firm touch. She knew he wasn't going to let go easily.

"I'm not going anywhere. You're most important now, Fern, and I make up my own mind about my life and my concerns. No one else does that for me." He shook his head. "I've been reading about what happens to victims of sex trafficking. How most victims are drugged with coke or meth or pills and so stoned they can barely say their name. They're farmed out as prostitutes, and if they dare to fight, they're beaten. These vicious men have made it as a business that makes more than 245 billion dollars a year globally from forced labor and sex trafficking. One woman…"

He released her hand and pointed at her. "One young, attractive woman like you can pull in probably around fifteen hundred a day, and that's a low estimate. It's likely they could make more than fifty grand in a month. One month."

The grim figures made her head swim. Fern gave a shaky laugh. "That sure beats my salary at the clinic. I had no idea I was worth that much money."

"It's not funny."

"I wasn't joking."

He looked so damn serious, ready to take on her kidnappers, the world, and she wanted to believe he could champion her. But she was no hero in a storybook.

Only a woman struggling to regain her life and memories, and hopefully, end this nightmare. Or at least prevent another innocent woman from entering it.

"Fern, we have to stop this. *You* have to stop this. I will do whatever I can to help you free yourself." He looked out the window. "Do you remember anything else? What about smells and sounds? You said the man who grabbed you smelled like pot. Anything else? Alcohol or cheap cologne? Maybe something they had to eat? Any sounds like ringtones or the van itself?"

Her temper simmered. She'd already done this with Jacob, with Ava, and Ryan was the only person who didn't pester her about remembering.

"I thought you weren't going to pressure me on this trip. Thanks, Ryan. Thanks a lot. Let's just go back to Dark Canyon."

"Giving up so easily?"

"I don't give up!"

He gave her a pointed look. Fern's insides knotted. Defense mechanism, she knew, her mind wanting to protect her from trauma. Better to forget than remember.

"We can go back, Fern. If you truly want that, I'll turn the Jeep around and we'll head back now. Might be for the best anyway. Having you out here in the open, I can understand how terrifying it is for you."

She blew out a breath. "I'm not terrified, Ryan."

She knew what he was doing, trying reverse psychology on her. Fern squeezed her hands. "Fine. Keep an eye on the street in case someone wonders what the hell I'm doing, or in case a cop comes along and writes a ticket for loitering. As if cops were around in this crummy town."

For so long, she'd tamped down the anger. Anger led to bad things. Fern bit her lip, closed her eyes and concentrated on her breathing as Ava had taught her. Deep breath. Count to five. Another deep breath.

No cell service, not much of a signal here in Oso. Ringtones? What a joke. The town council talked about erecting a new cell tower near downtown after merchants argued for it, and the weekly paper teased the meeting with a headline about ringtones finally being heard on southern Main Street…

"Ringtones," she breathed, her eyes still closed. "They… The other one, not Billy… When I woke up in the cabin where they held me, his cell phone rang. The ringtone was this…" She frowned. "This high-pitched whistle, and it kept going on and on. I remember thinking it sounded so familiar, from a television show or a movie that was popular."

"That's good. When we get a signal, we can ID it from YouTube. Unless you can imitate it."

Pursing her lips, she blew out a shaky rendition of the ringtone.

"Damn, I know that…that movie, I've seen it a few times. I know! It's from a movie I've seen. A really violent one."

What irony. A movie with violence, just as Fern had experienced violence. The bastards had kidnapped Fern and left her to starve and then burn to death in the little shack.

Quivering, she clenched her fists. "Every time I heard that ringtone, I wanted to scream. But I knew no one would hear me. I heard it recently, and it made me break out into a sweat. I didn't even know why!"

"Now you do."

She wanted to run. Hide. Scream out her frustrations. Her stomach roiled. This was wrong, all wrong, going back to her hometown. After all the work trying to control her reactions to what happened to her, she slid backward.

This isn't about me. I have to remember so no other woman gets hurt.

Fern drew in another shaky breath, the breakfast she'd recently consumed turning sour in her stomach.

"Let's drive the way I was walking home that night. It could trigger another memory. Drive slowly."

Ryan glanced at her as he started the Jeep. "I'm proud of you, Fern."

Proud. She didn't want pride. Nor did she want to be dependent on him. Even if she had feelings about Ryan, she couldn't stay with him for long. It could never work out. This was simply an arrangement of convenience for her, a safe place to stay for now.

Good old self-reliant Fern, too proud to admit you need anyone. Even now when you really do need Ryan.

Absently she rubbed her neck. Remembered how it stung when she got the ink, but the memory of when she got it remained hazy.

Something kept nagging at her. She wasn't merely walking home from work that night, but headed to another destination. But where? Businesses passed by, all familiar and yet strange. A pharmacy and small grocery store weren't far from her apartment as Ryan turned to head down her street.

On the corner was the Irish pub, the restaurant and bar where she'd scheduled a date with that cute pharmacy rep. Ryan barely passed it when she felt her stomach roil. "Ryan, pull over... please, now!"

Barely had he stopped when she flung open the door. Leaning out, she vomited all the contents of her stomach.

She felt two gentle hands pull her hair out of her face and

then rub her back. When she finally finished, she took the tissues he handed her and wiped her mouth.

Ryan fished out a bottle of water from the cooler in the back and uncapped it. She drank, the bottle shaking in her hands.

"I hate this." Fern set the water into a cup holder. "I hate not being in control of my life, my memories. Something's at the edge of my memory, and I know it's important and yet I can't remember it. I'm so frustrated with myself!"

"You know what we need right now? I know exactly what will make you feel better."

Fern shut the door. "Please don't tell me another greasy meal."

"Fun. Good, old-fashioned fun. The kind where you don't have to think, only experience."

She rubbed her throbbing head. "Please don't tell me your kind of fun involves anything requiring exercise or sudden movement. Did I ever tell you I get seasick?"

"We're miles from the sea, Fern."

"Doesn't matter. I can get seasick in a bathtub."

Ryan grinned. "No worries. Trust me, you'll enjoy this."

"That's what you said about the eggs and bacon."

"Ever been zip-lining?"

Moaning, she clutched her stomach. "That's your idea of fun, sailing over a thin line across a steep canyon? No. Big *N*. Big *O*."

"I'm kidding. Nothing risky. We could walk along the Animas River Trail, or go for a long ride on the Durango Silverton steam train—nah, scratch that, that's an overnight stay and a long train ride... Go shopping downtown or hiking in the canyons..."

Silent, she studied her hands. All normal activities for most people, fun things a couple would plan for a day trip. Plenty of people milling around, people who might recognize her.

People like her kidnappers. Automatically she tugged at the black wig covering her hair. It itched.

It was a barrier between herself and the world. A mask to hide behind, yet it provided little refuge. Feeling like she was on autopilot, Fern found herself nodding to all Ryan's suggestions.

No reason to think she wasn't safe. Surely he wouldn't lead her into dangerous territory.

"We'll skip lunch and have an early dinner. There's a bluegrass band playing—" he checked his phone "—at a popular restaurant downtown. The Bluegrass Meltdown isn't for another week, but this restaurant is hosting a few of the lesser known groups lined up for the festival. They also have lighter meals, like soup, that will go down easier than your breakfast did."

His brow furrowed. "Although they are more of a bar than a restaurant. Are you okay with eating in a bar?"

The question startled her a moment. Then she smiled. Few men would be so considerate. Few men knew she was a recovering alcoholic.

"As long as they have iced tea or soda water, I'm good."

Fern looked out the window at the quiet street housing her apartment complex. Such a deceptive scene, with a few shade trees along the sidewalk, and sturdy brick buildings. A good place to call home, with a playground close by. She could see a child swinging now, pushed by a young woman.

Except for those seeing the police work on the street after she'd been discovered, no one would suspect it had been a crime scene where she had been abducted and her life forever changed.

She rubbed the side of her neck and the tattoo. "Funny how the first time I planned to go to a bar in years, on a date, I get kidnapped. It was almost like fate intervening, preventing me from temptation…"

Fern stared out the window, put up a hand as Ryan started to speak. "The bar, the Irish bar, where I was supposed to meet Walter, the salesman I met at the doctor's office. I remember it like it was yesterday. My car had a flat so I walked home from work, but no, I was walking to the bar to meet Walter and listen to this amazing Celtic band. I figured the bar was a safe place to get to know him. And then…they got me."

Ryan's blue eyes widened. "What can you tell me about Walter. Tell me everything you remember." His voice was low and urgent.

This she did remember, seeing his handsome face as if he'd planted himself in front of her. Fern described Walter Landers, down to the blue-and-white-striped tie he'd worn and his gap-toothed smile that she'd found charming.

"Tell me everything you said to him. How well did he know you?"

"We got to talking in the office. Went for coffee together on my break at the café next door. Walter started talking about how he was adopted after being in the foster system for a few years. He was trying to track down his birth mother, one reason he was at the clinic because of a rare medical condition he had. That's one reason I connected with him."

His jaw tightened. "Let me guess. You told him you understood because you grew up in the foster system."

"Yes. He knew I was alone…had few friends, few people to check on me."

"Damn." Ryan exhaled a breath.

Insight struck her. "Ryan, do you think I was set up? It's too much of a coincidence that he asked me to meet him at the pub the same night they kidnapped me."

"I had the same thought," he said grimly.

Ryan glanced at his cell phone. "Signal's still crap. I'll text Jacob."

He fired off a text. Frowned. "It didn't go through. Let's visit this pub as long as we're here, and I can ask the manager about Walter Landers. If he lives in town, if he's ever been there before."

Touching her wig, she hesitated. No telling how long it would take for Jacob to get here to officially interview the manager.

Risky to do this. Fern looked at Ryan. Sure, capable and strong. He would never let anything bad happen to her.

Not if he could help it.

"Okay," she said in a small voice.

Minutes later, he pulled into the parking lot of the Irish bar. A Closed sign hung in the window. Relieved, she looked at her cell phone.

"I think they don't open until late afternoon. Maybe we should leave this to Jacob. I'm having second thoughts about getting out of the car. Someone might recognize me. Even with the wig and sunglasses."

Ryan's fingers tightened on the steering wheel. "I'm such an ass. I was so pumped up about following a lead I never considered how you felt about this. Sorry."

"Don't apologize. Let's go." She looked around. "I'd love to leave this town. Funny how it once felt like home, but no longer does."

He got it. "Want me to take the top of the Jeep off?"

The joy she felt lifted all her previous anxiety. Riding with the top down with a handsome guy. Some women might dismiss it as trivial.

Ryan couldn't have given her a better gift today.

After he put the top into a box in the back seat, Fern pulled off her wig and tucked it into the glove box. "Don't want it to go flying out the window. Someone might see it and think I lost my head. Ha."

He grinned. "More than likely an animal would use it for a nest."

He pulled out of the parking lot. "Time for some relaxation. Durango, here we come."

How long had it been since she'd had a fun outing? Since she'd been outside for a long drive through the twisting curves and canyons leading into Colorado? Fern had to admit she'd been obsessed with work and not her social life. Work was safe and reliable.

Work didn't dump you, or use you the way men could.

Not going to think about that now. I need to move forward. Enjoy the day, while this lasts.

After a while they were headed on 491 going south. "I have to warn you, this is a boring drive."

"As long as the company isn't boring, I'm good."

Wind whipped her hair. She fished in her purse and found a couple of hair ties and quickly pulled it back, braiding it. Now she could relax.

After a while the scrub, trees and wide open spaces proved soothing.

A few trucks rumbled past them, headed north. Fern's eyes began to close. They opened as Ryan snapped on the radio, singing along to the music he connected through Bluetooth.

A smile touched her mouth. "You have a terrible voice. Remind me to never do karaoke with you."

"Hey, I resent that remark." He puffed out his chest. "I'm in high demand. People pay for my singing."

"You mean pay to stop you from singing." Fern grinned at his scowl. "You know I'm kidding."

He heaved an exaggerated sigh. "And here I thought I could quit my day job."

"Sorry to disappoint."

Fern giggled at his downturned expression. "If you want to change careers, I'll support your decision. Even if it's wrong."

"Well, fine, I'll stick to singing in the car and the road."

"Lucky me," she teased.

The impish glance he gave her quickened her blood. "Be warned. I also sing in the shower."

An image of Ryan in the shower, soaping his body as he sang off tune came to mind. A heated blush ignited her cheeks. She stared out the window to hide it. Last thing she wanted was for her roommate to realize she fantasized about him being naked.

This was a platonic relationship. Ryan had a good heart, and she didn't want impose on him or make him feel uncomfortable.

They stopped at a roadside diner called Bufords. Fern raised her eyebrows as he pulled into the parking lot.

"Coffee stop," he explained. "Thought you'd like a soda as well, maybe a ginger ale, to quell your stomach."

So considerate. Fern's stomach tightened as she considered going into a crowded restaurant, but the thought of a refreshing soda tempted her.

"Soda's good. I'll leave the greasy burgers to you."

Smells of frying hamburgers and something Italian, maybe spaghetti, made her nostrils twitch. Though it was barely lunchtime, the wood tables were crowded with diners. Most of them were men. Judging from the big rigs parked in the lot, truckers as well. Maybe some locals.

Clean and bright, the diner had large windows overlooking the highway and dusty parking lot. A blackboard announced the day's breakfast and lunch specials. In the corner near a window sat a lone pinball machine, almost an afterthought.

The pinball machine looked vintage, perhaps from the 1980s. Fern forgot her anxiety. Oh wow, she hadn't played in months. But you never forgot your first love.

As they sat at a table close to the machine, everyone stared at them. Fern squirmed, wondering if this was a good idea. The place was probably local and everyone knew everyone and strangers…

A man entering the café lumbered over to their table. Tall and intimidating, he had a John Deere cap on his head, gray beard stubble shadowing his face.

"You a union man?" the man rumbled.

Oh dear. Fern's heart raced. She'd never been in a bar fight. Maybe they should leave.

Ryan's expression tightened. "Yeah. Union. I'm a firefighter."

The big man nodded. "Knew it. I'm Norm. Teamsters local 455. My brother is a firefighter, too. Unions always welcome here. Thanks for your service, brother."

As they shook hands, Ryan frowned. "How did you know I was union?"

"Sticker on your Jeep. Welcome to our little roadside stop."

"Thanks, bro." Ryan watched him walk off to the counter. The other diners nodded and returned attention to their meals. "Guess my dad put it there. Or my mom, more likely. She's prouder of me than Dad is, that's for sure."

Tension eased as the waitress came over, took their order. Fern asked for ginger ale, while he ordered a hamburger, fries and an iced tea.

"I envy how you put away so many calories," she told him.

"Don't. I have to work out later to make up for today." He patted his flat stomach.

"I look at a French fry and gain ten pounds."

"You don't need to lose weight."

Compliments made her uncomfortable. So did attention. She glanced at the pinball machine and brightened.

"Hey, I think it works. Do you have any change?"

Ryan fished out several quarters. "Go for it. Do you know how to play?"

The grin she shot him hid her secrets. *Oh yeah, I play.*

She plugged in the money, and the machine lit up, noisy and bright. She began to play, enthralled by this machine. Vintage eighties. The visuals were neon, sharp, and the layout of the machine doomed anyone who dared to stop and think about the next move.

He came over to watch.

"Timing is critical," Fern said as she maneuvered the right flipper to make a shot. "This machine is dope. So eighties and retro."

"It looks like one of my nightmares," he told her.

She laughed, loving this, the noise and the music energizing her. The futuristic music and electronic robotic voice sounded like old sci-fi movies. Flashing lights added to the thrill of play.

Fern crowed with delight as she juggled the flippers on the pinball machine. "I'm an expert. Stand back and pay homage."

By now a crowd gathered around, watching and cheering her on. Giddy with power and her success, she focused on the metal ball, loving the sharp ping of the bells, the points racking up. So much fun. She hadn't experienced this in months.

Ryan's wide grin, the cheers he added, emboldened her. Sure, a lot of bad things had happened to her and some days she fought her way out of the darkness, but having him around shone a beam of hope into her life.

For a moment, she lost focus and the ball slipped between the flippers, vanishing into the machine.

Cries of disappointment echoed. "Hey, you still got the highest score in months," one man told her.

"No one's played this in months," their waitress deadpanned.

She high-fived several guys congratulating her. A heady sense of triumph chased away all her previous trepidation. This place was remote and no one knew her. No history here or bad men lying in wait.

Slipping back into her chair, she drank heavily of the soda he'd ordered for her. Her stomach rumbled.

"I'm hungry. Say, can I get a BLT on rye?" she asked the waitress.

When the woman walked off, Ryan shook his head. "Less than an hour ago you were throwing up and now you want a BLT? You sure?"

"Yeah." She pushed back a lock of hair behind her ear. "It's like I got a second wind. Or my anxiety is gone. Funny, but this is the best place you could have taken me."

"If I'd known that you like pinball, I'd have taken you to the arcade in Dark Canyon. Used to hang out there growing up."

She beamed. "Something to look forward to."

He tilted his head. "You're a funny thing."

Somehow the remark didn't sound insulting, but rather like a compliment.

"I love playing. Pinball is hands-on, interactive and seems more challenging than video games, for me, at least. Pinball was one of the few things I could count on after my mom left me. You hit certain targets and it creates different fun reactions, depending on the machine. The bells and pings—it's noisy and challenging."

The smile he offered warmed her from the inside out. "Most of the women I've met enjoy shopping or hiking or competitive sports. They're always trying to act and look sophisticated. I've never met anyone as unpretentious as you, Fern. You're different. Refreshing."

Heat crept up from her neck to her cheeks. Ducking her head, she pretended absorption in her soda. "Maybe you haven't been hanging with the right women, Ryan."

"You have a point. Do you know how boring it is to watch someone shop for jeans and try on ten pairs? Enough time to play several vid games on my phone."

The waitress brought over their food. Fern dug into her sandwich with delight. Today turned out to be a great day, maybe the best she'd had in months.

Not because of the pinball, or even getting out of the house. It was all Ryan. She'd felt wrapped in wool, almost suffocated with concern and people worried about her memory and keeping her safe.

His company made her feel alive again.

Barely had he taken two bites of his burger when he groaned. "All this and I forgot to check my phone. Have to have a signal now."

Ryan pulled out his cell. A sheepish look came over him. "Ten missed calls! I turned down the ringer."

As he fiddled with the controls, his phone rang again. "It's Jacob," he told Fern.

"Hey, Jacob, sorry, man, I couldn't get a signal until we got to this café in Lewiston… Wait. What? What?"

Brow furrowing, he looked out the window. She had a sinking feeling again. All the previous joy evaporated like snow under a hot sun.

Ryan stood up and pulled several bills from his wallet. Cradling the phone to his shoulder, he mouthed to Fern, "Take the sandwich. We're leaving."

"I need a box," she began.

"No time."

Fern wrapped the sandwich in a napkin. He herded her to the door as their waitress started toward them. "Money for the check and your tip's on the table," he called out.

"Hey, you don't know how much you owe!" the woman called back.

Ignoring the woman, Ryan hustled her out into the parking lot. When they climbed back into the vehicle, he looked even more grim. "Check and see if anyone is following us."

Fern twisted backward. No traffic in sight. He was headed northeast again, toward Dark Canyon.

"Ryan, talk to me. What happened? Why are we going back?"

Still on the phone with Jacob, he ignored her. Ryan rattled off all the information they'd discovered today, including her description of the ringtone.

They'd been traveling fast for a few miles when he finally hung up. Ryan's expression hardened. Gone was the guy who'd smiled and made her laugh.

He was all business.

"My mom, sister and Jacob have all tried to reach me. There's new information Jacob discovered. It's bad."

With a sinking feeling, she braced herself. "Tell me. Shielding me from it won't help. I need to know."

He swore quietly as he glanced in the mirror. "Where the hell did that come from?"

Out of the corner of her eye, she saw a vehicle in the side mirror. Fern's heart raced. "Ryan, that blue van…"

Barely had the words left her mouth when they were rammed from behind.

Chapter 14

Palms tight on the steering wheel, Ryan focused on driving. He depressed the gas pedal to the floor, but the Jeep was an older model. Speedometer barely registered seventy.

Bam! Hit again from behind, he jerked forward. No one else on the road. If this kept up, they were toast. His mind sped through options. Fern, bless her, wasn't hysterical, but sat calmly, her eyes wide.

"Ryan, what's going on?"

Cursing again, he tried to speed up. "Jacob's team found preliminary info on the dark web. They have to verify it, but there's a reward of fifty thousand dollars—and the reward is also to kill whoever is sheltering you. The men who took you don't want witnesses."

Fern paled. She took out her cell phone and twisted around, taking photos of the rearview mirror.

Her voice quavered. "If that's them, Ryan, and I think it is, stop and let me out. Let them take me. Or try. I won't go down without a fight. You can call for help."

What? Grimacing, he jerked the wheel to one side as the van tried to hit them again. "I'm not letting you out, Fern. Over my dead body."

"Exactly. You're in danger. I won't see you hurt over this. Over me."

Willing to sacrifice herself to save him. Damn. His admiration, and fear for her, doubled.

He looked at the rearview mirror. "I've got to lose these assholes. Or slow them down until we can reach a police station."

No traffic on this road, other than them. Two cars passed them and the van slowed down. Obviously the men in the van didn't want any Good Samaritans following or reporting to the cops what they tried to do.

Then it was open road, no traffic and the van sped up, banging into them once more.

"We have to do something." Fern looked around. "Can we flatten their tires?"

Great idea. "My dad's toolbox is in the back seat. See what's in there."

She unbuckled her seat belt and climbed into the back seat, rummaging in the toolbox. "Ah, got it. Thank the good Lord your dad never cleaned out his stuff."

She uncapped the bottle of screws and unzipped the back window. "Let me know when."

Ryan depressed the gas pedal, putting a little distance between themselves and the pursuing van. "Now!"

Out went the screws onto the roadway. The van swerved to avoid them and sped up.

Fern bit her lip. "I'm sorry. I thought it would work."

He looked at her. "I'm sorry I brought you into this mess. I wasn't thinking. And your wig... You forgot to put it on. They may have recognized you in the café."

He twisted the wheel, going into the opposite lane to avoid the van slamming into them again.

"It's my fault. I got careless. I was enjoying being out with you so much I forgot I can't be like anyone else. Ryan, I never wanted to drag you into this, into danger! Please, let me out and whatever happens, happens."

Fierce anger filled him. Dammit, it wasn't right. Fern was

a lovely woman with a selfless attitude. Simply because she'd been alone and lacked family, they had targeted her.

He reached over and quickly squeezed her hand. "You are not alone."

Suddenly they heard the deafening sound of a truck horn. Ryan glanced in his mirror. "We've got more company."

To his amazement, the tractor trailer sped up and rammed the van from behind. The van jerked to the right and ran off the road.

The truck behind them sped up. Sweat poured down his back. Now what? Did Fern's kidnappers work in tandem with this guy, too?

A deafening horn sounded behind him. Fern twisted in her seat. "He's motioning for you to keep going."

After a few miles, Fern watching the truck driver the entire time, she told him to pull over at the next intersection. Ryan did, guiding the Jeep to the dirt road. He parked, but left the engine running. Wary, he glanced in his rearview mirror.

"If this guy is trouble, stay buckled up, just in case."

But he recognized the man running toward them. He recognized the green John Deere cap. Norm, the trucker from the café. Still, he remained ready to run if necessary.

"Hey. It's okay. I called for help," Norm said, holding up his hands. "I'm one of the good guys. We saw you bolt from the café, and then I saw that blue van. Same son of a bitch tried to run my friend off the road, so I climbed into my rig to see what was going on. And then he banged into you and I figured you needed help."

Ryan climbed out of the Jeep, along with Fern. He shook Norm's hand. "Thanks, man. I was afraid we'd end up in a pile of crushed metal."

No reason to explain to this guy, helpful as he'd been, what the real situation was.

But Norm gave him a long look. "When I saw what that van

was doing, I got the guy's plates. Called my cousin—he's a deputy in Grand Junction. Had him run the plates, and he told me the van is stolen."

Ryan remained silent. Norm looked at Fern, who kept staring at the ground.

"Not sure what's going on—that's your business. But the way you two tore out of the café, leaving a fifty-dollar tip for Mary, we knew there was trouble. And a brother always helps out another brother in trouble, so I followed you."

"Thank you," Fern whispered.

"They're long gone by now. Probably ditched the van for another stolen vehicle. But at least you're safe."

Understatement.

"There should be a sheriff's deputy here soon," Norm told him.

Ryan looked at Fern, pale and trembling. Talking to a strange police officer was not on the agenda. Trust ran low, especially now that he knew a price was on his head.

"We can't stick around. Have to get back. I need to make a call but..." He palmed his cell phone. "No signal."

"I've got a sat phone. Wife insisted on paying for it for these long hauls across the desert. She always worries." Norm went into the cab of his truck and came out with the phone.

Ryan dialed Jacob and explained the situation.

"If your vehicle isn't disabled, drive to..." Jacob named a gas station on the road back to Dark Canyon. "I'll be there, waiting for you."

After he handed back the sat phone, Fern suddenly disentangled herself from Ryan and ran to Norm, hugging him. "Thank you. Thank you for reminding me there are good people in this world."

The trucker looked embarrassed, and pleased. "Thanks. It's nothing. We have to look out for each other these days. You guys sure you don't need anything? How's your wheels? That guy sure wanted to run you off the road."

He walked to the back of the Jeep with Ryan, who winced at the dents the van had made. Not going to be easy to explain to his father how his favorite weekend vehicle needed repairs.

"Thank the Lord the spare tire absorbed a lot of those blows." Ryan ran a hand over the tire. "I can drive it, and that's all that matters now. We have to leave."

"I'll wait here for the deputy, tell him what happened." Norm gave him a long look. "I'll tell him it was a case of road rage that popped up and to look out for the van. You had a lady in the car to look after and couldn't stick around because you had to get back home in a hurry. The deputy will probably put out a be on the lookout for the van, and every trucker on the road will watch out for those guys."

Relief filled him. Norm wasn't pressing for details Ryan didn't want to give. "Thanks, man."

After shaking hands again with Norm, he climbed back into the Jeep with Fern. She waved at Norm as they got back on the road again.

When they reached the gas station near Dark Canyon, Jacob was in the parking lot, leaning against his black Chevy SUV. He wasn't alone. Officer Chayton Benally, the Navajo Nation policeman investigating her case, was there as well. She noticed the tribal police vehicle parked next to the black SUV.

With a grim look, both men came toward them as Ryan switched off the ignition.

She liked Chay. Engaged to Ava, he was brusque at times, but she'd glimpsed his kind heart and heard from Ava how tender he was with the baby they were adopting.

Today he wasn't kind. Chay scowled at them both.

"What were you thinking, going off like that in public where anyone could see you?"

He directed the question at her, but stared at Ryan.

"Fern was restless. She needed to get out of the house, and we stopped at Oso to try to trigger her memory," he told Chay.

Jacob was equally grim. "Fern could have been taken again. You could have been killed, cuz."

Ryan spread out his hands. "How was I supposed to know about all this? We couldn't get a signal on our cell phones."

"Exactly," Chay broke in. "There's many areas of the desert with dead areas. In an emergency, you're stuck."

"And we would call this an emergency," Jacob added. "Leave the investigating to us. You know better, Ryan."

Fern couldn't take this anymore. "Stop blaming Ryan. I'm the one who insisted on leaving. Because of Ryan taking me to Oso, I was able to recall some memories that will aid in your investigation."

Both officers glanced at each other.

"It was too risky." Jacob seemed calmer.

"The risk is already taken," Ryan shot back. "Now, do you want to know what we found out?"

"You tell them, Ryan. Give them my cell phone. I took photos of the van from the side mirror. I need to use the bathroom." Right now she felt like she was going to hurl once more. No amount of sketching, making lists or triangles would soothe her fractured nerves.

"I'll go with you. With what happened, you shouldn't be alone," Chay told her.

Fern sighed. "All right."

Leaving Ryan to tell his cousin Jacob what they'd learned, she trudged toward the gas station entrance. The restrooms were in back. Chay nodded at her.

"I'll be right here in the hallway."

Inside, she waited for the nausea to abide or resolve. Fern gripped the sides of the sink, staring into the dusty mirror. Pale, oh so pale, the face staring back at her. But she did it. She'd returned to Oso and, with Ryan's patient help, recalled important details of her abduction.

The time spent on the pinball machine seemed like years ago. She ran water into the sink, splashed her face and dried it with a paper towel.

By the time she emerged, the nausea was under control. So was she.

Chay escorted her out into the convenience store. "Need any food? Chips? Snacks? Water? Soda?"

"A ginger ale would be great." Thoughts of the uneaten BLT left in the Jeep sent her stomach roiling all over again.

The soda he bought her felt fantastic on her parched tongue. When they rejoined Jacob and Ryan outside, she felt somewhat normal again.

Bright sunshine and a cloudless sky greeted them. Such a gorgeous day, the kind you anticipated going for a long hike or even a simple walk along a scenic river like the Animas in Durango.

Not being chased down by evil men who wanted to take her prisoner and kill Ryan. The last thought almost made the nausea return.

Chay put a gentle hand on her shoulder. The contact settled her a little as she took a deep breath and looked at Jacob.

"Do you need anything from me?" she asked him.

"Ryan told us everything. I need you, and him, to be safe and stay home. Unfortunately the photos you took are blurry. No way to run a facial recognition." Jacob handed back her cell phone. "But the information he provided from your recalled memories helps. We'll check out this Walter Landers."

"He was short, about five feet, six inches, with sandy hair thinning in front, a little scar here." She pointed to her chin. "Gap-toothed in front, and he liked expensive suits. Italian silk, I believe. Dark colors. Oh, and he wore lifts in his shoes because one day he came in without them and was about my height."

As the men stared at her, she added, "He also liked wearing socks with golf clubs on them. So I believe he enjoyed playing golf."

Chay shook his head. "That's a tremendous help, Fern. Great description. I'll get going on this."

With a nod, he climbed into his patrol vehicle.

Fidgeting, Ryan looked impatient to be off. She understood. After the frantic rush on the road to escape the van running them off, nowhere on the road seemed safe. Only the walls of his house provided any security.

With a price on his head, though, was his home truly safe? What kind of desperation forced these men into offering to kill a man in order to get Fern back into their clutches?

Chapter 15

The good news was the information Jacob's team discovered on the dark web was incorrect. The reward offer had been vague, and after following up, Jacob's team discovered it was a dead end.

His mother, as usual, had taken everything to the extreme and thought Ryan truly had a price on his head. She'd never been a helicopter parent, but Sherry could turn overprotective if she thought one of her children was endangered.

The other good news was details Fern provided to the police could prove useful in tracking them down, including the cell phone ringtone and a description of Walter.

The bad news was the men were actively searching for Fern. Jacob had grimly informed him the van trying to ram them off the road fit the description of the same one used to abduct Fern.

The sheriff's deputies found it by the roadside, abandoned, and took it into evidence. But it looked stripped down, and they doubted they'd find anything useful, such as fingerprints or DNA evidence.

He wasn't happy about leaving Fern to go to work, so the next day he used his considerable sick time to take a day off.

Ryan began questioning his life choices. Not for the first time, he wondered if he should have agreed to quit the fire department and follow his dad into business.

Safer, for sure. More money. Oh yeah. No adrenaline rush

like he had now. No saving lives. At least his family would quit worrying about him.

Fern came into the living room, where he was reading an online article about new hazmat equipment.

"Cassidy Garner texted me and would like to see how I'm doing. Is it okay if she visits?"

Since the whole world probably knows where you live now, why not? But he clamped down that thought and offered a brief smile. "Sure. Does she want to have lunch here?"

"I don't think so. A quick visit."

Sure, a quick visit. Cassidy, Fern's nurse at the hospital, probably worried about her former patient, since Ryan had taken her out on a drive that could have sent her back to the hospital.

Or worse, to the morgue.

He set aside his tablet. "What's wrong?"

Oh, he knew her expressions by now. Fern was an open book when it came to showing her feelings, much as she tried to hide it.

"I spent a little time with Google, finding out what you do for a living, Ryan." Fern perched on the edge of a chair. "I don't know anything about fighting fires. So I thought I'd learn a little. I thought maybe it was dying from a fire or smoke inhalation, but it seems cancer is a biggie. I mean, who would think? But you come into contact with all those chemicals in smoke, and maybe even asbestos, and your chances of contracting cancer are significantly higher than most people."

Ryan said nothing, but he watched her, wondering where this was going.

"You keep saying you're just a guy doing his job. That's where you're wrong. You and the other guys are heroes, every time you rush off to fight another fire and put your lives on the line.

"But I have to be honest, Ryan. I'm starting to get feelings for you. You're incredible, and I owe you so much."

"You don't owe me anything." Damn, he didn't want her feeling as if he ran a bed-and-breakfast.

"Yet I can't help worry about you every time you go to work."

"Okay."

You don't want to get involved with a guy like me who may never come home after a shift. Because you've had enough men in your life who never came home.

She glanced down at her hands, as if unable to voice her thoughts. Finally she looked at him.

"I was only being honest."

"I get it. No worries." He'd heard plenty of the same from his last girlfriend, Kim March. She broke up with him when he almost bought it during a three-alarm fire at a local warehouse. He'd been on the stairs, starting upward, when he got blown down. Fortunately the hose crew doused him and got him out.

But Kim freaked out and declared she couldn't deal with the possibility of losing him. He'd appreciated it and tried to talk to her, but her mind was made up.

A couple of weeks later, he discovered she was more concerned about not having a date the night he worked that fire. There'd been an art gallery showing with many high-profile people there, and Kim was irritated he had to work and couldn't escort her.

Ryan knew he was better off alone.

Maybe Fern felt the same way.

He returned to his reading, and Fern vanished down the hallway, probably to work on her laptop.

An hour later, Cassidy showed up. With her blue eyes, strawberry blonde hair cut into a shag, and friendly air, she was attractive. Nice as well, but he wasn't in the mood to make friends.

She and Fern hugged.

"I'll be in my office, let you two catch up," he told them.

Before Fern started to protest, he went down the hall.

Seemed like only a short time later when Cassidy popped

her head into his office. "I wanted to let you know I'm leaving. Fern seems better."

Better? He could have killed her. "I guess."

"She does. In the hospital, she was isolated, and though her body healed, her spirit was low." Her smile dropped. "You okay, Ryan?"

"I'll be fine. Thanks for checking on her."

"Don't be hard on yourself, Ryan, for taking her out of the house. She needed it. Fern is tougher than everyone realizes. And she seems happy here," she said gently.

"I know how tough she is. But tough doesn't count when there's a killer out there and her kidnappers still running loose." He stopped short from saying, *and they almost got her.*

Thanks to his recklessness in thinking everything was cool, it was like an ordinary day out with a pretty woman. Not a kidnapping victim who had to disguise her appearance.

A victim who was recognized. That itself made him wonder.

How did they find Fern? Was he followed from Oso? Or worse, Dark Canyon itself?

With a scrutinizing look, she nodded and then left. He went into the kitchen to find Fern making sandwiches. "Turkey on whole wheat sound good?"

"Not really hungry," he admitted.

Fern gave him almost the same look as Cassidy. "You have to eat, Ryan. Please, don't blame yourself for what happened yesterday."

Was there anyone else to blame? But to keep the peace and make her happy, he helped himself to a turkey sandwich, managing to eat most of it and kill a bottle of water as well. Much as he longed for a beer, he hadn't kept any alcohol in the house because of Fern.

His desire for a cold brew mattered less than her comfort.

Fern pointed to the stairs. "I promised Cassidy I'd keep up with my exercises. I'll be downstairs, working out."

Nodding, Ryan began to clean up. His cell dinged a message. Jacob, with an update.

He called Jacob, and the news was mixed. The kidnappers had not followed him from the house. The plainclothes police officer monitoring the house ensured they were safe there.

Only some guys at the fire station, like Bob, along with Cassidy and Ryan's family knew where she stayed.

He wondered about that. "What if someone ran the plates on the Jeep? Is that how we were found?"

"More likely someone was tracking your truck because they had the license plate and saw you pull into your parents' driveway and then drive off in the Jeep. That's more probable. Once they had the Jeep's license, it was a matter of following you to Oso and the roadside diner," Jacob told him.

The idea of someone watching him at all times gave him the creeps. Worse, the kidnappers knew where Fern now lived. Her safety came first.

"Be cautious, Ryan. Don't trust anyone except family."

He hung up, deeply disturbed. Then he texted Mark, asking his cousin to come over and check on the security system.

Glad for the reprieve from his dark thoughts, Ryan met him outside a few minutes later.

Ryan clapped his cousin on the shoulder. "Come on in. If you're hungry, Fern made sandwiches and there's extra. No beer, but plenty of iced tea and water and even lemonade."

"Iced tea sounds great." Mark checked the cameras out front, and then they went inside. Mark made sure to lock the door.

After checking over the interior cameras upstairs and the DVR system, Mark seemed reassured. "Everything okay with the system?"

"System is fine. I'm the one who needs fixing."

"Talk to me."

"Let's go outside. Fern's downstairs, doing her PT. You just missed Cassidy. She came over to see how Fern's doing with her workouts."

His cousin's expression tightened. Ryan glanced at him. "You used to date Cassidy."

Saying nothing, Mark followed him outside, onto the patio. Ryan got it. A man had a personal life, and judging from his cousin's stiffness, Cassidy was real personal.

They sat at the patio table with two tall glasses of iced tea. A chill hung in the air, the weather at the fickle point of trying to decide to usher in spring or announcing winter still hung around, get used to it.

He updated Mark on the sitch with his truck being tailed, and the Jeep. "I'm thinking of renting a car."

"Might be a good idea, until they catch whoever did this."

Mark sipped his tea. "I had a feeling everything wasn't right with you. By the way, everyone in the family knows about your joy ride with Fern."

Damn. "Word travels fast."

"It's family." Mark shrugged. "They worry all the time."

Oh yeah, he knew it. "Speaking of family, I heard your dad is dating Susan Baylor. You okay with that?"

"I'm okay. Even if he married again, yeah. Dad deserves to be happy. Hope her pain in the butt ex won't be an issue, but he could."

"In what way?"

"Ken Baylor is harassing Susan. Forget about the fact they've been divorced for a few years." Mark scowled. "Never liked that guy after he moved into my neighborhood."

"Ken is a royal jerk," he agreed. "Maybe he'll lay off Susan."

"Doubt it." Mark sipped more tea. "So what about this joy ride with Fern?"

"I screwed up."

"Hard to imagine you doing something that risky, especially with someone else's life at stake, without taking precautions."

At least his cousin gave him that much credit, unlike his parents, who lectured him with texts all morning. "I did, but it didn't do much good in the end. And yeah, I'm feeling like I let Fern down, but it's more than that. Has to do with my career. Second thoughts. Maybe my family is right. It's too dangerous."

His cousin looked surprised. "That's out of left field. Never heard you talk like this, Ryan. Yeah, your job is risky, but you have training. You don't rush into a burning building without gear."

Ryan laughed. "Not without PPE and our PASS."

"What's that?"

"Personal Alert Safety System, which alerts if we're immobile for more than thirty seconds."

"Yeah, I remember the Twin Towers attacks..." Mark's voice drifted off.

They both fell silent for a moment, remembering the 343 firefighters killed in the September 11 attacks, and the devices that kept beeping in the rubble.

So many good lives lost that day.

Ryan cleared his throat. "My dad keeps thinking I should change careers. But how can I? This is my life."

"He worries about you being in a fire you can't escape."

Fires were living, breathing creatures. They provided heat and comfort during an icy winter, and could kill indiscriminately. It wasn't the flames that got people most times. People breathed in smoke, smoke mixed with godawful chemicals.

"Tell me about your work." Mark stretched out his legs. "What do you do when you get to a burning building?"

"Lots. Something most people don't understand is why we break windows if a building is on fire. It's to vent the building. Smash windows, let the smoke and gases escape. Increases someone's chances for survival, and by reducing the smoke, we can see easier."

"Most people think firefighters spray water and then enter," Mark said.

Ryan laughed. "Like in the movies? It's science, man. Water hits fire and heat and what do you get? Steam. It's not only the fire, but the heat and smoke, and all the smoke drops down, which is why they tell you to drop to the ground to avoid the smoke in a fire. It's black inside once you hit those flames with water. Like pitch-black until we vent the room or the building. We bring in hoses to work along the way, but it's a hell of a lot easier to enter and search before the hose is turned on."

He named a few other procedures he knew, and practiced, by heart.

Mark nodded. "So you know what to do if there's a fire. You've trained…"

"Always. We're always training, like you did in the army."

His cousin studied the back fence. "Let me ask you this—not why you want to quit. Why did you choose this job as a career? Don't give me the canned response—you wanted to be a hero, save lives, help humanity."

His cousin sounded a little bitter. Ryan drew in a breath. Most times he didn't want to talk about this, but Mark got it. After being in the army, his cousin showed little emotion. Mark asking him these questions could open his cousin up to talking about what happened, and why he came home.

"Yeah, I did, but it was more. Fires always fascinated me. I know some choose firefighting as a career for the adrenaline rush. For me, it's something more. Fire is beautiful and yet deadly. A beautiful killer, if that makes sense. I wanted to conquer it, defeat the enemy and beat it. Control it so it couldn't hurt anyone."

"Sounds like a military reasoning."

Not surprising, since many police and fire rescue personnel were ex-military. "There's times when I knew it was hopeless. You go into a burning house to rescue a kid, grab him out of bed and go for the other rooms, but the hall is burning. It's pure hell. No entry. You know whoever's in those back bedrooms is dead. The worst is a kid who was too little to save himself..."

Throat tightening, he managed to say, "It's a hard reality and you have to live with it.

"Then there are the saves you'll never forget because those are the ones worth holding on to when you're trying to sleep, wondering if it's worth it. Worth the risks, the women who want to date you because you're a firefighter and they love the glam, the excitement, but won't take a relationship to the next level. What's the point when there's a chance I'll go into a burning building and never come out? A lot of women can't deal with that risk of heartache.

"The saves where you see a kid's face covered in black soot and he starts coughing through the O2 mask and you find out later he made it and he's gonna be fine. His parents don't have to fund a funeral instead of a college fund."

Mark nodded. "I understand."

Mark didn't offer any information about why he understood, and Ryan didn't press him. Sometimes the work they did led them on a lonely path. Ordinary civilians usually couldn't comprehend the grueling work, hours and the emotional battles facing soldiers and firefighters.

"But all the training in the world—the gear, the hoses, the backup, the team who has your six—can't make up for the ones you lose, who are there so close and slip through your fingers. The ones who make you lose sleep at night."

Mark braced his elbows on his thighs. "The enemy within," he mused.

"A hard enemy to fight and control. I've been to fires where you know it's a lost cause, no matter how much water you use, how fast you arrive. The fire wins. Those are the bad days. When the bad days overtake the good, maybe it's time to reconsider."

"Like I did with my military career?"

His cousin sounded bitter. He knew Mark wouldn't talk now about why he quit the army and didn't want to pressure him.

"Maybe. If I quit, my mom will finally calm down, Dad will be happy and Ava less worried."

"What about you? Will it make you happy? Or miserable?"

Ryan thought for a minute. "I honestly don't know. Hard to say when this is all I've known."

"Your enemy within sounds easier to defeat," Mark mused.

He didn't want to walk down that road of self-examination, vanish into the darkness of his own thoughts. This was too serious, especially with Mark, who had his own demons to battle.

"Want to check out the bird feeder? Fern loves it."

Not batting an eye at the sudden change of topic, Mark accompanied him over to the bird feeder containing the camera.

He examined the feeder. "The solar panel should keep the battery charged, but if it gets low, use a charger."

"Fern's been taking care of it, makes sure to keep it full. She enjoys seeing the birds feed every morning and dusk."

"It's her, huh? Making you rethink your job."

Startled, he shook his head. "No, not really. I've been considering it..."

But the knowing look his cousin gave him made Ryan give up the excuses. "Maybe, in a way. I keep blaming myself for what happened yesterday, and what if they'd grabbed her?"

"They didn't." Mark glanced at his cell phone. "I have to run. Stop the self-blame. Won't do any good."

He wanted to tell his cousin to do the same, knowing that Mark had been through hell and back. Instead, he nodded. "Thanks, man."

When Mark left, Ryan leaned against the door and closed his eyes. His own demons were pretty damn nasty at times. But instead of seeing the face of Kate, the woman who literally slipped through his fingers last year and fell to her death, he saw another face.

Fern, terrified, as her kidnappers dragged her away once more, never to be seen again.

Chapter 16

That night, leaving his truck in the garage after giving Fern strict instructions to call Jacob if anything appeared out of the ordinary at the house, he took an Uber to the rental car agency. Ryan rented a compact vehicle and made arrangements to park it at the house where the plainclothes police officer kept watch.

With the car parked away from the house, he felt safer but still apprehensive about being watched. So when Cap asked him to cover a shift the following day when he was still off duty, he almost turned him down.

Yet he knew Cap wanted to discuss something serious when his boss said he didn't want to use a floater from the pool.

Ryan suspected Tom had other ideas in mind, such as lecturing him on his career flashing a warning sign.

When he got to the Dark Canyon station at seven the following morning, Cap was there waiting with a mug of coffee. Ryan accepted the brew and followed him into the glass-paned office.

Here it comes...

To his surprise, Cap handed him an envelope. "Got this yesterday. Congratulations. You've been awarded the city's Fire Service Recognition Award in honor of the work you did on the Pinyon Canyon Avenue fire last year."

Confused, he stared at the words on the page. "Cap, that wasn't anything much. I was doing my job. Like every other day."

"The mayor doesn't think so. Neither do your colleagues. Everyone at the house was asked to nominate someone, and they chose you."

Guilt flashed through him quickly as an out-of-control burn. Lately he hadn't been there for his team, his mind elsewhere. "I don't deserve this. There are others who've done much more."

"You're a good smoke eater, Ryan. You're courageous without being reckless, and you're a team player, through and through."

He heard the hesitation. "But…"

"We're worried about you."

We. Not merely Cap. "Why? What have I done? I pull my weight. I pitch in."

Ryan already knew the answer before his boss opened his mouth.

"It's this business with Fern Hensley. Having her move in with you. Ever since she did, you've been off."

Cap picked up a clipboard. "You showed up late for shift. Forgot to clean the hoses before you rolled them on your last run. There's other incidents, minor. I could go on."

"My personal business is mine. If I'm off, tell me. But don't you dare blame Fern or my personal life."

"I'm not blaming her. I feel bad for what she went through. But she's an outsider, Ryan. An outsider who carries risks to anyone sheltering her, like what happened to both of you yesterday."

Cap leaned forward. "I don't want to lose one of my best firefighters."

So that was the real issue. He wondered if Sherry had a talk with his captain and her worry trickled down, like a leaky dam.

He wasn't mad. Not yet. But getting there. The men and women of Dark Canyon Fire Department needed to butt out.

"I mean it, Cap. I'll stay focused. But Fern isn't the only victim here, and people seem to forget it. Ever think about that?

There's a killer out there, and kidnappers taking women to be sold into sex trafficking."

Lowering his voice, he locked gazes with Tom. "There's evil walking among us. Any innocent woman could be next. What if it was your wife, or your sister, or even your daughter? What would you do?"

"Anything I could to get them back," Cap said evenly. "I understand."

No, you don't. Tom was a good man, a hell of a firefighter and a good captain who cared about the men and women at the station, but he was loyal to the town and its people. Fern was an outsider. Cap stated as much.

For the first time, he realized how alone Fern must have felt even before the kidnappers took her. No one to lean upon, or close friends to call during times of trouble.

His heart beat faster as he remembered how she'd been lying on the cabin floor, overcome by smoke, nearly a victim. No one to even bury her.

Saying anything more to Tom would jeopardize his houseguest. Mark warned him. *Don't trust anyone but family.*

He stood, nodded. "I won't let you down again, Cap. No more mistakes."

"Good. Get to work. You're on cooking detail today."

Ryan started to head for the kitchen when a woman walked into the fire station and called out.

"Hello? I'm looking for Ryan Colton."

Recognizing her as the woman who'd taken the dog to the vet after the house fire, he walked toward her. "I'm Ryan."

"Carrie Armstrong." She reached out her hand. "I've been meaning to track you down, but I've been so busy with the spring hiking season in full swing."

"How's the dog? And the little girl?"

Carrie smiled. "Both are fine, thanks to you. But that's not why I'm here. I wanted to tell you something about Kate Mc-

Intyre. I didn't have a chance the other day because I had to rush Wobbles to the vet."

Ryan's chest tightened. He gave an indifferent shrug. "I tried to rescue her. I'm sorry for your loss."

Carrie's steady gaze met his. "It was a tragic loss, true, but that's not why I'm here. I wanted to tell you about Kate and how she shouldn't have been on the cliff that day. She was a beginner, and we never send beginners to that section of canyon. Also, Kate shouldn't have been alone, but with a guide."

This was news. Ryan frowned. "What are you saying, Ms. Armstrong?"

"I'm saying neither you nor I are at fault for her death. Especially you." The woman sighed. "I keep going over and over in my head why she was on the rock wall that day. Kate was depressed and thought rock climbing would help. She should never have gone by herself. We always make students sign waivers, but eventually, everyone has to take responsibility for their own actions."

He began to understand. "Thanks for letting me know."

Carrie nodded. "Well, I have to get back to work. I only wanted to let you know—in case you feel you should have, could have, done more."

For a moment, a haunted look came over her. "Sometimes I wonder if I could have."

"You didn't put her on the rock wall," he said gently.

She nodded. "And you did everything you could to save her. Goodbye, Mr. Colton."

He watched her walk out of the station, his thoughts jumbled.

Of all the mistakes he'd made as a firefighter, and most were minor, Kate was the one he regretted the most.

You have to move on.

As he headed for the kitchen, his mind wasn't on the mistakes he'd made on shift. It was how alone Fern had been.

Same as the other women who'd been taken.

There was a connection there. He knew it. Being in Oso, hearing how she had few friends, led a fairly solitary life, made him suspicious.

Fern had been targeted because she had no family. Few friends. No one would miss her.

As he watched the spaghetti sauce cook in the stainless steel pot, he called Jacob for an update on the case. Nothing new.

Extremely concerned, he called Fern. Phone went straight to voicemail. He texted instead, then called Officer Jenkins, the plainclothes police officer guarding the house today.

Jenkins promised to check on Fern.

The sauce began to bubble and boil. Ryan turned down the gas and tried not to worry. Impossible now.

Now more than ever, it was critical for Fern to recover her full memory so they could nail these guys.

None of the usual activities she'd undertaken since moving in with Ryan soothed her fractured nerves lately. Fern tried working on the computer, doing the lists Ava had recommended. Physical therapy, painting, reading, even her sessions with Ava here in Ryan's home proved ineffective.

Ava had suggested relaxation might help trigger important memories in the cabin. The pressure on her to remember had doubled since another woman had been kidnapped.

She needed to move forward. Ryan's generous offer to stay with him had been a step in the right direction. Now she'd fallen backward and wondered if she could recover.

Numbers made sense. Coding was numbers and logic. Fern itched to get back to work and scanned for medical coding jobs. But the terror and grief clawed at her, and she knew work was impossible.

Trapped in fear, she wanted to escape the pit. She wanted her old life back, the solitary, reliable Fern who paid her bills on time and worked to the point of obsession. The Fern who enjoyed seeing bright smiles on patients when she explained how their illness would be paid through insurance.

The horrific experience of being taken against her will, bound up with zip ties, her body left on the rough wood floor, then the acrid stench of smoke stinging her eyes and nostrils...

Rebuilding her life would take time. She understood that. Yet until she recalled all her memories, Fern knew she'd never become whole and happy again.

She felt like a mosaic with missing parts. Every time she felt a little joyful, like riding with Ryan in the vehicle, something happened to smash it once more.

Tomorrow night was dinner with Ryan's parents. She wondered if it was a good idea. Would they scrutinize her over what had happened? Be worried their only son was endangered by sheltering Fern?

Fuss over Ryan while blaming her? She got it. Ryan had a caring family. A slew of Coltons, from cousins to aunts and uncles, who loved him.

I'm alone.

Maybe I'm better off staying here alone.

How could she entertain stepping outside the house when her kidnappers were roaming free? Yet inside Ryan's house she felt trapped, except when he was present.

With Ryan around, she not only felt safe, but energized and alive. However, Fern knew her presence meant a threat.

The kidnappers wouldn't hesitate to kill him, and her, together. Maybe even set another fire, hoping they'd both perish.

You don't have any money, not enough to leave. You have no place to go. What are you going to do? Until you become whole again, and stable with your memories intact, you're stuck.

Folding her laundry as she sat on the guest bed while Ryan worked a shift, she made triangle patterns with her socks. The patterns soothed her. Repetition of familiar shapes.

Shapes helped clear her mind. They made sense in a way the

world did not. Shapes were reliable. Predictable, unlike people and their motives.

A faint memory pricked her mind. She'd never done this as a child when feeling threatened or scared. Hiding in the closet, clutching her favorite, worn stuffed bunny, she learned to be quiet and still, lest she invoke her mother's rage.

Or worse, William's anger.

Fern went still. Why were triangles so important and what drove her to create these shapes? Much as she liked numbers and her job of coding, geometry had never been her best subject.

She closed her eyes, trying to evoke memories. Shapes were important. Stop signs were red octagons. Yellow railroad signs were circular. Brown trapezoid signs indicated a national recreation area.

Yellow pendant signs warned motorists not to pass.

Her eyes flew open. *This is ridiculous. I'm trying to remember triangles and all I can recall is my driver's ed class.*

But as she returned to folding socks, she kept making triangle shapes. Fern stared at the white ankle sock she'd formed into a triangle.

This had to mean something and wasn't merely self soothing.

Her conscious mind might have forgotten plenty, but her subconscious kept repeating the pattern.

Ava told her during a session how tricky the subconscious was, and how your mind would never make everything crystal clear in dreams. Fern admitted to having dreams of being naked. Ava explained it had nothing to do with actually being naked, but feeling vulnerable.

If anyone has a right to be vulnerable, it's me.

Maybe the triangle represented something from her kidnapping. Abandoning the laundry, she went downstairs to the basement and her sketch pad. Fern took the charcoal pencil and began drawing triangles.

Nothing.

After returning upstairs, she went into Ryan's office and switched on her laptop and began surfing the web. Triangles, triangles. What did they represent?

Absorbed in the deep dive she'd undertaken, she was surprised to hear her stomach grumble. Fern glanced at her cell phone.

Almost two thirty! She'd forgotten to have lunch. Time for a break, maybe mix up a green salad with chicken to make up for the tacos Ryan had brought home yesterday.

In the kitchen she set about making her lunch, shaking her head in amusement at the junk food in the refrigerator. Ryan was equally bad at snacking. Forget about nutrition. *We've got our own food pyramid. Mexican food at the bottom, followed by sugar and snacks and...*

The bowl she held slipped from her loosened fingers and crashed on the tile floor, shattering. Fern barely noticed. Her mind kept screaming a warning.

Not a triangle. A pyramid.

Not a pyramid such as those in ancient Egypt or the Mayan ruins. A corporate kind of triangle/pyramid.

"Hierarchy," she said aloud, staring out the kitchen window. "Who's at the top of the food chain?"

Willing herself to remember, she gripped the sides of the sink and closed her eyes, forcing herself to think about the terrible little shack where she'd been imprisoned. Smells of male body odor, grease and the oil lamp that burned because there hadn't been electricity. Drugged and feeling as if she were hallucinating, everything had been a daze, but shortly after they'd taken her to the shack, Billy and his partner had talked when she wasn't quite so out of it.

Before all the drugs had infused her system and she could barely think straight.

Oh, they'd been clever not to mention names in front of her, but not so clever to leave out all the details. She had been lying on the floor, eyes closed, pretending to be unconscious but listening all the while.

"Billy, how the hell are we gonna hide this one from the boss? He'll skin us alive if he finds out we took her on our own."

"If he finds out. He ain't gonna find out. He thinks he can order us around because we're at the bottom of the food chain, but we'll show him. This one ain't going to Mexico. I've got a bead on a buyer in California who wants her for some wealthy guy overseas. Gotta up the price."

"Yeah, well, the guy at the top of the food chain won't like it. Selling this one won't get us that much money, not as much as his cut, dammit."

"Maybe we can recruit others to do it for us. Make our own secret pyramid scheme." A rough laugh, grating on her nerves.

Fern's eyes opened. That was why she made triangles. Her conscious mind had wanted to forget everything to protect her, but her subconscious knew the importance of the symbol.

"The triangle is a pyramid, a central power structure, and Billy and his friend violated that system. They were at the bottom, grabbing women to abduct and sell in Mexico, but the real power was at the top of the food chain. Someone in authority, the real leader with decision-making ability. I was never meant to be part of the regular shipment of women out of the country. Billy and the other guy took me to sell on their own," she said aloud.

Excited and hopeful for the first time in days, she picked up the broken bowl, dumped it into the trash and danced around the kitchen.

"I remembered, I remembered!"

Fern scrolled through her cell phone to call Jacob and hesitated. Instead, she called Ryan. The call went straight to voicemail.

Without leaving a message, she hung up.

Though she knew Jacob needed to know, she felt more comfortable telling Ryan first. He was the reason why she recalled these important details. Ryan gave her a place to feel safe and relaxed.

If only she could recall the other man's name, that would help even more. Billy had been more bossy and the leader of the pair. The other man had been physically stronger, intimidating. He growled a lot, sometimes snarled like a big predatory cat.

A tiger. No, more like a lion. Lion... She closed her eyes. "Horoscopes," she muttered aloud.

Her eyes flew open again. "Leo. His name is Leo!"

Immensely pleased with herself, she did not hesitate and dialed Jacob's number. His phone also went to voicemail.

After leaving a detailed message of what she remembered, Fern hung up.

Next she called Ryan again and told him that she remembered.

He whistled. "That's terrific news. Do you remember everything?"

Phone gripped in her palm, she recalled details of the kidnapping, the whispered voices, the hateful sting of the needle when they drugged her.

"Everything," she told him.

"Excellent. Hey, I have to run, but we'll talk later. Jacob will want to debrief you. You okay with that?"

"I can handle it. No worries," she told him.

After Ryan hung up, Fern thought about it. If Jacob wanted to come over and question her with ruthlessness, she could take it. *I'm strong enough now.*

Strong enough to leave Ryan's house. I can't be a burden to him any longer.

After tomorrow night's dinner, she'd tell him.

Chapter 17

The last time she'd been at this house, Ryan had "borrowed" his father's vehicle and they'd snuck away. How happy she'd been to get out on the road, free with no worries!

Plenty of worries now. Fern smoothed down her navy-blue skirt as she climbed out of the rental car. Paired with a sensible powder blue blouse with long sleeves and low-slung heels, her hair worn loose around her shoulders, she knew she looked good.

This dinner wasn't about looking good, however. She wanted to assure his family there would not be any trouble from her.

She was determined to enjoy herself and this dinner. It had been so long since she'd socialized with others, she worried she would not fit in.

As if reading her mind, he glanced at her. Whistled. "You look terrific, Fern. Really pretty."

"Thanks." She grinned. "You're pretty as well, especially with that tie."

Laughing, he fingered the tie she'd bought him online, a blue tie with fire hydrants. It provided a whimsical contrast to his plain white shirt and dress pants.

With Ryan at her side, confidence returned.

"Mom is informal, but Dad, well, he's a hyper businessman." Ryan shrugged.

She understood. The dress code provided a cushion against parental scrutiny and criticism.

As they walked up the driveway to the imposing house, he clutched her hand. Simple human contact that felt reassuring. Fern sensed the occupants inside noticed her through the floor-to-ceiling living room windows that afforded stunning views of the distant purple mountains.

"My father can be hypercritical as well, though deep down, he is a good man. Parents, you know?"

Time for a little self-reflection. "Actually, I don't know," she confessed as they reached the front door. "My mother was great at criticizing, but far from a good parent. Fortunately my foster parents made up for her neglect."

He stopped, turned and rubbed her shoulders. "Are you nervous about this dinner?"

"No." She studied his brilliant blue gaze and sighed. "Yes, a little."

"We don't have to do this. If you want, we'll go home right now. I'll make an excuse to my parents and Ava."

"No." She looked at the frosted glass doors etched with the Colton monogram. "This will be good for me, Ryan. And I don't want you giving up time with your family over me."

It took all her courage to walk through the double doors into the entryway. Her low heels clicked on the black-and-white-marbled tile. Wealth and luxury radiated in the sweeping staircase, polished furniture as elegant as pictures she'd seen in magazines, and a crystal chandelier hanging above their heads.

Fern remembered the two-room squalid apartment where she'd lived with her mother, with its peeling wallpaper and scuffed linoleum flooring.

You're out of your league, kiddo. Try not to gawk.

Ryan's warm hand in hers loaned her strength. He wasn't

his parents. Dedicated to saving lives, he lived in a house with secondhand furniture and enjoyed it.

Tension slipped from her as he led her inside to the living room.

Ava sat on the white-and-blue-striped sofa, smiling at an older man with bushy gray hair as he cooed to a baby in his arms. The older man resembled Ryan. She recognized Chay next to Ava. Another man she didn't recognize lingered near the marble fireplace. Tall, with a muscular build and short light brown hair that looked windblown, he had an intense air.

Must be a Colton, she thought. Ryan had the same dynamic intensity.

Sure enough, Ryan brightened as he spotted the man. "Noah. I thought you were working."

"For a chance at your mom's prime rib, I can take a break," the man shot back, grinning.

"My cousin Noah," he murmured to Fern. His voice dropped. "Noah does search and rescue with his dog, Dancer. He's the one who alerted me to your presence in the cabin."

Another Colton to thank for saving her life. Their gazes met, and Noah gave a brief, friendly nod.

I owe him my life as much as I owe Ryan.

Comforted by the presence of these two stalwart, protective men, Fern relaxed a little. She nodded back at Noah.

"Where's Sabrina?" Ryan asked.

"She was busy, but sends her love."

An older woman came into the hallway, wiping her hands on a dish towel. Ryan hugged her, and she hugged him back in obvious affection that made Fern wistful.

"Ryan. You finally made it. You must be Fern."

The woman smiled, holding out her hand. "I'm Sherry Colton. Welcome to our home."

Her handshake was firm, but not overbearing. "Please, make

yourself comfortable. Ryan, you know where the bar is. Can you serve Fern?"

Sherry's smile was warm. "We have wine, prosecco, bourbon, vodka, scotch, whatever you like."

"Thank you. I don't drink."

No surprise on Sherry's face. "Ryan, we have soda in the minifridge under the bar and cold water. Excuse me, but I have to get back to dinner."

They watched his mother scurry down the hallway and vanish into the kitchen.

A blonde woman in a simple but expensive black sheath and heels Fern knew were designer sat in a chair away from the rest of the group. She had a shrill voice, mentioning a newly opened Asian fusion restaurant in town. With her thin face, model-good looks and long blond hair, she commanded attention.

So many people, more people than she'd encountered in months. Fern drew in a calming breath. Ava noticed her, and her beaming smile fed her confidence.

"Fern! You look amazing. So glad you made it." Ava waved.

Chay nodded at her with a brief smile. Fern was glad of his company. Chay was quiet and reassuring.

Introductions were made. The blonde was Kim March, the Coltons' neighbor who had grown up living next to Ryan and Ava.

Ryan's father seemed friendly enough in his greeting as he handed the baby to Chay, who handled her like a pro. He came over, shook hands with his son and smiled at Fern.

"Nice to meet you, Fern. Welcome to our home. I'm James Colton."

Ryan gave his father a level look. "Dad, I thought this was a family dinner."

His father shrugged. "You know your mother. She loves company. She saw Kim earlier today, and Kim asked about you.

Your mother figured one additional place setting wouldn't hurt. You haven't seen Kim in months."

Ryan's expression tightened. Fern swallowed hard against the emotions rising in her throat. She saw the way Kim looked at Ryan, as if he were dessert and she craved sugar.

A woman noticed these things.

I should have stayed home.

"I haven't seen her in months on purpose, Dad," he murmured with a furious edge in his tone.

But he put a hand at the small of Fern's back and guided her forward with a proprietary smile.

"Everyone, this is Fern. She's living with me."

Making it sound like they were lovers instead of introducing her as his houseguest was intentional. She glanced at the blonde again, who frowned.

Unsure of what Ryan's endgame was, Fern decided to play along for now. She squeezed his arm and stepped closer to him.

Everyone acted friendly enough, but Kim eyed her like something she'd stepped into with her designer heels. Then she offered a wide smile, which never met her dark eyes.

Fern had dealt enough with women like Kim. They were constantly sizing up anyone thought to be competition, and angling how to get rid of them.

I'm not the competition, Kim. And I've already had people try to get rid of me, in ways that would make you scream endlessly.

Fern automatically moved her gaze elsewhere, not wanting to give her any more attention than she deserved.

Ava and Chay stood. "We're going to put Ella Grace down for a nap," she explained. "Ryan, why don't you and Fern catch up with Dad and Noah?"

They took the seats vacated by the couple. Noah remained by the fireplace, sipping a drink. Ryan turned to her.

"How about a ginger ale?"

"Sounds good. With ice, please."

"I'll get it." Noah headed to the elegant hand-carved bar in the corner. "Beer for you, cuz?"

"Cola is fine. On the rocks."

Noah blinked, but left and returned with two drinks. Kim kept smiling at them both, but the facial gesture seemed strained.

"It's good to see you, Ryan. Your mom tells me you've been quite busy," Kim said.

"I have."

Though polite, the edge in his voice told her Ryan hadn't expected this visit, nor did he welcome it.

"Kim and I used to date," he told Fern. "A long time ago."

"Not that long ago," Kim said, with a laugh as fake as her long eyelashes. "We had good times. Ryan and I used to hike a lot in the canyon. Remember Rye?"

Kim spoke with the proprietary tone of an ex who knew Ryan well.

"Yeah, we did some hiking." Ryan turned to her. "Speaking of hiking, weather's supposed to be great next week. You up to a short exploration of Dark Canyon wilderness? Won't be a long walk. Only a short one to stretch your legs."

"Maybe. I wouldn't want to hold you back."

On a hike or anything else.

"You won't. It'll be fun, and I know an easy stretch of the canyon. I won't let you overdo it."

His look was warm, as if they were boyfriend and girlfriend.

"Have you done a lot of hiking, Fern?"

This from his father, who looked at her as if Ryan had brought home a stray cat and the man couldn't decide if the cat was going to claw him or purr.

"A little, before…" Her voice trailed off. Oh damn, this was all wrong. She did not want any of them to think her weak. Find a chink in the armor she'd worn to protect herself, and jab deep inside.

She sipped the ginger ale to soothe her throat and continued. "I've done some rock climbing, when I had time. In my hometown there's an indoor sporting center with rock climbing, and I'd practice there when I could. Nothing too steep, but enough to train myself for the real thing."

"Rock climbing is dangerous..." his father began.

"Training is important," Noah cut in. "Those canyons can be tricky. Smart of you to know that."

She held back what she truly wanted to tell Ryan's dad. Life is risky. You never know from one day to the next what will happen. No matter how much you plan, bad things happen. Make the best of each day you're above ground.

But maybe his father, with all his money and responsibility, couldn't understand that. Still, she did appreciate his desire to protect his children. His family.

I have no family.

Usually the realization made her sad. Tonight, for some odd reason, it strengthened her. As Ava always told her, she'd survived many horrid experiences and come out the other side with her spirit and her strength intact.

I am a survivor. I have taken what life threw at me and emerged from the grinder as myself.

Kim turned to her with another wide, fake smile. "Fern, how did you and Ryan meet?"

Panic rose up. Struggling for answers, she glanced at Ryan. But to her surprise, Noah spoke up.

"You might say I found her first and introduced Fern to Ryan."

Grateful for the save, she nodded at Noah. "Noah brought us together," Fern told Kim.

No details necessary.

Ryan covered her icy palm with his warm one. "Fern's amazing. She's a terrific cook, and we enjoy being together. She also copes well with my long absences when I'm on duty."

"Well." The long-drawn-out word sounded flat. "Being a firefighter's girlfriend was challenging, Fern. I hope it doesn't bother you as it bothered me. I constantly worried about Ryan never coming home."

The woman gave a long sigh. "I never understood why you choose firefighting instead of working in your father's business, Ryan."

"Neither did I," his father commented. "The offer is still there when you're ready to get a real job."

Beside her, she felt Ryan tense. Noah's frown was directed at Kim, but she sensed this was a long-standing family argument.

"Ryan has a real job, Uncle James. Same as me," Noah said.

"There's no future in it and certainly limitations when it comes to income," Kim interjected.

Enough of this criticism. Didn't anyone recognize Ryan's bravery and the importance of what he had chosen as a career?

Fern locked gazes with Kim, ready to go to battle.

"Ryan's work is critical," she told Kim. "He's essential to Dark Canyon. The town is fortunate to have men like him, and Noah, to keep people safe. Some people choose careers that give other people a chance at life, at their own futures, and that means more than making money."

Kim recoiled as if Fern had slapped her. Ryan squeezed her hand.

"I see your new girlfriend likes your lifestyle, Ryan," his father said diplomatically.

But the truth would come out, eventually. Tired of the games, Fern leaned forward. "I'm not his girlfriend. Ryan was kind enough to reach out to me when I didn't have a place to live, and I accepted his offer to stay with him."

"How long have you been staying with Ryan, Fern?" Kim drank her wine.

"A while," he interjected. "Fern's settled in quite nicely."

She flashed him a grateful look.

On the other hand, the hostility on Kim's face warned the woman was not over the breakup with Ryan.

"I've never seen you around town, and I know a lot of people. Ryan is a generous person. It's good you don't have to pay rent and he lets you stay there."

Kim made it sound like she sponged off the man. Fern's temper rose. Before she could speak, Ryan did.

"For someone who was never interested in my life when we broke up, Kim, you certainly are interested now."

Relief filled her. He'd swiftly turned the convo around. Kim shrugged. "Only an observation. It is your life. I was merely curious. I'm glad you moved on, Ryan. I have. Did you know I'm seeing Chet Powell? He's the new chef at Fusion Up. We're talking about moving in together."

"Good for you," he said evenly.

"Perhaps you and Fern can join us for dinner sometime. Chet is an excellent host."

Not in my lifetime. Ryan acknowledged the offer with a slight shrug, indicating his indifference.

This certainly had turned from a friendly family gathering into awkward city.

Relieved when Sherry came into the room to announce dinner was ready, she accompanied Ryan to a dining table that seemed larger than her childhood home. Fern swallowed her anxiety. Determined to see this through, she joined Ryan at the table.

The appetizer of shrimp cocktail was excellent. Fern made an effort to taste every dish. By the time they started on the prime rib, Kim was still chattering about her past relationship with Ryan and asking pointed questions about Fern.

Fern made noncommittal answers but sensed Ryan's growing fury.

Across the table, Ava's worried gaze met Fern's. With the smoothness of a man accustomed to commanding conversations, Ryan turned to his sister. "Ava, tell me how Ella Grace is doing. I can't wait to hold her after dinner."

Talk turned to the baby, turning attention away from Fern. She managed to focus on her dinner, smiling now and then, but feeling tongue-tied. This was all so normal for them. Her? She never had family dinners around the table. Arguments had always turned violent. Fern learned to never speak up.

Until she lived with the Englehearts, Fern barely knew how to act at the dinner table. Sometimes she'd hidden underneath it to escape the flying cutlery her mother threw at William.

The fights and the loud voices...

The prime rib was tender and rare, the new potatoes excellent. Fern helped herself to a small piece. She drank heavily from her water glass. Others, except for Ryan, sipped red wine.

Though stressed, she wasn't tempted by the wine or the expansive liquor collection. Fern felt firmly in control.

"Kim, how is your new job at Colton Holdings?" Sherry asked. "James tells me you're not only managing the office, but you've been handling a few new clients."

With animation, Kim began chatting about the properties she'd signed on to sell through the business. James said little, focusing on his meal.

So that was why Sherry invited Kim. Not that it made Fern feel any more relaxed. Ryan's ex-girlfriend had direct ties to the family business.

Sherry steered the conversation, asking Noah about Sabrina as well as his work, and chattering about baby Ella Grace. Fern ate as she listened. Her throat tightened as Sherry explained to her that Annie Ross, Ella Grace's birth mother, had been found dead in the Dark Canyon Wilderness. Her friend and roommate Lori had been helping Annie raise the baby in Wilson, but after Annie's suspicious death, Lori wanted Ella Grace to be safe, so she left the baby at the fire station.

Lori had told them some details of Ella Grace's background.

Ava and Chay planned to legally adopt the baby and the name Ella Grace honored Annie.

Fern remained quiet, glad no one shot any more questions at her.

Only when James directed his attention at his son did she grow tense once more.

"Ryan, it's never too late to quit the fire department and join me at Colton Holdings. I could use your help. I'm not getting younger, and it will take you a while to learn the business."

"You're too young to retire, Uncle James," Noah said lightly.

"I'm not looking at retirement. I am looking forward to the future of this company and our family." James gave Ryan a level look.

Suddenly Ryan seemed fascinated by cutting his prime rib into tiny pieces.

"You'd love working at Colton Holdings, Ryan. Your father is right. You can make much more money in real estate. A career at a firehouse?" Kim gave a dramatic sigh. "It's unlike being a sous chef, where you can work your way up to exclusive restaurants."

"James, now is not the time," Sherry chided.

"When is it the time, Sher? We barely see him anymore because he's always working, and when he isn't working, he's never around."

James talked around his son as if Ryan were invisible. She sensed Ryan struggling to hold back his temper for the sake of the family dinner.

Turning back to Ryan, who remained quiet, James raised his fork and jabbed it in his direction.

"I accepted your choice when you graduated from the fire academy. You needed action and excitement. Now you're getting older, Ryan. It's time to think of your future. Turn to a career where you use your brains, not brawn."

Fern's grip on her fork tightened as she carefully set it down.

She hated being the center of attention. Always had. Better to stay quiet and demure instead of drawing people to her. Fern knew she was a product of her disturbed childhood. She'd worked hard to overcome shyness and learn to assert herself.

In crowds, though, and parties, she still struggled to make her needs known and socialize with strangers.

Ryan's family gathering sounded like a perfect way to slide back into the ordinary world once more. Unfortunately, this wasn't a typical gathering, not with his ex-girlfriend there.

If this makes you uncomfortable, think of how Ryan must feel.

She wanted to put her arms around Ryan and shield him from past hurt and his father's criticisms. Sherry seemed adoring and eloquent and devoted, loving with James and her children.

His father, on the other hand, was a strong patriarchal type who liked to control things. Understandable, for a businessman like James Colton who headed probably a multimillion-dollar company. But the man's attitude about Ryan's career made her bristle.

Fern knew she had to say something in Ryan's defense. Dedicated and courageous, Ryan had done much for not only her, but the entire town of Dark Canyon.

Galvanized into action by her feelings for Ryan, though she had a habit of shunning any confrontations, Fern lifted her chin and faced James Colton.

"You should be proud of your son for the lives he's saved. Ryan is a selfless, dedicated firefighter. It takes brains, quick thinking as well as physical strength to be a first responder. His integrity and compassion for others, putting their needs before his own, should be lauded. Not condemned."

Silence filled the air. Even Kim blinked in apparent surprise. Noah, with a wide grin, clapped.

"Well done, Fern. About time someone took up our cause."

James turned to his nephew. "Your cause?"

"I'm in search and rescue. Ryan and I are colleagues in keeping this town's citizens safe."

Kim gave her long hair a graceful flip. "That may be true, but I agree with James. Ryan, when we were together we barely had time to share meals. If you weren't working you were training."

Enough of this dogpile. Fern gave a wide smile to Kim, as fake as the woman's nails. "Training is imperative. You should see him sweat as he works out in the basement. All those muscles."

The purr in her voice sounded almost foreign to her. Ryan looked amused. Distress pinched Kim's thin cheeks. She looked stricken, like a child given the opportunity to choose rum raisin but picked plain vanilla and regretted the choice.

With diplomatic grace, Sherry interjected. "You and Ryan are excellent at your jobs, Noah. By the way, how is Sabrina? Please invite her over. I have a new piano composition I've learned, and I'm planning a recital."

"Bring the earplugs," Ryan advised with a grin.

Sherry gave him a withering look while Ava joined in. "Ryan, stop teasing."

"I'm not. Love you, Mom, and you're amazing on the piano, but your choice of music and mine don't agree."

Lively discussion began on music choices. Fern ate her green beans, marveling at how Ryan's mother did her own rescue—a skillful turn of topics to save the family dinner.

When the dishes were cleared, Fern and Ava helping while Kim kept discussing the *mar-ve-lous* dishes her new boyfriend created, Sherry invited everyone into the living room for coffee, tea and dessert. Chay took Ryan to the nursery to spend time with his new niece.

Noah bid everyone goodbye. Sabrina had texted him she was home, and he was anxious to see her.

When Noah left, Fern politely excused herself to go outside for fresh air. As she stepped onto the back porch, a cool breeze washed over her, drying the sweat trickling down her back. Bracing her hands on the railing, she stared up into the starry night.

Here, she could breathe again. Ryan's parents clearly loved him. But the tension between Ryan and his father triggered old memories about her own childhood.

Not that William was a father, or even a father figure. Her mother's drunken boyfriend had been too self-centered to care about Fern, except when he got mean and needed a target for his sarcasm and cruelty.

The French doors behind her opened. Fern stiffened as James joined her by the railing.

"There you are. I need to explain myself to you."

"No, you don't. It's your family."

His father gave a wry smile. "Can't have you walking out of here, thinking I'm a terrible parent. I'm not, Fern. I love my son. Both my children. I am proud of them."

James stared into the darkness. "I worry about Ryan. Every time sirens scream down the street, I'm afraid one day he may not return. It's one reason why I want him to join me in the business."

Fern touched his sleeve. "You're devoted to your company. Can't you see Ryan feels the same about his firefighting career? You have to trust he's making the right decisions when facing a fire. If not for him, I'd be dead. I owe him my eternal gratitude. Men and women like Ryan, and Noah, and all first responders who put the needs of others before themselves, deserve our thanks."

James nodded. "I understand and appreciate your taking his side."

"I appreciate you not mentioning to Kim the circumstances of how Ryan and I really met." There. She stated it.

"It's none of her business, though I can't say I'm surprised she sided with me. Most of Ryan's previous girlfriends did as well. Not you."

"I'm not his girlfriend."

Another wan smile. "Could've fooled me. Excuse me a moment."

After James went inside, Ryan joined her. Fern smiled. "How's Ella Grace?"

A wide smile touched his face. "So tiny and cute. Holding her is like holding a piece of heaven. Ava and Chay are great parents."

Ella Grace is fortunate. Fern shivered, as she remembered her own childhood.

"Cold?" he asked softly.

She shook her head. "I had an interesting talk with your dad."

"Yeah? I bet. I apologize for Mom inviting Kim. She didn't think it would be like this. I had no idea she was working for the old man."

"It's been an interesting evening," she agreed, emphasizing interesting. Like interesting such as the old curse – May you live in interesting times.

"Dad hiring Kim puts even more pressure on me." Ryan jammed a hand through his neatly combed hair. "Mom told me he had to hire her because he's shorthanded. He'll never stop reminding me of obligations I have to the family business."

He snorted, his blue eyes, so much like his father's, filled with turmoil. "I'm tired of fighting him, Fern. He's never accepted my lifestyle choice."

Compelled to defend him, Fern gripped his hand. "It's a lifestyle choice any parent would be proud of, Ryan, while stressing them out each time you respond to a fire. But it's your life. I can't see you settling into a desk job and barking out orders to subordinates."

The intensity he radiated seemed to fill the air. His fingers curled around her as if he cherished her support. "I'm not a desk jockey, Fern. Never have been. You understand. Why can't my father?"

"Because he's your dad." Her voice gentled. "As much as it bothers you, you're blessed to have a father who loves you enough to care about what happens to you."

As the words came out of her mouth, James came outside once more. Heat suffused her face. Before she could stammer an apology, Ryan's father held up a hand.

"I came outside to let you know Sherry's crème brûlée is worth every calorie and you should both enjoy it. Thank you for defending me, Fern. She's right, son. I do care and I do love you, and every time I hear sirens, it sends my heart racing because that could be you headed into danger. Never coming home."

Shadows danced on Ryan's face, showcasing his tight jaw. "Dad, we constantly train, all the time. I'm a professional, and yeah, there's always a risk, but teamwork and training reduce the risk."

James put a fatherly hand on Ryan's shoulder. "I understand. That won't keep me from worrying, or stop me from keeping the door open in case you change your mind and want to join me at Colton Holdings."

Sensing this was an opportune time for Ryan to privately talk with his dad, Fern murmured excuses about stepping inside to help Sherry with dessert.

Ever the hostess, Ryan's mother told Fern she had everything under control and did Fern want to try it? Fern agreed and sampled a small piece at the kitchen table. When she finished, Sherry insisted on cleaning up.

Her eyes lit up as Fern told her how delicious the dessert had been.

Next, Fern headed to the living room. But Kim was there, talking with Chay and Ava.

Making polite small talk was too difficult right now, especially with Kim trying to one-up her. Maybe she could give it a go, for Ryan's sake.

Seeing her, Kim got up and motioned to the hallway. "Fern, may I have a word?"

When they were out of earshot of the others, Kim faced her. Gone was the superior smirk. Kim looked stricken.

"I'm not one to gossip, but I thought you should know something. I was in the kitchen, and Sherry and Ava were talking about you." Kim pushed a lock of hair behind her ear, exposing a perfect round diamond stud.

So tasteful. Pretty, unlike the words Kim told her.

"Sherry said she hoped you would move out soon and take the offer of the rental house she and James set up for you. It's an expensive home with a view of the mountains, with 24/7 security, and if the contract isn't signed soon, they'll lose the offer. They still had to discuss it with Ryan."

Fern's heart sank.

Kim didn't look spiteful or filled with glee. In fact she seemed apologetic. "I'm sorry, but I thought you should know… I see you didn't. Not that I was eavesdropping. I simply happened to be nearby."

Her voice trailed off. "I'm sorry to be the bearer of bad news."

Sorry? You should be dancing. Yet Kim did truly look contrite. At least Ryan's ex didn't know the full story or why his family wanted her out. For that she felt a pinch of gratitude.

So that was how they really felt about her. Nothing personal. No. They only wanted Fern to leave Ryan's home and stay at the luxurious, impersonal house James and Sherry would rent, along with 24-7 security.

"Thanks for telling me."

Kim nodded and went toward the living room.

Dryness coated her throat. Fern didn't know whether to

leave, slamming the door behind her, or maintain a polite attitude and stay.

Leaving would upset Ryan. She couldn't do that to him. Not in front of his family. Later, when they were alone, they could talk in private.

Fern headed down the hallway to the guest bathroom to splash water on her flushed face.

Instead, she heard a faint cry from a darkened room. Fern went toward it. The nursery Sherry and James had set up for baby Ella Grace.

On a white dresser, a duck-shaped lamp glowed softly in the darkness. The new grandparents had gone to great lengths to make the bedroom welcome for Ella Grace. From the white changing table, to a comfortable rocker by the window, to the baby-safe crib.

In the crib, the baby whimpered.

Years of caring for younger foster siblings had taught her well. She checked the baby's diaper. Dry. Ella Grace continued to fuss, so Fern picked her up and cooed.

Ella Grace felt so tiny and fragile in her arms. Fern shifted her weight, humming a nursery rhyme as she rocked from side to side.

"You're so blessed, Ella Grace," she told her in the darkened nursery, only the light of the whimsical yellow duck lamp casting cheerful shadows across the room. "Your mom left you when you're too little to remember. Instead you have Ava and Chay, good people who cherish you. Your Uncle Ryan thinks the world of you. Your grandparents love you, all the Coltons will love you. You'll grow up happy and protected, and you'll never know the heartache of watching your mom walk out the door, screaming for her to come back and waiting in the dark for hours, crying and wishing she would return."

Comforted by the rocking motion, the baby yawned and closed her eyes. Asleep.

Setting Ella Grace carefully in her crib, she tucked the pink blanket around her. "Sleep well, sweet baby."

As she turned away, Fern caught sight of a silhouette in the doorway. She stiffened, recognizing Sherry.

"I heard her fussing and wanted to set her back to sleep. I only wanted to help." Hard to keep the defensive note from her voice.

But as she stepped out into the well-lit hall and partly closed the door, she noticed the wetness on Sherry's cheeks.

Ryan's mother wrapped her arms around Fern. "I'm sorry all those things happened to you, Fern. I didn't know."

Uncomfortable and yet feeling as if she'd crossed an important threshold, Fern briefly hugged her back. "It's not something I tell people."

Not even your son.

Sherry stepped back, wiping her eyes with her hands. "I didn't mean to eavesdrop. I was only going to kiss her goodnight."

Funny how eavesdropping was a common activity tonight in the Colton home. Fern managed to gather her lost composure. Ryan's parents would never know how much it hurt to realize they wanted her out of his home.

"I'm glad Ella Grace has you as a grandmother, and family who cares." Fern meant it.

"How old were you?"

"Ten. It was a long time ago." Fern started down the hallway, hoping Sherry would stop asking her about her childhood.

Sherry made sympathetic sounds. "How can a mother abandon her child like that sweet baby? It's so horribly unfair."

Sensing this was more about her than Ella Grace, Fern stopped short. She looked at Sherry. "Life isn't fair. The pain, well, you learn to live with it and survive. You become clever at wringing out each little bit of joy, like a dishrag, thirsty for each drop. I was fortunate to have good foster parents who cared. They helped me get through it. You never get over the hurt. But you do move past it, and it makes you grateful for all the blessings sent your way."

Ryan's mother didn't ask more questions, but she squeezed Fern's hand before releasing it. "I understand what Ryan sees in you. You're quite special, Fern."

"He's the one who's special. I'm blessed he came into my life."

Because it was a good time to introduce the subject and Sherry could tell her in person about the rental house, she added, "I'll always be grateful for everything he, and Ava, have done for me. But I think it is time I should look for lodgings elsewhere."

"Nothing could prepare us for what happened the other day when you both were out in James's Jeep. I will admit, I was terrified when I thought my son was in danger." Sherry studied an elegant nail. "I also discussed with my family about lodgings for you elsewhere, where you would be safe."

Fern's stomach roiled at the admission. Hearing it from Kim was one thing. Confirmation from his mother was something else. A definite admission that his family didn't want her around. She got it. Who would want a woman with a target on her back that extended to their only son?

"But I see how Ryan looks at you, Fern. How he acts around you, in a way he never did around Kim."

Sherry made a dismissive wave. "Kim may be an ambitious career woman, but she was all wrong for Ryan, and they both knew it."

"I don't think I'm right for him," Fern said softly. "I won't impose on him anymore. He's been wonderful to me."

They'd reached the hallway's end, blocked from going farther by Ryan. He'd overheard.

"Let's get one thing straight, Fern. You're not an imposition."

"I've been your guest far too long, Ryan."

"I'll be the one to decide if you're overstaying your welcome." He spoke in his clipped, commanding voice she sensed he used while fighting fires. "Not my family or anyone else. You're staying, Fern. Even if you don't like it, Mom."

Beneath her expertly applied makeup, Sherry flushed. "Don't be rude, Ryan."

"It's not rude to state the facts and how I feel. Fern is my guest in my house, and I won't have her pressured to move out."

The hardness of his voice, the protective way he bristled, made her glad he was on her side. But she'd seen how much his family loved him and couldn't be a burden any longer.

If something happened to Ryan because of her, Fern would never forgive herself.

"I can't do this, Ryan. I'm endangering you."

Turning, he cupped her cheek with a tenderness that nearly made her weep. "I can take care of any threats, Fern. You're not moving out on my account."

His gaze narrowed as he eyed his mother. "Or anyone else's."

"I agree," Sherry said softly. "It's between the both of you. I'll talk with your father, Ryan, and assure him."

Anxious to take the focus off herself, Fern gestured to the nursery. "Ella Grace is adorable. I picked her up when she was crying and she went straight back to sleep."

Talk turned once more to the baby. Ironic how such a small, innocent child could defuse tension.

A little while later, Ryan announced he had an early day and they said their goodbyes. Fern thanked Sherry again for the delicious dinner.

It wasn't until they were driving away in the rental car that she could relax a little. However, there remained the predicament of her presence in Ryan's house.

Streetlights showcased downtown businesses, where pedestrians shopped the stores on Main Street. Soon they were headed to the other side of town, away from the upscale homes where Ryan had spent his childhood.

Fern found her voice as they neared his neighborhood.

"I won't be a wedge between your parents, or anyone in your family, Ryan."

Her protests were met with a wave of his hand. "Listen to me, Fern. I know the Coltons can be intimidating. Dad can steamroller over anyone interfering with his family, and Mom, well, she can lose all social graces if she believes any of us are threatened. But it's my life. My choice. I want you to stay with me.

"If you choose to move out because you're tired of me, that's different."

Tired of him? "Never," she said fiercely. "On the contrary, you make me feel alive again, Ryan. In a way I've never felt, even before the kidnapping. My life was ordinary. Safe and dull. You woke me up and helped me to step outside my shell and the barriers I put around myself, ones I didn't even realize were there."

He pulled into the driveway of the house where the plainclothes officer stayed. Ryan shut off the engine and turned to her.

Making a humming sound deep in his throat, he cupped her cheek. "You've done the same for me. You're so different from the superficial women I've had relationships with in the past. You never take anything for granted. I adore the way you seize each day and are so grateful for it."

Fern closed her eyes against the gentle brush of his thumb on her flushed skin.

"I mean it, Fern. You championed me in front of my family, and that takes tremendous courage. My father can be intimidating."

Her eyes flew open. "Intimidating, perhaps. He loves you, though. You have a family who cares about your welfare, Ryan."

Not wanting to say any more, her throat tight, she slipped out of the car.

When they were inside his house, the dead bolt securing the door, Ryan headed into the living room. He patted a spot beside him on the faded sofa, nothing like the silk-covered one in his parents' house.

"I can't stay here anymore, Ryan," Fern told him, refusing to hold his hand, much as she longed for the comfort of his warm touch. She folded her hands into her lap, staring at them, willing herself to say the words.

"I'm a complication in your life. I don't belong here. I appreciate—oh how I do! I appreciate all you've done for me, giving me a place to stay, but I've decided to accept your family's offer of a rental home, with security, until the kidnappers are caught."

Ryan shifted closer to her on the sofa, the springs creaking beneath him. "You're not complicating anything. How the hell did you find out about the rental home?"

"Kim told me she overheard your family discussing it."

His expression turned dark with fury. "It's a family matter and none of Kim's business."

Hastening to reassure him, she looked up. "I'm no cheerleader for Kim, but she wasn't being mean about it. I think she wanted to warn me. But it doesn't matter. I was already considering moving back to my old apartment in Oso. Maybe not getting my job back, but there's remote work I can do…"

Slashing the air with his hand, Ryan scowled. "No. You're not going anywhere. Not unless you feel uncomfortable being here with me, Fern. No one is going to make you leave. Your old apartment? That's a stupid idea."

Now her temper began to rise. "Stupid idea? What's stupid is staying here, where everyone in your family scrutinizes me, where I'm a guest and keeping you from living your life. No privacy, and worse, my presence means you're a target as much as I am!"

Tears rose in her throat, much as she tried to fight them. This was so wrong, so difficult. She'd started to fall for Ryan, and she needed to bolt. Couching it in other reasons was safer.

Whenever she cared for someone, they always left.

Shadows in the living room seemed to deepen as the night darkened the windows. Ryan went over and drew the blinds. Grateful they were no longer showcased to anyone outside, like a painting hung on a wall, Fern continued.

"I won't see you get hurt on my behalf, Ryan."

There, it sounded noble, neatly tied up like a Christmas package, with a shiny red bow and paper. Even though inside the box remained empty.

"You're lying, Fern."

Moving closer, he reached out and took a strand of her hair between his fingers. "I can tell. I know you well enough by now. That little nervous tic in your cheek, the way you can't look at me."

Oh, he knew her well. Ironic. The one man she desperately needed to leave before she did something stupid like fall in love with him knew the hollowness of her words.

Too late. *I'm already falling in love with you.*

She had to convince him. "I'm not your responsibility, Ryan. Your responsibility ended the moment they put me into an ambulance."

"I know."

"Then let me go." Fern's voice cracked. "Before you get hurt, too."

Gently, he tugged her hair. "No."

The memory of smoke filling her lungs, ties biting into her wrists as flames devoured the weathered walls of that cabin, flashed through Fern's mind. She shuddered.

"Please." Her voice dropped to a whisper. "I'd die if anything happened to you. You have others who love you, care about what happens to you."

"No, Fern." The word was said in a swarthy growl of command, brooking no argument.

This time he released her hair and drew her into his arms, a shelter she desperately wanted. "You have someone who deeply cares about you. Me."

Hot tears stung her eyes. He became a blurry visage. "I'm all wrong for you."

"You're right for me in ways I don't quite understand myself. All I know is the thought of you leaving is killing me. All the other women I've had relationships with, well, when they walked out the door, it hurt only my pride. Not my heart."

With a happy skip, her heart beat faster. "Ryan…"

Gently, he pressed a finger against her wobbling mouth. "I care about you, Fern Hensley, and it has nothing to do with your past or saving your life. If you tell me you don't feel the same about me, I'll help you pack your bags and arrange for you to stay elsewhere with armed security guards. But God help me, I'm falling in love with you."

Though her mind argued this was a horrible idea and she needed to leave, her heart thrilled at his words. Always in the past, logic and reason won over silly emotions.

Not tonight. For the first time, she wanted to leap into the unknown and damn the consequences. Tomorrow she might have regrets. They both might. But tonight she deserved this closeness, this tender intimacy.

Lonely for too long, starved for affection, she craved his touch. Only Ryan's touch. It filled her with wonder as his stunning blue gaze met hers.

"What's your answer? Do you want to leave?" he asked softly.

Fern slid her arms around his strong neck as if saving herself from drowning. "No."

Fern's heart pounded against her ribs as his fingers tangled in her hair. A tantalizing scent of his cologne, the brush of his night beard against her warm cheeks filled her senses as their mouths met. A small voice in the back of her head screamed this was not right, she had to stop it now, but she silenced it. Ryan capturing her in his arms, his strong body against hers, felt right.

His mouth moved subtly against hers, inquiring, hesitant as if he feared pushing her too hard. Fern responded with an open mouth, her tongue darting inside the cavern of his. The kiss, deep and moving, sealed their fates.

When they finally broke apart, breathless, Fern's eyes remained closed for a moment longer, her lips slightly parted. When she opened them, the vulnerability she felt remained, but the passion and sheer want in Ryan's eyes soothed it.

"I've wanted to do that for so long," she whispered, her voice trembling slightly. "I was afraid you didn't feel the same way."

Ryan traced the curve of her cheek with his thumb. "How could I not?" The words came out in a hoarse voice, as if he struggled with his own emotions.

They fell into another kiss, deeper this time, unspoken longing pouring out between them. Sofa springs moaned beneath them as Ryan pulled her closer, his heart's frantic hammering echoing her own. Books, magazines and a coffee mug scattered on the table before them spilled to the floor as she kicked out her feet to lie supine against his firm weight.

The noise broke them apart. Amusement danced on his face. "Oops. Forgot how small this couch is. Not exactly room to maneuver here."

Fern sat up, managed to stand and grabbed his hand. "I know a better place."

Following her down the hall, he balked at her bedroom door. "No. Mine is bigger."

With an urgency meeting her own, he tugged her toward his bedroom. Fingers trembling, Fern stripped off her stockings, shoes and clothing, stopping at her panties. She gave him an uncertain look.

He stopped unbuckling his trousers. "What's wrong?"

"Are you sure you want this?"

Ryan gave a rueful look downward. "Oh yeah. With you, absolutely."

He blinked. "Birth control?"

"Condoms?"

A sheepish grin as he opened the nightstand drawer. "Take your pick."

Charmed by his adorable confession, and emboldened by the heat in his eyes, she chose one.

Fingering the foil packet, she hesitated. "Ryan, it's been a long time for me. I don't want to disappoint you."

Stripped down to black boxers, he came forward and took the condom from her hand. Ryan dropped it on the nightstand. "If you feel uncertain or need to stop at any time, tell me."

Gently he pushed a lock of hair from her face. "I want you, damn, I want you so much I can barely breathe. But I get it if you're not ready or you get scared."

His understanding, twined with the desire in his eyes, took her own breath away. She trusted him, and knowing he would follow her wishes, even if she needed to stop, made her pick up the condom and tear off the foil.

"I'm more than ready, Ryan. Now, get naked."

A wide grin touched his mouth. He shrugged out of his boxers and her breath hitched. What a body.

Lean, like a finely tempered steel cord, with muscles roping his arms and legs, his flat abdomen showing the results of all those workouts in the basement. But it wasn't his body, or his impressive erection, that made her step toward him.

The emotion on his face told her he not only desired her, he cherished her. Ryan was willing to let her make the moves. Empower her.

Release control to her.

After being abducted and treated like a commodity, her kidnappers thinking only of using her for someone's sex slave, his consideration edged aside the hesitation and fear. Emboldened, she dropped to her knees with the condom in hand.

First, though, a small taste...

Ryan's eyes closed. He fisted a hand in her hair and groaned, the sound music to her delight.

She kept doing it, but in the back of her mind a little voice taunted her. Fern stopped, drew back.

He glanced down. "You okay?"

She gave a small nod. Nothing was going to ruin this moment. Not her fears, nothing.

Ryan reached down, helped her to her feet. The tremor running through her couldn't be disguised.

To her amazement, his arms wrapped around her and he held her. Not tightly, but close enough. It was such a warm, comforting gesture, Fern melted into him. For a few moments, they stood in each other's arms, enjoying simple human contact.

She wanted this.

She wanted him.

Encouraged, Fern broke away and palmed the birth control. Her fingers stroked his erection, and then she bent down and rolled on the condom. He was willing to concede to her every need.

Now she had to show him what those needs were.

Ryan was a good soul who cared. His courage and willingness to help others fueled her passion for him. He helped her to believe in people once more, and fed her hope the world could be a good place.

As he cupped her face, his expression filled with tender concern, she tunneled her fingers through his hair. "Every time I'm afraid or think bad things will happen, I push back those thoughts remembering you. You make me brave, Ryan. God help me, I think I'm in love with you."

A small smile touched his face. "Me, too. You make me out to be better than I am. I'm only a guy who happens to be crazy about you, Fern Hensley."

"You're so much more." She caressed his jaw. "So much more. Same way I am not a delicate, fragile woman. I've been through a lot, true, but I'm not made of glass."

Ryan touched his mouth to her cheek. "Far from it, sweetheart. You're a diamond that can cut the thickest glass, and I'm damn lucky to have you in my life."

The mere touch of his lips against her skin sent ripples of need shuddering through her. "Then let's stop talking and get to it," she whispered.

"There's only one thing standing between us, sweetheart."

"What?"

"Your panties."

Fern glanced down and groaned. He laughed, pulled them off and gently pushed her back onto the bed.

Their lips met in the briefest of kisses. Then they touched again, and, oh God, it felt truly like a miracle. Fern felt alive, more alive than she'd been over the past few months. His mouth was firm and warm, a promise of more than mere sex.

His kiss felt like a pledge of love.

As he grazed the side of her throat, dropping a kiss and lingering over the hateful tattoo there, she felt absolution. For what? Fern didn't know. But with every sweep of his mouth, gone was her trepidation, replaced with burning desire.

Ryan made her feel whole.

Ryan made her feel treasured.

Not as a prize to be sold, but a woman he adored.

As they kissed, she felt a deep connection to this man. Not simply because he pulled her out of a raging fire, but because their bonds ran deeper. Fern couldn't explain it. She only knew to follow her heart for once, instead of listening to her head.

Fern looked up at him, sliding her arms around his neck. "Don't hold back, Ryan. I need you. I need everything you have to give to me."

A brief smile touched his mouth, then Ryan covered her naked body with kisses, his hands fisting in her hair. A shiver born of sexual awareness seized her as she tested the granite-hard muscles of his shoulders with her fingers. The spark between them caught and flared. She turned her face to where his shoulder met neck, put her mouth on the flesh there and tasted the tangy salt of his skin. Smelled the musky spice of him.

Ryan kissed the tiny hollow of her throat, the movement of his mouth increasing the hot throbbing between her legs. She twisted beneath him. His hand drifted to the curve of her hip, then dipped between her thighs.

Fern jerked upright in shocked pleasure. He quieted her with a soft murmur, pushing her down, and she felt his finger slide between her feminine folds. Smooth as silk, he glided back and forth, creating tendrils of coiled tension.

She was soon a wound spring, ready to release the fires he stoked with each caress, ready to feel the full burn with erotic pleasure.

This was what she'd hoped for, searched for, in a lover. A man willing to give her pleasure before his own and fulfill her needs first. A man who truly cared for her, not only for sex.

Still, it meant losing control. Letting go.

"Shhh," he murmured. "Just let go. Surrender to it."

"Yes," she whispered.

She did just that. All tension within her exploded, and she wailed as it burst from her center and from her throat, shattering her consciousness as if it were glass. And when her eyes fluttered open, she saw Ryan looking down at her with deep satisfaction, and with a hint of male pride.

"Now," he murmured, and pushed open her trembling thighs.

This wasn't merely sex, this was something more, and they both felt it.

She sensed him holding back, and yet he quivered with need.

Time to let him know she wasn't fragile glass. Fern wrapped her legs around his hips and coaxed him farther. Ryan caged her with his body and wrapped his arms around her, holding her tight as his mouth met hers. The kiss was a maelstrom of unleashed lust. He took her mouth with fury, his tongue plunging inside with masterful strokes. Tasting her, taking all and leaving nothing, building her fervent and growing ardor.

Pausing, he glanced down to gauge her reaction. Any fear or hesitation, she knew he'd stop.

Assuring him, she opened her legs wider and arched her hips upward.

"Do it," she told him in a breathless whisper. "Please. I've wanted you for a long time."

He nudged his lean hips between hers. The breath caught in her throat. She arched upward. A promise lingered in his passion-darkened eyes.

Ryan lifted the long mass of her dark hair and kissed her neck. He ran his tongue over her skin. "Don't be afraid," he murmured. "I promise, I'll take good care of you."

Fern opened her legs wider, the ache between them exquisitely sharp, demanding to be filled. Wide-eyed, she watched Ryan settle closer. The silky hair on his muscled chest rubbed against the sensitive, hardened crests of her nipples. He rose above her, gaze fierce, his shoulders blocking out the view of the ceiling. She felt the demand of his erection.

Ryan slipped forward, beginning to penetrate. Then, with a soft murmur and a powerful movement, he surged forward. Fern gasped, and then lifted her hips as they began the dance.

The delicious friction twined with the smoky heat of his

gaze. Fern ran her nails across his back as he pumped furiously inside her.

She wanted more. Fern wriggled and arched impatiently, wanting all of him, wanting him gasping in need as much as she. He smiled, and his hips began to piston, his sex sliding in and out until his breath became rapid pants. Then he stiffened above her, and Ryan threw back his head and shouted her name, the cords in his neck strained.

Ryan collapsed with a heavy sigh, burying his face in the pillow beside her. She stroked the sweating, quivering muscles of his back, and her legs cradled him tenderly. When he shifted his weight off of her, Fern instinctively curled next to him, putting her head on his shoulder. Her eyes slowly closed, and her breathing deepened. She felt sleepy and oddly comforted by Ryan's arm about her waist.

She, whom men had abducted to be used as a commodity, marveled at the feelings flaring between them.

If only it would last. Tomorrow might look different. But for tonight, she'd cherish lying naked in his arms, feeling loved for the first time in years.

Chapter 18

When Fern woke the next morning, sun streamed into the bedroom. Yawning, she rolled over and touched an empty pillow.

Blinking, she forced herself to wake up. Fern sat up. Ryan was gone. Joy over last night faded into disappointment.

A cream-colored note sat on the pillow. She picked it up.

Good morning, sleepyhead. Much as I wanted to stay here, I had to work. Didn't have the heart to wake you up. Text me later. Love you. Ryan.

Well, as love notes went, it wasn't literature, but the PS made her smile.

PS. I'll carry the memory of being in your arms, such perfection, and this time I *mean* perfection, through the day. Hope you don't have trouble walking, sweetheart, after the workout I put you through.

The PS was accompanied with the drawing of a grinning figure surrounded by flames and holding a fire hose. The figure had devil horns. Fern laughed. Typical Ryan. Well, they had awakened during the night to make love two more times, each time leaving them breathless once more.

She quickly showered and dressed. When the coffee was

brewing—was it really after ten o'clock?—she fired off a quick text with hearts and fire.

He texted back several smiley faces and added he had to rush out to a call.

Always working, always rushing into danger. Fern set down her phone and poured coffee. Sitting at the kitchen table, she couldn't help her secretive smile.

The sex had been amazing, emotional and everything she'd ever hoped for in a lover.

So perfect it scared her.

Her smile faded.

Her pragmatic mind warned this relationship with Ryan couldn't last. He'd leave her, like everyone else eventually did. She was struggling to get her life back together, always looking over her shoulder because her abductors wanted her dead. Who could maintain a relationship, faced with that?

Knowing it was fear talking, Fern thought about calling Ava. Normally such a dramatic event, having sex for the first time in months, after the trauma of being kidnapped, would be an event to discuss with one's therapist.

But when the therapist was the brother of your new lover? Fern laughed.

What a conundrum.

Best to discuss her feelings with Ryan. She didn't need a third party.

What she truly needed was an update from Jacob on the case's progression. Had the clues she provided, when she regained part of her memory, advanced anything?

She dialed his number, only to get his voicemail. After leaving a message, Fern hung up.

Dressing in comfortable yoga pants, a loose T-shirt and sneakers, she went downstairs to work out.

Though she hated that Ryan had to work today, perhaps it was best they both had their time apart to deal with the turbulent emotions of last night. Maybe Ryan didn't feel the same way, but Fern doubted it because it had been so real, so raw and passionate.

Ryan was honest and not the kind of guy who would sweet-talk a woman into having sex. He lived life to the fullest.

The rest of the day passed quickly as she showered, then did laundry, putting fresh sheets on both beds, cleaned up the house and worked on the laptop. Medical coding was coming back to her, and she felt confident she could get another job, probably a remote one, with a new doctor's office. Or even a local hospital.

She typed up a new résumé and began looking for jobs online.

A new life. New hope and possibilities. But would Ryan be part of it?

Fern took a break finally around dinner. She made a light chicken casserole, reasoning it could be frozen for Ryan when he returned home. He didn't care if it wasn't pretty enough for a cooking show or some influencer's Insta.

Fern stopped cutting up vegetables. Knife hovering in the air, she stared out the kitchen window.

Ryan lived every day with a vibrancy and vitality few men she'd known ever demonstrated. Ryan didn't care about her looking perfect with makeup, or what clothing she chose to wear. He cared about her, her feelings, who she was, including her past.

Her phone rang as she popped the casserole into the oven. Jacob, judging by the ringtone.

The news was not good. They had no leads on the case, despite the clues she'd given them. But Ryan's cousin had questions, as well as some information.

"Your date you were going to meet the night you got taken—Walter. You didn't know him well?"

"No. I'd met him at Dr. Sonder's office the previous day

when he came there to sell something, maybe medical equipment, no, I think it was drugs. Did you find him?"

"He doesn't exist."

Knees weak, she sat on a kitchen chair. "He sure did exist when he asked me to meet him for drinks."

"There's no trace of him." Jacob's deep voice sounded almost like a growl. "He's gone. No one in Oso recalls seeing him. Not even your former employer. The receptionist said he arrived one morning, the morning you had the day off, and asked when you'd return because he wanted to discuss something with you. Tell me everything that happened."

Her stomach roiled. "He came into the office, and we struck up the convo about Irish history because I was reading a book about Ireland. He asked me to meet him at the Irish bar that night to hear this terrific band from Ireland. Only to meet him for drinks... I thought it was safe."

Jacob's next words sent a chill down her spine.

"There's no history of a Walter Landers. The man doesn't exist. Looks like everything was a ruse. He was targeting you, Fern."

"Are you saying he set me up?"

"I believe so. We figure Billy and his partner went rogue on the top guy organizing this sex trafficking ring and wanted a woman they could sell on their own to make quick cash. But they needed help. So they found you through the foster system, did some checking and then had Walter lure you to the bar so they could gauge a time when to take you."

Sweat broke out on her forehead. Stupid. So stupid of her, and trusting. The one time she agreed to meet a stranger, look what happened.

"I always took my car to work. Parked in the lot out back, and if he was watching me, he must have known which one was my car. Maybe even followed me home," she said slowly. "But that morning I had a flat so I walked. It wasn't far. Wal-

She knew enough not to touch the menacing note, much as she wanted to rip it off the door and ball it up. Burn it in the fire pit.

Instead, she dialed the number of the officer staying a few doors down.

Paul Jenkins immediately answered, and when he heard the problem, he announced in a clipped tone he would be there immediately.

Barely had she hung up the phone when it texted a message Officer Jenkins was outside.

Fern opened the door. Brown hair cut military short, square-jawed, Officer Jenkins wore jeans and a T-shirt, but the pistol on his belt meant business.

She pointed to the note. Even though he was there with her, she couldn't bring herself to read the words. They were burned into her brain.

LEAVE BEFORE SOMETHING HAPPENS TO YOU FERN.

He frowned. "Why did you open the door?"

"I thought I heard a bird. There wasn't much noise, and if a bird was lying there, stunned, I wanted to save it."

As reasons went, it sounded lame, but the rugged police officer actually smiled.

"My wife does the same thing. She loves the little birds that visit the feeders in our yard."

He turned his attention to the note. Fern hugged herself against the night's chill as Jenkins studied the front stoop and the note. Cradling his cell phone, he gestured for her to go inside. He joined her a few minutes later, closing and locking the front door behind him.

"A unit will be here shortly to dust for evidence and take the ter texted that the bar was a short walk from the office as well and parking was limited. He said he would meet me there but to text him when I left the office so he didn't have to wait alone."

Jacob snorted. "And he suggested it was such a brisk, cold night out and you had been working inside all day, that you also walk."

Fern covered her face with one hand. "Yes. How stupid of me. He must have been the one to flatten my tire."

"You're not stupid," he said in a gentler tone. "You were deceived by a pro, and meeting him there was a hell of a lot safer than him picking you up in his car. You did the right thing, Fern."

"At the wrong time." She couldn't help her bitter laugh.

"It is what it is. If there are other important details you recall, call me. If I'm not around, leave a voicemail and I'll get back to you right away."

"Thanks." She hung up.

His pragmatic words reassured her.

She settled into the living room to watch television. YouTube had several videos on Ireland, and the green, lush landscape and lilting music soothed her ragged nerves.

Halfway into a video, she heard a noise at the front door. Not a knock, but something that banged against the wood.

A bird? Thinking of the birds out back flocking to the feeders, knowing birds sometimes crashed into windows and doors, Fern went to the front door. If it was a bird, perhaps she could save it.

She opened the front door.

No stunned bird on the doormat that read Welcome.

As she went to close the door, she saw a note taped to the wood. Words painted in blood red.

Fear skidded down her spine. Fern struggled to calm herself. She counted to five, took a deep breath. A whispered scream came out.

note. They'll take care of it. With your permission, I'll check the security footage on the DVR."

She escorted him to Ryan's office. He opened the cabinet, plugged in the code she found in the drawer and began reviewing the footage. Fern hovered in the doorway.

"Is someone threatening me? Could it be the kidnappers?"

"Maybe. But criminals like that rarely announce threats. They only act on them. Don't worry. Might be neighborhood kids pranking around."

"The note doesn't seem like a prank, but a threat."

"We're treating it as such. Because of what happened with you and Ryan on the road, knowing the kidnappers are still at large, we're taking precautions."

Jenkins had a kind, fatherly air, and his even voice took the edge off her fear.

"Would you like me to stay the night, until Ryan gets home from his shift? Does he return tomorrow morning?"

Fern managed a nod. Dead tired on her feet, yet unable to relax because of the threat outside, she knew sleep would be fleeting.

"Thank you, Officer Jenkins." Fern waved in the direction of the kitchen. "The fridge is fully stocked, and there's snacks and some leftover casserole I froze if you get hungry."

"I already ate, thank you."

"I'm headed to bed."

An hour later, nestled in Ryan's big bed, she couldn't sleep. Snug in her flannel pajamas, she clicked on the remote to watch television. Much as she hated seeing the news, Fern felt she had to find out what happened in the outside world.

The local news was grim. She sat up, sheets twisting in her hands.

Another woman had been reported missing, and this one, like her, had been formerly in the foster system. No witnesses to her abduction, but grainy footage from a traffic cam showed her struggles as two men took her off the street and shoved her in the back of a light-colored van.

Billy and his mysterious accomplice had a new vehicle and new victim.

Fern switched off the television. Another woman. What would happen to her? Would she also be left to die inside a burning building? Or shipped off to another country to be sold?

I can't sit here and let this happen. I have to do something to help.

The euphoria felt last night making love with Ryan had vanished. Back to reality. Fern stared at the dark television screen.

She pulled on a soft flannel robe and went to find Officer Jenkins. He sat on the living room sofa, working on a laptop. Looking at the sofa, remembering how she and Ryan had kissed there, made her throat close tight.

Such a sweet memory. *I hope I never lose that one.*

Jenkins glanced up. "What's wrong?"

Fern perched on the edge of a chair. "I watched the news and heard another woman was kidnapped."

"Yes." Jenkins closed the laptop. "We released the news to the media in hopes someone saw something."

Her hands tightened on her lap. "Do you think it's the same men who took me?"

"Could be. Unless the operation has expanded."

Fern saw her life stretching before her like a ribbon. In the not distant past was the love and desire Ryan expressed for her. The future was filled with threads unraveling. Until these men were caught, more women would suffer.

She would never get her life back, have a chance for the happiness she deserved, until they were caught. Sometimes you had to leap out in faith to do the right thing.

Even when you put your life on the line.

Ryan risked his life each time he went on a call. He'd made it his career. Knowing this fed her courage.

Fern looked up, letting her hands relax. "I want to propose something to the police, to Jacob and the other investigators on this case."

Expression neutral, Jenkins told her, "Go on."

Here we go. "I'd like to offer myself as bait in an operation to lure these bastards and finally catch them. Before another woman is kidnapped."

Chapter 19

Ryan was not happy when he got home the next morning and discovered what Fern planned.

Officer Jenkins had left, telling Ryan about the note. Unfortunately there were no fingerprints. The excellent security cameras outside had shown images of a person dressed in shapeless black taping the note to the front door and then running down the street. The figure wore a black hat and a mask, hiding his features from the camera.

"No." Ryan shook his head. "Listen, I've had a rough shift. Calls all day and night, no time to sleep. With some of our guys sent to fight the wildfire at the edge of the reservation, we were shorthanded all night. All I've had is two granola bars eaten in the truck on the way to accidents. We'll talk about your idea later, Fern."

Knowing he was tired and needed sleep, Fern didn't want to push it at first. But time slipped away and she had to take action, before more innocent lives were ruined.

"I can't talk later, Ryan. I'm angry. Furious."

Unable to sit, she paced the living room, wearing out his Berber rug. "Before they took me, I was living a normal, maybe solitary existence. Never bothering anyone, never breaking the law. Hells bells, I didn't even have a traffic ticket!"

He blinked at her use of curse words. Of course as curse

words went, they were mild. Seldom had she ever cursed. Always trying to be the good girl, please everyone else.

Fern tired of putting others' needs before her own. She needed to do this, had to do something instead of hiding in his house.

"What gives these jerks the right to take women and sell them like merchandise? As if our only value comes from our bodies? Stripping away all our identities and everything we've ever loved?"

Knowing it would be impossible to stop, she raged on. It was as if all the pent-up fury from the time she was little until her kidnapping boiled to the surface, a volcanic eruption of emotion too long suppressed.

"My whole life has been about being meek and quiet, afraid to speak up, fearing either I'd get chastised or no one would love me. Well, you know what?"

Fern took a deep breath. Ryan sat quietly on the sofa, listening. Not saying a word, not rebuking her the way some men might or rolling his eyes or trying to interrupt.

He kept looking at her, his expression encouraging her to continue. So she did.

"I'm worthy of love. I have a voice, opinions, and I matter! I deserve better than the fate those, those, those..."

"Assholes?" he offered.

A tremulous smile touched her mouth. "Yes. Better than what they tried to force out of me. I deserve better than what William and my mother gave me. I deserve to be happy."

Knowing she had to convince him, Fern went to Ryan and sat beside him and took his warm hand into her trembling one.

"I can't be happy here, hiding out like a prisoner, knowing there's something I can do to help, Ryan. I won't be happy until those men are caught and I can finally get my life back. Until I know other women will be safe as well. The only way

I can help is to offer myself as bait to trap them, with the police waiting nearby."

At his frown, she rushed on. "I have to do this because I'm the only victim who's still alive and they're after me. They want me, Ryan. The police will ensure I'm safe. Can't you see? This is my one chance to make everything right. My chance to do more than hide away as if I'm the one who did something criminal."

Fern took another deep breath. "My chance to help prevent this from happening again. Regaining my memory about Billy and Leo didn't help the police. This will."

He looked tired and worn-out. Part of her hated doing this to him when the man clearly needed rest. But if she didn't speak now, Fern knew she'd lose her nerve.

He gave a longing glance at the hallway, where his bed and much-needed sleep awaited.

"Well?" she asked.

"It's about time you got angry." He squeezed her hand. "With everything you've endured, your anger is more than justified. I'm proud of you, Fern."

No one had ever expressed pride in her. Warmth spread through her at his praise.

Then he shook his head. "Despite that, I don't want you to offer yourself as a sacrificial lamb to catch the kidnappers. Can't you see that? It's way too dangerous. You have no police training. Let an undercover policewoman do it."

Sliding her hand out of his, she bristled. "An undercover policewoman isn't who they're after. I'm the one they want. I have value to them."

Ryan's jaw tightened. "You talk about value? You have value more than as enticement for two desperate criminals, Fern. I won't let you do this."

"You won't let me?"

The words came out slowly as she digested their meaning. Everything in the past came rushing back.

Her mother, refusing to allow her to go to school.

William, laughing at her powerlessness over his occasional slaps.

The foster parents who wouldn't let her save her money to buy a pretty backpack, but took every cent she made from babysitting.

I've survived a hard childhood, abuse, alcoholism and a kidnapping. I'm not going to take it anymore.

Fern stood up. "You can't stop me, Ryan. I love you, and I'll always love you, but you have no claim over me."

Rubbing a hand over his face, he sighed. "It's been a bitch of a shift, Fern. I'm going to bed, and we'll discuss this further when I get up. Please, make sure to stay inside and keep the doors locked. You hear anything or see anything threatening, wake me up immediately."

"You need your sleep."

"I need you to be safe."

He headed toward his bedroom.

Staring after him, she felt her entire body tense, her throat close up. She loved Ryan. Loved how he cherished her.

Cherishing her didn't mean he had the right to tell her what to do.

For too many years, she'd lived according to other peoples' rules and standards. No longer.

It felt freeing, acknowledging her independence. Fern knew Ava would be happy to see her finally stand on her feet.

Even at the expense of defying her brother.

She had to do this to help Jacob and the investigators catch Billy and Leo. No matter how much it might cost her with Ryan.

After managing to catch only four hours of sleep, Ryan woke up groggy and still tired. Too agitated to try to rest, he showered and dressed in blue sweatpants and a Dark Canyon Fire Department T-shirt.

Fern wasn't in the kitchen but sitting outside on the patio, watching the little birds fly in and out of the feeders. Though he'd asked her to remain inside, he couldn't blame her for being out on this beautiful spring day.

Reassured she was okay, he made fresh coffee and sat at the table, rubbing a hand over his weary eyes.

Offering herself as bait to the police to catch the kidnappers sounded like an excellent idea on paper. Yet he knew everything could go south in a heartbeat.

Much as he trusted his cousin Jacob and the other police, he couldn't trust them with Fern's life. The note deeply worried him. Someone threatened her, and he wanted to find the person and rip them apart for that threat.

The greater threat was Fern herself, wanting to put her life on the line.

As he took a bracing sip of caffeine, he thought about how much she meant to him. How horrible it would be to lose her. He wasn't a poet, hell, he had trouble writing a fire report, but she stirred something inside him. Something deep and permanent. Never one for hearts and flowers and mush, Ryan finally understood why some guys fell hard and deep in love.

I'm headed there myself.

Taking his coffee, he went outside to join her.

She glanced up as he sat at the table. "Good morning. I can make you lunch, or breakfast, if you're hungry. I thought you'd get more sleep, though, so I don't have anything ready."

He sighed. "Honey, I told you when you first moved in, you're not here to cook. Or clean. I don't want you to feel obligated."

Fern gave him a long look from those incredible hazel eyes. In the sunlight, he could see flecks of green and caramel among the brown.

"I don't feel obligated. It's my pleasure, Ryan. I like taking care of you and making sure you're comfortable."

Normally he'd bask in her assurance. Not today.

"I'd feel more comfortable if you'd drop this idea of offering yourself as sacrificial bait."

"I would argue, but you only woke up and it's cruel to debate before your first cup of coffee."

Ryan scowled. "It could be my second cup."

"Doubt it. Your shirt is on inside out."

He glanced down and groaned. Then looked up to see her impish smile. Ryan set down the cup, pulled the shirt over his head. He paused, seeing the glow of interest on her face as she stared at his chest.

"Like the view? I can leave the shirt off," he teased.

Amused, he watched a delicate flush tint her cheeks. Fern swallowed. "Um, wouldn't want you to catch a chill."

Before he could respond, she added, "Though I'd be happy to keep you warm."

Warm? He was heating up now, and it had nothing to do with the shirt he put back on. Ryan's hand covered hers. For a moment they sat in companionable silence, the sweet intensity between them building. So hot, like arcs of electricity shooting into the air.

Much as he longed to take her hand, lead her back inside, march her down the hallway to the bedroom and make love to her again, Ryan knew they had to talk.

He withdrew his hand, swigged the rest of his coffee, prepared to gird his loins in a different interaction with Fern—convincing her to drop the idea of being bait.

A loud ringtone with a man singing about a fiery love sounded inside. Fern glanced at the house.

"Is that your phone?"

Ryan raced inside to grab his cell on the kitchen table. Seeing the name on the screen, he groaned again. Damn.

"Colton," he answered. "I'm off shift."

"Not anymore." The smooth voice of his captain dashed all

his plans. "We've got a level one hazmat at Mountainview Avenue, potentially turning to level two."

He rubbed a hand over his face. As senior hazmat technician at the Dark Canyon Fire Department, he had to respond. "What's the situation?"

"House fire, one-level single-family residence, pool chemicals inside. Lots of chlorine. Guy ran a business on the side."

Ryan blew out a breath. Pool chemicals were especially dangerous in a fire and, ignited, could release toxic gas. Chlorine alone was corrosive and could damage skin and eyes.

He needed as much information as possible.

Most household fires were deadlier than the average public realized. Plastics and normal household chemicals all could release dangerous vapors. Bleach mixed with ammonia made chloramine gas, which could be fatal.

Pool chemicals, with their high levels of chlorine, ah man...

"Police on scene now," his lieutenant told him. "We're on our way."

The truck was already responding. Dark Canyon had its own special hazmat response truck, outfitted with gas meters, suits, boots and everything they needed in case of a chemical spill.

Or worse.

He gauged the distance from his home to the station and realized he'd never make it in time. "Pick me up on the way."

Now he had to tell Fern, delay their discussion. Work came first. Saving lives came first.

As he headed outside once more, Ryan had a fleeting wish that for once his needs and hers came first.

Chapter 20

Gone again. *Better get used to it if he's going to be in your life.* Much as she wanted that, Fern wasn't certain about any kind of permanent relationship with Ryan.

Discussing her idea of being bait in a sting operation had to be put off. How could they talk if Ryan was off saving lives?

Listless, she ambled about the kitchen, debating on making dinner. The fire was riskier than usual, he'd told her, with chemicals mixed in. He might be gone for hours.

Maybe she'd bake something. Cookies or brownies. Comfort food. No, she needed veggies. A nice salad. And then she'd bake something sweet for Ryan.

She had promised Ryan she would not do anything rash, such as embark on this mission to offer herself as bait. Not until they could sit down and have a heart-to-heart.

It was going to be a rough talk. But she had to convince him she'd be fine.

Fern went into the kitchen, took a paring knife and began cutting vegetables.

A knock came at the door. With Jenkins gone, Fern felt wary about answering. Maybe it was Jenkins, checking on her. She glanced at her phone. No messages.

Knife in hand, she paused.

"Police. Miss Hensley, we're here to check on you."

Huh. She peered out the peephole. An officer in a uniform framed the round hole.

"Badge, please."

A gold shield was held up.

"Just a minute."

As a precaution, Fern called Jenkins. No answer.

Then a text came from Jenkins. Have to leave. Fire near my family. Worried for my pregnant wife. Told the department to send a replacement.

Sympathy filled her. She glanced at the peephole again. Maybe this was the replacement officer. The man did have a gold shield and a uniform.

As she unlocked and opened the door, a ringtone sounded. Fern froze.

The whistling theme from the movie *she remembered well.*

"Oh God," she whispered. "No. Please, no."

With all her might, she tried to shut the door, but the man on the outside pushed it in, sending her toppling to the floor. Screaming, she scissor kicked, trying to get away.

"Hello, Fern. Remember us?"

Never could she forget that deep voice with the cruel laugh.

No, not again, not again. Please. Fern's scream died in her throat as she clawed at the floor, trying to find purchase, kicking her legs, willing them to move, move, move!

Like her nightmare, she was immobilized. Fern gasped for breath and tried to crawl away, her heart in her throat, her pulse hammering, but someone grabbed her legs and pulled her.

Outside. Where she'd have no control.

She'd read about this—never let the criminals take you to a second location because they'd have more control over you there. Do everything you can to fight them.

The knife! She rolled and swiped at her attacker, who dodged the blow and laughed again. Fern got a good look at his face.

His craggy face with the scar on his chin, the beady, bright blue eyes that looked soulless.

Billy. She tried to swipe at him again, but he dodged.

Then he stomped on her hand. Pain exploded, bright and sharp. She whimpered and released the knife.

"You're coming with us."

As they dragged her out onto the stoop, she managed to fumble for the knife. Fern sliced her hand, leaving blood on the concrete.

A sign for Ryan to find.

Then the knife was wrested from her hand. She felt a painful, hateful prick of a needle and everything went dark once more.

Upon arriving at the scene, Ryan realized an incident command post had already been set up. He was the senior hazmat tech.

Ryan shrugged into his breathing equipment and gear, donned his orange boots and duct-taped the suit to the boots so nothing could get inside.

Along with the two other hazmat techs, he trudged to the porch. Orange flames shot out of the garage, where most people stored chemicals. Radio chatter and static blared as he assessed the situation. Clutching the specialized gas meters, they went inside.

Upon entering, he swept the gas meter over the area. The meter could detect C12 in parts per million. But it showed nothing.

Fire had caught at the back end of the house. Ryan and the others emerged.

"Gas meter is negative," he radioed to the incident commander. "We'll check the back and the side."

They did so, seeing piles of junk, auto parts, but no pool chemical containers. Something was off. He reported their findings to the incident commander. No hazardous chemicals.

Ryan used protocol to decontaminate, just in case. As he shed the hazmat suit, he watched his team train water on the flames.

This call was different. Ryan felt it in his bones. His mom used to say he had good instincts about danger. She'd called it his "sixth sense."

He'd used it to his advantage on the job. It tingled now, like a feather stroking his spine.

Fire engulfed the home's back. At any time, the fire could jump to the front rooms.

House was an older wooden structure. Damn, he hated these kind of fires, hazmat or no hazmat. Wood went up like kindling in a hot campfire. The burning structure could also collapse.

No self-evacuation, which could mean no one at home. Or worse—someone trapped inside.

"Who called it in?" he demanded of the incident commander.

"Guy who lives here. Pete Sanders."

After donning his fire gear and boots and helmet, Ryan whipped his head around. Definitely needed to talk with the homeowner.

Neighbors had gathered around to watch. One woman screamed out, "Old Pete Sanders is still inside! He lives alone."

He had a sinking feeling about this one.

"Does he own a pool cleaning company?" Ryan asked. "Store chemicals?"

The woman shook her head. "He's retired and hoards car parts and other stuff."

Lieutenant Sims ordered Ryan, Mike and Bob inside. Ryan gripped an axe.

"Mask up," Sims ordered, and led the way.

"Fully engulfed," the lieutenant announced into his radio.

"Fire department, Mr. Sanders, call out," Ryan yelled through his mask as he entered the house.

To his relief, the hoarding was limited to piles of old newspapers and they could navigate through the room. But old newspapers were a firetrap.

Flames had already caught on the ceiling and advanced down the hallway, a tunnel of hot orange. The home was a tinderbox. Other firefighters had already vented the roof to let the heat and smoke escape.

They broke open doors, could see little through the acrid smoke.

"In here," someone screamed from behind a closed door. "Help me."

The door was jammed. He struck the wood with his axe and broke through. A man was on the floor, trapped by a fallen dresser.

Ryan reached him, pulled him free.

"Rye, what's your twenty?" the lieutenant's voice crackled over the radio.

"I'm okay," he radioed back. "One victim, coming out."

Ryan scooped the man over one shoulder and struggled out into the hallway.

The guys already had a hose on the flames, battling the fire inside as he ran out with the victim. As he went to place him on the ground, the man grabbed his coat.

"Who—who are you?" he asked, coughing.

"Try not to talk," Ryan said gently. "I'm Ryan Colton, the firefighter who rescued you."

"Colton...you're the one. My wife...still inside, basement," the man rasped. "Cathy. Help her. Please."

The other firefighters helped him place the man on a stretcher. Guy had burns, had inhaled a lot of smoke.

Ryan called out to his lieutenant. "Lieutenant, I'm going back in. Wife's in the basement."

"Not without backup."

"I'm right behind you," Bob yelled.

Breathing equipment in place, axe and heat detector in hand, he was already racing inside as the guys trained water on the flames. He tugged open the basement door, and he and Bob ran down the rickety stairs. Tremendous smoke filled the air. No sign of the wife, not even a sig from the heat camera.

Glancing up, he saw the ceiling ready to go.

"Rye, get out of here," Bob radioed as he ran for the stairs.

"One last sweep," he radioed back.

Just as Bob made it up, the ceiling collapsed near the stairs. With the stairs gone, Ryan ran to a basement window. Now the basement was on fire, reaching the piles of newspapers stacked neatly throughout. The papers caught, smoldered and burned.

Ryan tried to open the window. Painted shut.

Now he knew why his sixth sense tingled.

I'm not going to die in here. It's not my time.

Using his axe, he smashed the basement window and cleaned out the glass. Narrow, it would be a tight fit. Already he felt heat at his back reaching for him.

He radioed for help. He tossed his axe and thermal camera outside. Mike and Bob were there as he hauled himself up, and they pulled him through the window.

"Rye, you okay?" Bob asked.

Tearing off his mask, he nodded, breathing in fresh air.

Lieutenant Sims came over, led him to Nick, who handed him an O2 mask as Ryan sat on the back of the truck.

The sinking feeling overcame him. Lost another person. He tried but, damn, almost bought it himself.

"Couldn't find her."

The lieutenant clapped his shoulder. "Damn good thing you're fit. If you were Bob, you'd never have cleared that window."

"Hey, I resent that remark." Bob grinned, his face crinkling with concern. "I thought you were right behind me, Rye. Damn, I'm sorry."

"I'm good," he assured him, coughing.

Nick checked his vitals. Ryan tried to remove the O2 mask, but Nick replaced it.

"No dice. You may have breathed smoke."

Ryan removed the mask again. "I'm fine. Need to check on your patient."

The man lay on the stretcher, barely conscious. "Mr. Sanders, your wife, Cathy, are you certain she was in the basement?"

Eyelids fluttered. Sanders looked at him, removed the oxygen mask and rasped, "I'm sorry. I needed the money. He promised a lot of money to get you here. Said you were the hero type who would go after her."

"Who is he?" Ryan demanded.

But Sanders fell unconscious.

Ryan's guts tightened as he glanced at Nick, who gestured to the ambulance. "Gotta go."

As the ambulance growled away, he looked around. It didn't make sense. He'd searched the basement, no signs of life. Only newspapers and boxes and piles of clothing.

Seeing the wide-eyed neighbors, he went over to them. "You said Sanders lived here. Where's his wife?"

"Wife?" One woman shook her head. "His wife left him fifteen years ago. He's lived alone ever since."

His heart raced in a panic as he walked back to the truck, feeling as if his head were going to explode. He took his personal phone, dialed Fern's number.

No answer.

The bad feeling increased. Ryan radioed his lieutenant. "Lieutenant, I have to get home. Something's wrong."

"Go," he ordered. "Take our command vehicle. I'll clear it with the incident commander."

Not needing a second authorization, Ryan sped off toward the SUV. He raced homeward. When he reached the neighborhood, all seemed quiet. Ryan parked at the house where Officer Jenkins stayed.

Exhausted and yet running on adrenaline, Ryan looked for Jenkins. Usually he sat on the porch, reading a book and drinking coffee.

No one there.

Though it wasn't a reason to be alarmed, combined with the circumstances of the fire he'd fought, the absence raised the hairs on his nape. Maybe Jenkins had to leave. But the police officer would have called for backup.

Something wasn't right.

The man might be at the house, like last night, staying there to guard Fern. Yet Fern would have told him.

Warned him to give the officer a heads-up when Ryan walked through the door, lest he get a gun in his face.

An older model black sedan pulled up to the driveway and Officer Jenkins parked and got out. The worry etched on his face echoed Ryan's.

Then it clicked. He'd been so busy with the scene, securing everything, the man on the sidelines looking familiar, and yet he'd ignored him because he had a job to do…

"You were at the fire," Ryan told him.

Jenkins nodded. "Had to go. Got a call there was a hazmat sitch in my neighborhood, and I needed to evacuate my family. I texted Fern what happened and told her the department would send someone else here to take my place."

No one had. There was no plainclothes officer guarding his house. Guarding Fern.

Like him, Jenkins had been lured away from keeping Fern safe.

He walked quickly, his boot heels clicking on the sidewalk, echoing the beat of his rapid heartbeat. Fern had to be inside—she was okay and promised she wouldn't leave. Promised she'd wait for him to come home. No way could she change her mind and not tell him.

Jenkins was running behind him.

Please be there. Please. Words became a frantic chant, the way he'd used to wish away the monster in his dark closet at night.

Before he grew into an adult and discovered life's real monsters hid in plain sight and not in your closet.

Ryan was running now, pummeled by adrenaline, all exhaustion gone, his arms and legs pumping. Breath coming in and out in little gasps, he finally reached his home. Fern's sanctuary.

"No, no, no," he moaned.

The front door stood ajar. Blood smeared the front stoop, tiny droplets as if Fern had cut her hand. Or worse.

Ryan ran through the house, screaming her name.

No answer. Nothing but the frantic beat of his heart and his own harsh breaths.

Fern had vanished.

Chapter 21

Panic squeezed his throat. Ryan stared at the blood on the stoop. Fern was hurt.

Jennings reached the house and squatted down, studying the blood. Calm and collected, the officer was pragmatic.

The love of his life was missing. Ryan took a deep breath and counted to five, took another deep breath to calm the hell down. He was useless like this.

Fighting fires took professionalism and stuffing your emotions way down inside. He had to do the same now to help Fern.

"Fern's smart." The police officer pointed to the blood droplets. "She left a clue."

Puzzled, he looked down. "How is that a clue?"

"Tells you she was forced. She didn't walk off on her own. There was a struggle."

Suddenly he realized with all her talk about leaving the house, striking out on her own, this clue was quite important.

"I could have come home and assumed she left because she wanted to leave," he said. "Because she'd been talking about it."

Jenkins nodded. "Who else knew Fern talked about leaving?"

"My family. They found a rental for her. Mom, dad, my sister, her fiancé, Chay, and you…"

His voice trailed off as he stared at Jenkins.

The man stood up, nodding. "Let me call this in. Don't touch anything. Go into the house and pull up the security footage."

As he headed to the office, Ryan texted his cousin Jacob, telling him what happened. Jenkins didn't seem as trustworthy now.

He scrolled through the footage and was dismayed to find the front door cameras had been blacked out. Jenkins joined him in the office.

"Spray-painted over to hide their faces and the abduction," the officer explained.

Anger wouldn't help Fern now. Answers would. He narrowed his eyes at Jenkins.

"Fern was under your protection. You were supposed to watch her, and only you knew she'd been talking about leaving the house and living elsewhere. In my book, that makes you a suspect."

The older man met his gaze with a level look. "I know it looks bad. But I was set up, same as you. We both were called to a fire to get us away from Fern."

Now Pete Sanders's words made sense. He called Nick for a report on the fire victim.

Nick answered immediately. "I was going to call you, Ryan. Sanders is on a vent. Guy kept apologizing before they vented him about taking money to lure you to the fire."

Ryan thanked him and hung up. He didn't have time for understanding or convos. Ryan kept scrolling through the security footage, hoping and praying something, anything, would show up.

Hearing Jacob call out, he ran to the front door. His cousin looked grim.

"Fern's gone." Ryan relayed what happened and cursed the fact he'd been lured away from protecting her. He should have known something like this could happen.

"Hey." Jacob put a hand on his shoulder. "Easy, cuz. It's

not your fault. Let's focus on what happened, how we can get her back."

Giving a brusque nod, he jerked his head at the door. "You heard about the threatening note. I'll show you the security footage."

As Ryan came to the footage of whoever left the note, Jacob frowned.

"This person... Whoever left the note is left-handed. The way he tossed his head, combined with the slim physique. This isn't a man, and I highly doubt it's the one who took Fern."

Ryan studied the footage closely. The head toss, pert and sassy, a person, no, a woman accustomed to turning her head, displaying long, silky blonde hair.

"Left-handed." Ryan clenched his fists. "Son of a... I think I know this woman. It's my ex-girlfriend, Kim, who lives next door to my parents."

Jacob's jaw tightened. "I'll have her brought in for questioning."

"No time. We'll go visit her right now."

Every minute counted. The more time wasted, the farther away the kidnappers took Fern.

A patrol unit took them there, lights and sirens blaring to speed to the quiet neighborhood. Ryan was out the door, barely giving the officer time to park. Jacob caught up to him as Ryan was about to pound on the door. Anger shot through him, a vicious, deep anger that made him want to kick the door down, demand answers.

"Let me handle this."

Ryan nodded, stepped back. When Kim answered the door, he could see the surprise and panic flare on her pretty face.

"You know why we're here?"

"No, I..." Kim stepped back and bristled. "It's an odd time for a social visit, Ryan."

Typical Kim, turning a situation around as if she were the one offended.

"This is far from social," he snapped.

Her eyes went wide as Jacob once more put a restraining hand around his arm. Good thing he did, because Ryan was ready to charge into the room.

Jacob pushed forward, blocking Ryan. "Fern Hensley has been abducted. We're here about the note you left on my cousin's front door."

Managing to sidestep Jacob, Ryan watched her carefully. He knew Kim well enough to know when she lied. Guilt and then fear crossed her face.

"You left the note." How he managed to speak calmly was a damn miracle.

"I—I—"

"That's right, Kim. It's always about you. Always has been. Ever wonder why I broke up with you?" He gave a derisive snort. "She doesn't care about Fern, Jacob. Only her own hide."

Jacob's gaze glinted, as if he'd digested Ryan's information and gleaned valuable information. "It's best if you're honest with me now, Miss March. You're facing trespassing charges and more, and this is your chance to mitigate any further damage."

"I didn't hurt her. I didn't know she'd been kidnapped, I swear it!" Kim clenched her hands in her lap. "It was only a joke…"

"A joke?" This time Ryan couldn't remain quiet. "You left a note threatening Fern on my front door and you call it a joke?"

She didn't meet his furious gaze. "I—I was jealous. When I saw her with you at the dinner, how close you both were, and I heard your parents wanted her out, well, they wanted her gone, too!"

Incredulous, he stared at her, wondering how the hell he'd ever become involved with Kim. "You were jealous? You have a boyfriend."

"He's not like you! No one is like you, Ryan. I miss you, and when I saw Fern was with you, living with you, I thought the note would scare her into leaving. I didn't mean any real harm."

Tears filled her eyes, but they weren't tears of regret or sorrow. No, not over Fern. Kim only cried for herself, because she was scared of the consequences. Such privilege. Her entitlement was a sharp contrast to gentle Fern, who cared for others and had a good heart.

They were wasting time here. Ryan glanced at Jacob. "She had nothing to do with Fern's disappearance. She doesn't know anything. I can tell."

Jacob nodded. He looked at Kim with disgust. "Ryan, do you want to press charges against her for trespassing?"

"Not now." He turned back to his ex. "If I ever see you around my property again, I will have you arrested. In the meantime, I suggest you look for another job. When my father discovers what you did, he won't want you around, either."

"But Ryan…"

Kim's beseeching look didn't pull weight on him anymore. Disgusted, he stormed away.

When they returned to the house, Ryan got a call. Tempted to ignore it, he knew he couldn't.

Jacob, talking to the police officers dusting and securing the crime scene, saw his distress. "What's wrong?"

"Brush fire. Dark Canyon Wilderness. Have to report to the incident commander. They need me to help create a fire line. They're already doing back-burns to keep it from spreading."

Never had he felt this helpless, not even when Kate McIntyre slipped through his gloved fingers. Back then, he'd been too much in shock. With the disappearance of Fern, the woman he loved, and aw, hell, he could admit it now, he felt out of control.

He wanted to help, rush out and try to find her. And when he found the sons of bitches who took her, there would be hell to pay.

Jacob nodded. "Go. Do what you do best, Ryan. Your job, keeping people safe. I'll deal with this."

"Promise you'll call or radio dispatch with any news, and I mean any news, about Fern?"

"I promise."

As Ryan headed to his car, he knew Jacob would keep that promise. Coltons always kept their word. They were family, and families counted on each other when times were rough.

This was one of the roughest times he knew, and he needed his family support as much as the public needed him to deal with this brush fire.

Fern roused from unconsciousness to a smoke-filled inferno burning nearby.

Blinking hard, gasping for air, she struggled out of the narcotic-filled daze to look at her surroundings.

No weather-beaten shack this time. No flames consuming dry wood walls, coming closer. Looking around, her eyes watering, she realized she lay on rocky earth. Canyon walls surrounded her. Smoke filled the air, acrid and harsh. Close by, a wildfire burned.

She struggled to sit up and realized her wrists and ankles were restrained once more by zip ties. Billy and Leo had dumped her here near the wildfire, probably to let her burn. Finish what they had started and failed back at the cabin.

At least this time they hadn't broken her leg or beaten her. Maybe they were in a hurry, or thought her too weak to fight for her life.

I am not going to die here.

They'd tried to kill her once, and a brave, commanding firefighter had rescued her. No rescue for her now. Fern knew she was on her own.

Coughing, she peered into the smoke-filled air. The wildfire encroached on the canyon, shutting off access. Though she'd pressed the GPS locator on her necklace so police and Jacob could track her position, Fern wasn't certain it would work. The distance might be too far.

She had to find a way out, and if no help was coming, she'd do it alone.

You're not alone.

Ryan's voice echoed in her memories. He'd been there time and again for her, steadying her when she felt ready to falter, reminding her she had courage and strength.

He admired her.

Respected her.

Loved her.

I'm not going to die here. Not when I have so much to live for and I was given a second chance.

Love was worth fighting for—hells bells, she was worth the fight.

A tiny stream trickled nearby. Leo and Billy were in such a hurry to dump her, they'd failed to check out all the surroundings. On her hands and knees, ignoring the pain from stones cutting into her legs, she crawled over to it. She found a sharp stone sticking out from the ground.

With some effort, she sawed back and forth with her wrists, grimacing as the stone cut her skin. She did not stop.

I need a little help here. Fern glanced skyward.

Her luck turned. The zip ties Billy and Leo used were old and they snapped. Fern pulled her wrists free, then tore off her blouse and wet it, tying it around her mouth and nose like a mask.

The shirt would act as a filter from the smoke. Ash would not get through the fabric, clogging her lungs. At least for now.

Ryan had told her most fire victims died from smoke inhalation.

Next she went to work on her ankles, using another stone to saw through them. Finally her ankles were freed.

Fern wet the shirt again and coughed, then retied it around her face. She thought of the sign she'd left Ryan at the house, managing to cut herself to leave blood on the stoop so he'd know something was wrong. He would not assume she left him and went elsewhere.

Wind blew, carrying arcs of sparks and more smoke. Then it shifted, showing a tall structure in the distance.

A fire tower.

If she made it there, she might have a chance. Ryan told her the towers were stocked with water, food and firefighting equipment. It looked out of the range of the wildfire.

He'd given her the little pocket compass as a gift to find her direction in life. Now it would guide her to the tower, hopefully, toward survival.

After removing it from the necklace, she held it steady. The fire tower was north. North like the North Star, the only star in the sky that never moved.

Steady and true, like Ryan.

If I get out of this, I'm making a fresh start. With Ryan, if he'll have me. Stop thinking like that. You will get out of this.

Fern stood on shaky legs, willing herself to walk forward. Willing herself to climb over rocks and navigate the canyon, toward safety.

Toward life.

The Dark Canyon Wilderness was about forty-five thousand acres of prime Utah backcountry. People came from across the country to navigate the desert and forest, take in the ancient cliff dwelling ruins. The canyons and mesas were quiet, peaceful, and the topography shifted from forest to desert. You could lose yourself out here, or as Ryan found at times, find your purpose.

One of the most popular hikes was the forty-mile loop, beginning at the rimrocks of Cedar Mesa sandstone, where hikers moved downward more than two thousand feet to a dry streambed. It was a challenging hike, and he'd done it plenty of times.

Always wary of flash flooding, Ryan knew the trouble times were the summer and fall thunderstorms, but since the canyons were broad, the danger wasn't as severe. Still, it helped to be alert and aware, especially when spring brought occasional flooding. So far, they hadn't had to rescue any hikers inside the fire line, and he was immensely grateful for that.

In summer, temperatures could reach over a hundred degrees. Now, in April, they were tolerable, that is, if one embarked on a hike.

Outfitted in firefighting equipment, pounding the soil, Ryan sweated as if the temperatures were summer.

Working a fire line called for different skills than a house fire. Ryan's shoulders ached from digging a trench down to the bare soil to remove brush and other vegetation that could feed fuel to the fire. They'd created an anchor point, where the fire was the coldest. Smoke swirled around them, but at his vantage point, he could easily see.

If they contained the fire, it wouldn't advance to homes on the edge of the wilderness.

A spring rain sure would come in handy now, but though clouds scudded overhead, they weren't counting on it.

Without words, he worked with his team, his mind focused on the job, trying not to worry about Fern. With relentless determination, he kept at it until he heard a call from dispatch that had nothing to do with the fire.

"Ryan. We got a ping on Fern's necklace. Over," Jacob's voice crackled over the radio.

Ryan whipped his head around. "Where?"

"Edge of the Dark Canyon Wilderness." Jacob gave the GPS coordinates. "We're going to send a team in there."

As he plugged in the coordinates to his cell, his flare of

hope turned to a sinking feeling. *At least we found her. There's a chance.*

Memorizing the coordinates, Ryan went to the mobile command set up nearby. He consulted the satellite tracking app the incident commander used to give orders to those fighting the blaze.

A chill raced down his spine. Sons of bitches had dumped Fern at the edge of the fire. Right where the flames were racing.

She didn't have a chance.

By the time rescue reached her, she'd be dead.

He spoke into his shoulder mike. "Jacob, I'm only about two miles from that location. I'm going in."

"No."

"No choice. I'm here. You're not. No one else is. You don't know the terrain like I do."

The slick rock and the sand would make hiking to her a bitch, and minutes counted.

"I'll radio you when I find her. Colton out."

The incident commander lifted up his helmet and studied him. "Colton you do this, it's against orders."

"Have to, Chief."

The man, burly and rugged, gave a brief smile, outlined in his soot-stained faced. "Not my orders. Someone's orders."

His captain gazed at him. "Not my orders, either, Ryan. Go get her. Radio if you need help. We need to stay here. But we've got your back."

Ryan struggled against the emotion clogging his throat. These men and women were his family as much as Jacob and the other Coltons. He nodded. "Thanks."

"But you're not going in alone." Tom shook his head.

On this he would not compromise. "Look, I'm not asking anyone else to risk it to retrieve Fern. You're needed here."

Tom grumbled, but lifted a bulky item off the folding table. "Here. Take this. It's all we can spare, but it will help. Use it to track her and then radio back your coordinates. Battery's running low. Keep the drone turned off until you get closer to her last known location. We'll keep in touch with you and radio back hot spots and the advancing fire line."

Ryan took the drone and the remote. He'd trained with this drone for wildfire fighting and knew it was an older model. It didn't have infrared for sighting hot spots, but it would help to scout ahead for Fern's location. "Thanks."

It was a lot to carry, but the drone was critical.

After consulting with the GPS and making sure his sat phone worked, he checked his gear. Emergency pack with medical kit, navigation guide, headlamp, communications radio, rogue hoe. His hardhat and Nomex flame-resistant shirts and pants, gloves and boots would protect him. Ryan grabbed two additional NIOSH-approved N95 masks.

Fern had nothing to protect her.

He marched into the wilderness, toward Fern.

He only hoped he wasn't too late.

Chapter 22

Fern had doused all her clothing and hair in the little creek and struggled to walk to the fire tower. But the rugged terrain and the soft sand made hiking difficult. Stopping to rest, she looked around, wondering if she was walking directly into the fire. Hard to gauge from the smoke and the wind blowing in her direction.

Well, if I burn to death this time, at least I'll have tried to save myself.

She wiped tears from her eyes, telling herself it was from the acrid smoke, not thoughts of her life ending.

Think of Ryan. He risks his life all the time to save people, rushes into burning buildings without a thought for his own safety...

Ryan also has training and wears protective clothing, her cynical self added.

Fern laughed and coughed. She could almost hear Ryan's voice in her head, agreeing.

Then his deep, stern tone urging her forward, to keep moving. *Don't stand still. Don't give up.*

An odd whirring noise sounded overhead. Blinking back tears, she looked up.

A black drone flew overhead, zipping along the canyon. Her heart leaped with joy. Ryan had shown her a vid of such drones and how firefighters used them to scout out the fire's location, fight the flames themselves and even locate stranded hikers.

"Hey!" Fern waved her arms, coughed and screamed again, trying to get the machine's attention and whoever operated it. "Help! I'm here!"

Suddenly the drone dropped from the sky a few feet away, crashing on the soft sand.

Despair nudged her. Maybe the smoke got to it, or the battery died. But surely whoever operated the remote would have seen her.

Unless the remote's battery died as well.

"Please," she whispered. "Please, someone come. I don't want to die here."

She began the bargaining stage so familiar to her after dropping to rock bottom during her drinking days, before her foster parents brought her to Alcoholics Anonymous. *If you get me out of here, God, I promise I'll be good. I promise I'll make something of my life. I promise to help others.*

"I promise I won't run away again like before, and I'll stick with Ryan and see where we go," she said aloud, and then coughed.

Smoke swirled, a grayish fog, and cleared. Out of the clearing walked a figure in soot-stained yellow, with dark trousers, a white hardhat. An N95 mask covered his face.

Fern blinked, not wanting this to be a hallucination caused by the drugs Billy and Leo had given her.

She waved her arms again. "Hello! I'm here. Help!"

"Fern?" the figure asked.

Stunned, she stood in disbelief as he raced forward. The figure tore off his mask, revealing the features of someone she knew well.

Someone who had saved her from the hell in the cabin, and once more reached her side.

"Ryan?" A sob rose in her throat.

"Fern. Thank God."

Never had she hugged anyone so tight. Then, brisk and professional, he looked around. "Got to get out of here. Fire's advancing and the wind is shifting."

He fished two more N95 masks out of his pack. "Here, put this on. It will help filter the smoke."

She pointed to the distant fire tower. "I was headed there, thinking maybe someone was up there."

"Not now, but good call."

He consulted the tablet-sized remote in his hands. "Drone battery is dead. We'll have to hoof it to the fire tower and use the radio to keep abreast of the fire line."

Ryan spoke into his shoulder mike and received a transmission of crackling noise that reported the fire's position.

"Colton out." He looked at Fern. "Fire's blowing to the west, away from the tower. If we can make it to the tower, there's equipment there. Oxygen masks, water and, best of all, a radio that has a more powerful signal."

"Thank you." She coughed, her eyes watering from smoke, and emotion as well.

He set the remote down on the ground. "Have to leave this and the drone here. Too much to carry."

He gazed at her. "Can you walk?"

Fern nodded. The drugs they'd injected into her had mostly worn off, though her legs felt like rubber. But she'd run out of here if necessary.

"Let's go."

Brisk, professional, the air of command in his voice. She'd never seen him at work, not like this. Taking charge, compelling her forward, focused on getting them out.

The sand beneath their feet made it difficult to walk, her shoes sinking into it like quicksand. Every few minutes Ryan's radio crackled, giving him updates on the fire line and the battle being waged to contain it.

Thigh muscles bunching and burning, she began to wheeze. Maybe the narcotics hadn't left her system after all.

Ryan hooked an arm around her waist and helped her walk through the sand and navigate the boulders in their way. Finally they reached the tower. She looked up at the steep ladder. Though it was a series of switchbacks, allowing one to rest at landings, it was a long way up.

"Can you make it or do you want me to pull you up?"

Fern shook her head. She was making it on her own.

"I'll be right behind you."

Slow going, dragging herself up, one step at a time. At each landing, she stopped, struggling to breathe. Ryan let her rest, not pushing her, but she knew, judging from the dizzying feeling, she needed oxygen.

Finally she reached the top. Ryan pushed past her and helped pull her upward to the walkway ringing the tower office.

Arm around her waist, he helped her inside. Huge windows allowed excellent views of the entire Dark Canyon Wilderness. There was a cot, binoculars, extinguisher, propane stove, radio with a headset, even a mini refrigerator. Best of all, a small cabinet, from which he pulled out a portable oxygen bottle. After she pulled off the N95 mask, Ryan slipped the plastic oxygen mask over her face and opened the canister.

He set about calling on the radio, giving the incident commander their position.

Finally he returned to her side, after securing two bottles of water from the supplies.

Fern breathed in the oxygen, her head clearing. She blinked, her eyes still watering.

Springs creaked as he sat on the cot with her.

"Now we wait."

She removed the mask. "What are our chances?"

"Good. They'll get to us." He didn't look at her. Jaw rigid, he stared at the windows before them.

"The tower's not manned these days, except when they can find someone willing to work for very low pay. Not necessary, anyway, not with the tech these days like the drones flying overhead to spot fires. It's mainly used to aid stranded backpackers who get lost or injured," he said.

"Will you get into trouble for leaving that drone?"

His mouth twitched in a faint smile. "Trust you to worry about me, after all you've been through. Nah. I'm good."

The smile vanished. "As long as you're safe, and okay."

"Thanks to you."

His jaw went taut. "When I thought of those bastards taking you, leaving you to burn to death again…"

He looked away.

Fern touched his arm, needing this connection and reassurance, for both of them. "I'm here. I'm not going to die, Ryan."

Glancing at her, he gave that faint, almost haunted smile again. "No. You're a tough one, Fern Hensley. Strong, resilient. I counted on that when I heard you were missing again. Put the mask back on, honey. You need that O2."

Ryan stood and paced the tower's small interior as she put the oxygen mask on again. "Soon as you feel strong enough, and they have a safe area overhead for the helo, we can leave. Smoke's too thick right now."

Bracing his hands on the desk, he stared out the window. "I hate this canyon. Too easy to get caught here."

Something else bothered him. Her intuition warned it wasn't her or their precarious situation.

Fern removed the mask. "You've been here before."

He didn't seem to hear her, as if lost in his own thoughts. "I let a woman die out here."

She felt a gut punch at the words. "Tell me."

Maybe it was her voice, raspy from the smoke, or he simply needed to unload. Whatever the reason, Ryan began to talk.

"It was about a year ago, in the spring. I'm a rock jock, you know? Loved to climb, always did it when I could. The challenge, it's great and keeps me going."

He snorted. "Something Dad never understood—the physical need to get out and get moving in nature."

Fern put the mask back on and listened.

"Cap always liked having a rock jock on the team, came in handy for rope rescues when the park rangers in Dark Canyon got overloaded or couldn't get a rescue in time. Well, last spring, I got a call. We got a call. Stranded hiker rock climbing on the Sundance Trail."

He pointed out the window. "The trail is amazing to hike. You descend about twelve hundred feet into the canyon. Then you're surrounded by these terrific rock walls, just pressing against you, with a stream in the middle. Done it many, many times. Thought it would be a piece of cake."

Shaking his head, he gave a grudging laugh. "Me and my assumptions. Well, we got there, with all our equipment, ropes, harness, you name it. I put on my equipment and climbed up to rescue her. She was dangling from a rope that wasn't secured right."

Fern watched him.

"Her name was Kate. Kate McIntyre. Terrified. Frozen in place, couldn't go up, couldn't go down. Her anchor was coming loose, and I knew it wouldn't hold. Only one anchor. Should have used at least two. Dammit, I secured three anchors to get to her!

"I reached out to her, secured her to the line. I told her not to move, I would do all the work. I told her everything was going to be okay."

Fern didn't need to guess the ending. The haunted look on his face told her everything.

Ryan checked the oxygen canister. "She was twenty-four."

She removed the mask. "A year younger than me," Fern mused. "Was she an experienced climber?"

He blinked, as if the question startled him, then motioned for her to put the mask on again. "No. I found out a few days ago from her instructor that Kate was a beginner. She wasn't experienced enough for that climb. Her parents said the same thing at her funeral, but it doesn't matter."

"Do they blame you?"

As he shook his head, she breathed in more oxygen, then removed the mask.

"Why do you blame yourself if her family doesn't, either? You did your job. You tried to rescue her. You didn't push her off the cliff."

"I didn't save her!"

Fern looked at him calmly. "I never took you for a martyr, Ryan Colton."

His gaze narrowed. "I'm not."

"Then let it go." She spoke softly, coughed. Took in more oxygen. He needed to hear this, needed her words. Months ago, this brave man risked his life to save hers.

Now she needed to save his—from any more guilt.

"You rushed into a burning cabin to save me. What if you were too late? Would it have been your fault?"

Ryan looked away. "No. The wood was weathered, shack was nearly engulfed when I arrived. It was timing. Luck."

"Would you have blamed yourself if I died in there?"

He rubbed a hand over his face. "Fern, the comparison isn't the same…"

"Of course it is. Different scenarios, different outcomes, but you acted the same in both. You did your job to the best of your ability. So what makes mine different from Kate's?"

"I…" Ryan looked away. "You were nearly unconscious. Restrained. I saw you tried to crawl away. Tried to save yourself."

"And Kate? I'm sure she tried to save herself as well. Or did she?"

Silence hung in the air for a minute, broken only by the wind rushing outside the windows, the crackle of the radio. Ryan finally met her gaze.

"I was on the ropes, and I had the carabineer and harness ready to secure her. I told her to remain still. I could see if she moved, she'd fall."

He spoke slowly, reciting the memory as if they were back there in the canyon, his equipment prepared to save the stranded Kate.

"She clung to the rock wall. Didn't even scream. Just looked at me as if she'd already given up. I begged her not to give up, I was almost there, so damn close.

"Kate told me it didn't matter anymore. I couldn't help her. I begged her to hang on. I reached for her, tried to pull the harness around her, kept telling her she was going to be okay."

Ryan swore softly. "She told me it would never be okay. Never told anyone what she said. Not even my captain. Or the chaplain when we talked."

"You held it all inside, because that's what guys like you do. Never show your emotions." Fern understood.

"She struggled and started to slip. I grabbed her hand, told her to hang on."

Fern held his hand, giving him her support, her love. "Kate did not."

Gripping her hand, Ryan didn't say anything for a moment, as if digesting her words.

"She let go."

"And you didn't."

Slowly her words seemed to permeate through to his mind. Ryan squeezed her hand.

"I didn't."

"You did everything in your power, everything you'd trained for, to save Kate."

Finally he looked up. The sorrow lingered in his gaze, but the haunted look vanished. "I did everything."

Fern slid her free hand over his soot-stained cheek, her heart swelling with emotion. "Ryan, something I've learned over the years, when I struggled with drinking, when I remembered how vicious my mom's boyfriend was to me, how my mom walked out with him instead of staying to care for me, her only child. We're all responsible for our lives. You can try to save someone with all you've got, but all the wishes and equipment in the world won't rescue someone who doesn't want to be saved."

"Kate did," he said slowly, closing his eyes. "She wanted to live."

"How can you know that for certain? You tried your best." Fern caressed his cheek. "You reached out to her in her moment of need. You said and did everything right."

His eyes opened, and she saw the pain in them. "Then why couldn't she hold on?"

"Because she couldn't. It's time for you to let go as well. You can't save everyone."

He gave a short, bitter laugh. "That's what Cap says. We can't save everyone."

Fern put his hand over her heart. "But those of us you can and do save, they make it worthwhile. We're the ones you have to keep fighting for, Ryan."

For a moment he closed his eyes again, as if relishing her touch, her understanding. Maybe as if he sought forgiveness, but for what? There was nothing to forgive.

Knowing he needed her support, Fern clasped his hand. "You did everything, Ryan. You did what you could. What you're trained to do."

Noise crackled from the radio. Ryan squeezed her hand, went to the microphone. He listened.

"Colton out."

Finally. Relieved, he motioned to Fern. "We can leave now."

The smoothness of his expression assured her Ryan finally made peace with his past. She knew the feeling. Life sometimes handed you a heap of trouble, but with the right people along the way, you could free yourself.

She only hoped they could get out of here the same way and move forward.

Chapter 23

Ryan wasn't happy with Fern descending the ladder, even taking it slow. The helo would be here soon, and the smoke might blow in their direction, making rescue difficult, if not impossible.

With the drugs still in her system, he knew she couldn't hike out. Even with the right equipment, she might not survive. Wildfires were tricky and, with a shift of the wind, could send flames in their direction.

The helo would safely airlift her to the hospital.

"I'll go first down the ladder and help you," he ordered.

"No, I'll go first before I lose my nerve. I'll be okay with you behind me."

Much as he disliked the idea, he recognized the stubborn lines on her forehead. Part of him wanted to lift her over one shoulder and jog downward.

Part of him was damn proud of her for surviving once more.

But if she insisted on doing it her way, well, there were precautions.

Ryan removed rope carabiners and climbing rope from his pack, then put a safety harness around her waist and a rope. With one of the carabiners, he secured it to his belt. Next he wound a length of rope around one of the sturdiest poles at the top and attached a strong climbing carabiner.

They went outside, onto the walkway, and began to descend

the ladder. Fern was directly in front of him, easing her way down, one rung at a time.

Going too slow, but they still had time. In the distance, he could hear the helo's whirling motor.

"We're gonna make it, honey. You can do this," he encouraged.

Leaning heavily on the railing, she was too unstable. The railing was only a support and rickety...

Suddenly her feet slipped and the railing snapped. Fern screamed and dropped. The rope securing them pulled hard, nearly spilling him as well.

Dangling hundreds of feet in the air, Fern grappled for purchase. Ryan clung to the ladder. He tugged off his glove and reached out a hand. "Grab my hand," he yelled.

"I can't reach!"

"You can!"

Fingers wriggling, she managed to clasp his hand. He couldn't let go. Not going to let go, not going to watch her fall to her death.

Like Kate had. No. Not going to lose her. Not now, not ever. Not after all this.

"Don't you dare let go," Fern screamed at him. "I'm counting on you, Ryan Colton."

Something in his chest eased. Guilt? Relief? He wasn't sure. Didn't matter. "Never," he yelled back.

Ryan swung her around so she directly faced the ladder. "Hook a foot around the railing."

Working with her, talking softly, he got her to steady herself. Fern's eyes squeezed shut.

His mind raced over solutions. In the past, he'd used a Munter hitch on a belay system to lower stranded climbers to safety. The adjustable knot was easy to tie, and self-regulating. Best bet to get Fern down. Her legs couldn't take the strain of climbing the stairs.

Fern was secure for the moment. He opened his pack and began setting up the belay system.

"I'm going to lower you down."

He prayed this would work. Dimly he remembered the rope training Cap scheduled for him.

This has to work.

Ryan glanced overhead. The helo hovered, lowering down a basket. Knew they couldn't hold that position long. Slowly he lowered Fern down. To his relief, she didn't scream or kick or struggle.

Her trust in him was absolute.

Fern's feet touched ground. Relief flooded him. He quickly released her, then rappelled downward. Soon as he reached the bottom, he released the ropes and slung her over one shoulder.

Her lack of protests worried him. He jogged over to the basket, motioning for them to lower it farther. Then he strapped Fern in, making sure she was secure, and gave the thumbs-up to the rescue personnel waiting above.

Not until she was inside the helo did he relax a little. They lowered the safety harness for him. He strapped himself in, and they raised him up.

Smoke swirled around them. "Gotta go," one of the medical technicians yelled above the roar of the chopper. "Wind's shifting."

"I'm in. Let's roll," Ryan yelled back.

He gave a worried glance at Fern, lying so pale and still as oxygen was administered.

Then they were off, flying out of the canyon, in the direction of the hospital.

Toward medical help. He prayed they weren't too late.

Waiting had never been his strength. He knew he lacked patience, even though he'd acquired more of it after years on the job.

Firefighting patience was one matter. Family matters were another.

He'd paced these hospital corridors before. Usually for family, like when they were kids and he'd roughhoused with Jacob and Noah. That one time when Jacob ended up here in the emergency room. All because Ryan had been a little too rough as captain of the pirate ship and made Jacob walk the plank. When Jacob resisted, Ryan gave him a little shove and Jacob landed on the ground. Sprained wrist, not the broken bone they all feared.

He'd caught pure hell for that later, but the waiting to hear if Jacob was okay was worse than the tanning on his bottom.

Waiting to hear if Fern was okay was much, much worse.

Gathered in the hallway with him were a few firefighters and his friend Nick Malone. Nick had gone to the cafeteria to fetch him a much-needed coffee. Ryan had shrugged off medical treatment. Running on fumes and little sleep, exhausted beyond belief, he cared only about Fern's condition. She seemed so fragile, lying on the stretcher as they airlifted her to the hospital and rushed her to emergency treatment.

Nick came toward him, holding a small cup of coffee. Expression grim, he handed it to Ryan.

His stomach roiled. "What's wrong?"

"Not sure if I should tell you this…but one of the guys told me there was a bad wreck on the highway. Two men in a van going fast. They crashed. One died on impact. The other is here, at the hospital."

Ryan uncapped the lukewarm brew, took a bracing sip. At least it was strong, even if it tasted like old socks. "Anyone we know?"

He honestly couldn't take any more bad news today.

"Not really, but someone Fern knows well, unfortunately," Nick said evenly.

It didn't hit him at first. He was so tired, Ryan couldn't make the connection. Then he looked at the anger on his friend's face and knew.

The coffee cup fell from his shaking hand to the floor, spilling liquid over his trousers, boots and the floor.

Ryan stared at him. "Who is it? Which one of her kidnappers?"

"Billy. Leo's dead."

Billy. The man who thought to end Fern's life, left her to burn to death first in the cabin and now in the wildfire. The man who broke her leg. Tormented her. Wanted to sell her as a sex slave.

He managed to speak calmly. "Here, in this hospital?"

Nick nodded. "I did a little snooping. He's conscious, but not speaking to anyone. Clammed up tight. Knows he's in trouble. Right now he's in ICU under heavy guard."

Not heavy enough. Ryan turned to head to the elevators when he spotted his cousin Jacob headed in his direction.

Always intuitive, Jacob stopped him, caught his arm as if he sensed where Ryan was headed.

"Let go." Ryan scowled.

"You heard."

"Yeah, and I owe him a visit for what he did to Fern."

"Easy. Billy's not going anywhere. There's several officers making sure of that."

"Let them stop me."

He wanted to march into Billy's room, punch him, maybe break a few bones and worse, for what Billy had done. Make him pay. Let him know Fern was not alone, never alone, and when you hurt someone loved by a Colton man, you had better make peace with your maker, fast.

"Don't. You're needed here. Fern needs you."

The words calmed him a little. "Has the bastard said anything?"

"No. He's refusing to say anything."

"I could get him to talk." Ryan raised his fists.

"I get it. I do." Jacob placed himself square in front of Ryan. "You have to let the system do its work, Ryan. Concentrate on Fern. She needs you. Please. For her sake."

He tried to control his raging temper, nodded. Ryan managed to speak in a controlled tone. "Nick told me they crashed."

"Courtesy of myself and others. We forced them off the road."

The news made him calmer. Jacob was in control.

"How is Fern?" Jacob asked.

"Don't know. Doc's in with her now. She suffered a lot of smoke inhalation, again, and the drug in her system left her weak and might have caused more damage than we realized."

Anger boiled up, bright and fierce, all over again. "They injected her with ketamine. Not enough to knock her out, only enough to make her disoriented and woozy. But it adversely affected her respiration, and combined with the wildfire smoke…"

Words died in his throat. He couldn't continue, couldn't face the possibility of Fern not recovering from this.

Not after everything she'd endured. *Please, let her live. Let her be okay.*

Jacob looked as if he'd like to deal Billy a little justice of his own. "I'm familiar with the effects. Ketamine is used as a date rape drug. Enough of it can kill."

He felt sick, thinking about how close Fern had come to both.

Jacob studied him. "You okay now? Promise you'll leave Billy to us?"

Ryan nodded. "As long as you promise you'll do everything you can to give Fern and the other victims justice."

"Trust me on this. I want justice for Fern and the other women as much as you do." Jacob's voice carried a deadly edge.

Still, he couldn't relax. Not until Fern was fully recovered and out of this hospital. That reminded him…

"Pete Sanders, the victim in the hazmat fire I saved—got any updates?" he asked Jacob.

His cousin's eyes narrowed. "Burn unit thinks he is not going to make it."

"Sanders apologized, said he got money to lure me there," Ryan told him.

"We believe he started the fire and called it in as a chemical fire to get you there, but it got out of control. Whoever targeted his house and gave him money knew Officer Jenkins lived only two doors down and worried about his pregnant wife."

"And they knew I was the senior hazmat technician and would be there. A chemical fire that posed a real threat to the neighborhood would also tear Jenkins away from guarding Fern," Ryan mused. "Who would know Jenkins lived there?"

"Another cop, maybe. Jenkins knows a lot of police from many departments all over. He used to work in Provo and then Moab before moving here."

Damn. "Fern said Billy dressed like a cop and showed what looked like a police badge at the door, which is why she opened it. Could Billy have gotten both from a cop?"

Jacob shrugged. "Easy enough to fake both these days. You can buy cop outfits and fake shields online. Still…"

His cousin's tight expression echoed the worry in Ryan.

The doctor came out of Fern's room. Judging from the cautious smile, it was good news, but Ryan couldn't relax until he knew Fern would be all right.

"She's young and strong. Smoke inhalation is serious. It can weaken the heart and cause cardiac arrest, but she was smart in tying the shirt around her mouth to mitigate it."

The doctor gave him a stern look. "Now that you know she's going to be all right, you get yourself checked out. Can't have something happening to you."

Ryan promised he would, soon as he checked on Fern.

Before anyone could stop him, he went into the emergency room bay where she was lying. Fern was awake, looking pale, but her face broke into a smile upon seeing him.

He took her hand, glad for the feel of it beneath his own.

She removed the oxygen mask. "Is it over?" she asked, her voice hoarse and thick.

Gently he replaced it. "It's over, sweetheart. No worries anymore. You're safe now. For good."

If he spent the rest of his life insuring that would happen, he'd be a happy man.

Chapter 24

Two days later, Fern was released from the hospital into Ryan's care. Being free from the antiseptic atmosphere wasn't her only concern. Knowing one of her kidnappers had been in the same hospital had been upsetting. She'd found out by accident after overhearing a nurse.

Fern trusted the justice system would take care of Billy. As Ryan kept telling her, she had to focus on herself now.

Officer Jenkins had stopped by the hospital to check on her and apologize for abandoning his post. Fern told him no apology was necessary. If she had a family and they were threatened by a hazardous fire, she'd have done the same.

While in the hospital, Jacob had updated her on the case. The house across the street from Ryan's home had been arson. Investigators found the gas can used in the fire had been purchased from a hardware store in Oso by a man who looked like Billy.

"We believe Billy and Leo set the fire to lure Ryan out of the house so they could grab you. They didn't count on the ammo going off, or the large police presence. Got scared off," Jacob had told her.

The good news was Jacob and his team had finally tracked down Walter, thanks to matching prints the man had left at Dr. Sonder's office. His real name was Timothy Simpson, who had a record for larceny. However, when police went to his apartment in Oso to arrest him, Simpson was dead.

Suicide, Jacob informed her grimly.

Now, as Ryan escorted her into the house, he gave her a questioning look as she stepped inside. Fern braced herself to feel anxiety—for this was the place where she'd been abducted.

Instead, all she felt was comfort. She gave him a reassuring smile as he closed and locked the door behind them.

"It feels good to be here again, with you." She meant it.

The familiar scent of his home—coffee, the tang of spices they both enjoyed, and Ryan himself—embraced her. A weight lifted off her as she headed for the living room.

The sofa where they had first started making love. Fern took a deep breath. Such joyful memories pushing aside the bad ones.

As she sat on the sofa, stroking a hand over the fabric, indulging in those memories, Ryan stood before her. His eyes lit up when he gazed at her, and his smile was welcoming and warm.

"Hey," he said softly, taking a step toward her. "You okay?"

Fern nodded, her eyes not leaving him. She felt a surge of emotion, something tender and almost overwhelming. "Yeah. I... I'm good," she said, her voice trembling just a little.

The house was quiet, but it felt full. Full of peace and security and love, love Ryan brought with him in his big, commanding presence.

She gazed at the walls, worn sofa, bookshelves crammed with reading material, the big-screen television. Everything felt right.

Ryan's house felt more like home than her apartment. More like home than anyplace she'd ever called home.

For a moment she remained still, soaking up the peace and quiet, letting it fill her up. She'd been to so many places in her life—places that never truly felt like home. The hospital had been sterile and cold, and her apartment was merely a place to sleep at night. But this felt like it was made for her.

Ryan sat down beside her, close but not too close, giving her space to breathe but offering quiet comfort all the same.

"Found a good ink shop in town, if you still want to remove this?" He gently touched the dollar sign tattoo on her neck.

Throat tight, she nodded. "I was thinking a good artist could turn it into something pretty, so it wouldn't leave a scar."

The scars inside would take longer to heal, but time would help. Belle, her sponsor, assured her of this. She'd phoned Belle in the hospital and told her everything, including the news she had yet to share with Ryan.

"I have a surprise for you," Ryan said.

He'd heaped gifts upon her at the hospital. A warm blanket his mother gave him for Fern. A favorite mug. A stuffed animal to hug.

"Another one?"

"This one you can't unwrap. I'll go get it."

He vanished down the hallway and returned with a box, placing it in her arms.

A soft whimper came from inside the carton. Fern peeked inside. "Bumper!"

"His foster parents agreed you saved him, so you should be his new owner," Ryan told her as she lifted out the puppy and discarded the box.

The puppy licked her nose, and she laughed. Ryan's wide grin echoed her own feelings.

"Smart dog. He's already worming his way into your heart," he teased.

She set Bumper down, watching him explore his new territory. "I hope he's housebroken. I wouldn't want him ruining your carpeting."

"I'm told that was the first thing they taught him." Ryan rubbed the back of his neck. "Been meaning to tell you, but wanted to wait until you were stronger. Noah, Mark, Ava and I went to your apartment. You lost the lease, so we moved your stuff into storage. Sorry."

Fern shrugged, feeling oddly lighter at the news. "No great loss."

"We can help you find a new, pet-friendly rental in Oso, if you want. If you planned to try to get your job back or another one there."

Ryan looked away. "Although I was hoping…"

His voice trailed off. Then he studied Bumper, sniffing the carpet. "Better put him outside."

They went outside, watching Bumper lope across the grass and bark enthusiastically at the birds at the feeder.

"I know it's not your home, but I wanted to formally ask you if you'd move in with me. I'll understand if you're not ready."

So much like Ryan. Honest and direct. No games, no manipulation.

Time to level with Ryan. "I've been studying medical coding again to refresh my skills. I've been applying all over, and I have an offer of full-time remote work with a large medical practice near Salt Lake. It would mean in-person meetings there, but only for two days a month."

"Salt Lake. Wow. That's quite a distance."

"But worth it. My old job gave me a high recommendation. The human resources director told me they wanted me to start next month. Remote work means I don't have to live in Oso anymore. I can live wherever I wish."

"And what do you wish?" he asked softly.

"I always thought I was supposed to be looking for something…something out there—" she gestured at the mountains "—something I had to find. But I think I was just looking for this. For somewhere I could feel like I belonged."

Fern removed the paper from her jeans pocket. The list was the most important one she'd ever jotted down. "I made a list of things I'm looking forward to. Your sister suggested this when I was in the hospital. A list for my future. So I could find my new direction in life."

Ryan's deep blue gaze remained steady. "Am I on the list?"

She handed it over, her heart thudding hard. "You're at the top."

Barely scanning the paper, he set it down on the nearby table. Ryan reached out, his hand brushing against hers lightly. His voice was low, steady. "You don't have to look anymore, Fern."

Fern's heart skipped a beat. The words settled inside her, filling that empty space. She felt something in her chest shift— a quiet, contented warmth that had been missing for too long.

Barely able to speak for the tightness in her throat, Fern nodded. "I don't need to search for direction anymore, Ryan. I've finally found my way home. It's right here with you."

The joyful smile on his face assured her of that future. Fern went into his open arms. His kiss was deep, soulful and promised passion.

She no longer needed his compass or any kind of GPS.

Fern knew she was exactly where she was meant to be—here with Ryan Colton, the love she'd searched for her entire life.

* * * * *

Get up to 4 Free Books!

**We'll send you 2 free books from each series you try
PLUS a free Mystery Gift.**

FREE Value Over $25

Both the **Harlequin Intrigue®** and **Harlequin® Romantic Suspense** series feature compelling novels filled with heart-racing action-packed romance that will keep you on the edge of your seat.

YES! Please send me 2 FREE novels from the Harlequin Intrigue or Harlequin Romantic Suspense series and my FREE gift (gift is worth about $10 retail). After receiving them, if I don't wish to receive any more books, I can return the shipping statement marked "cancel." If I don't cancel, I will receive 6 brand-new Harlequin Intrigue Larger-Print books every month and be billed just $7.19 each in the U.S. or $7.99 each in Canada, or 4 brand-new Harlequin Romantic Suspense books every month and be billed just $6.39 each in the U.S. or $7.19 each in Canada, a savings of 20% off the cover price. It's quite a bargain! Shipping and handling is just 50¢ per book in the U.S. and $1.25 per book in Canada.* I understand that accepting the 2 free books and gift places me under no obligation to buy anything. I can always return a shipment and cancel at any time by calling the number below. The free books and gift are mine to keep no matter what I decide.

Choose one:
- ☐ **Harlequin Intrigue Larger-Print** (199/399 BPA G36Y)
- ☐ **Harlequin Romantic Suspense** (240/340 BPA G36Y)
- ☐ **Or Try Both!** (199/399 & 240/340 BPA G36Z)

Name (please print)

Address   Apt. #

City   State/Province   Zip/Postal Code

Email: Please check this box ☐ if you would like to receive newsletters and promotional emails from Harlequin Enterprises ULC and its affiliates. You can unsubscribe anytime.

Mail to the Harlequin Reader Service:
IN U.S.A.: P.O. Box 1341, Buffalo, NY 14240-8531
IN CANADA: P.O. Box 603, Fort Erie, Ontario L2A 5X3

Want to explore our other series or interested in ebooks? Visit www.ReaderService.com or call 1-800-873-8635.

---

*Terms and prices subject to change without notice. Prices do not include sales taxes, which will be charged (if applicable) based on your state or country of residence. Canadian residents will be charged applicable taxes. Offer not valid in Quebec. This offer is limited to one order per household. Books received may not be as shown. Not valid for current subscribers to the Harlequin Intrigue or Harlequin Romantic Suspense series. All orders subject to approval. Credit or debit balances in a customer's account(s) may be offset by any other outstanding balance owed by or to the customer. Please allow 4 to 6 weeks for delivery. Offer available while quantities last.

Your Privacy—Your information is being collected by Harlequin Enterprises ULC, operating as Harlequin Reader Service. For a complete summary of the information we collect, how we use this information and to whom it is disclosed, please visit our privacy notice located at https://corporate.harlequin.com/privacy-notice. Notice to California Residents – Under California law, you have specific rights to control and access your data. For more information on these rights and how to exercise them, visit https://corporate.harlequin.com/california-privacy. For additional information for residents of other U.S. states that provide their residents with certain rights with respect to personal data, visit https://corporate.harlequin.com/other-state-residents-privacy-rights/.